"About your fee—"

"I don't have a fee."

"I pay for whatever services I receive."

"I don't take cash from stalking victims." Awareness of her alluring body heated his blood. He'd like to have her in his debt. He'd really like to have her in his bed. Thaw the ice, rev her engine, but now would definitely be a bad time to let her know what he was thinking. Especially since the frigid glare she gave him said she suspected exactly what he was thinking.

"How about a trade?"

She tilted her head to one side. "A trade?"

"I get rid of your stalker, you give me a honeymoon."

"Pardon?" Her voice had risen slightly, and the corners of her mouth twitched.

Seeing her fight a smile convinced him that heat pulsed beneath her icy veneer. "You've got the Honeymoon Hideaway at Elk River, right? Fancy cabins, room service, moonlight and romance. I could really go for that. Can you set up a honeymoon for me?"

"I could...." She relaxed—Daniel nearly melted into a puddle beneath his desk. "Are you engaged to be married?"

I'm going to marry you. "Not yet. We'll just keep it open-ended."

Dear Reader,

Sexy and sweet, tough and tender. These are the men of ELK RIVER, COLORADO. The men who still stand tall and know how to treat a woman. The men whom Sheryl Lynn writes about with emotion and passion in her new duet.

You may remember the legendary Duke family of Colorado, whom Sheryl first introduced in a duet called HONEYMOON HIDEAWAY a few years back. These titles—#424 *The Case of the Vanished Groom* and #425 *The Case of the Bad Luck Fiancé* as well as last month's #514 *The Bodyguard*—are still available. Send $3.75 ($4.25 CAN.) each for the first two titles, $3.99 ($4.50 CAN.) for *The Bodyguard*, plus $.75 shipping and handling ($1.00 CAN.), to Harlequin Reader Service: 3010 Walden Ave., Buffalo, NY 14269, or P.O. Box 609, Fort Erie, Ontario L2A 5X3.

Happy Reading!

Debra Matteucci

Senior Editor & Editorial Coordinator
Harlequin Books
300 East 42nd Street
New York, NY 10017

Undercover Fiancé
Sheryl Lynn

TORONTO • NEW YORK • LONDON
AMSTERDAM • PARIS • SYDNEY • HAMBURG
STOCKHOLM • ATHENS • TOKYO • MILAN • MADRID
PRAGUE • WARSAW • BUDAPEST • AUCKLAND

For my favorite future superstars: Jennifer, Emily and Mikey Campbell; Abby and Tristan Manus; and Justin Murphy. Don't grow up too fast, but when you do, get out there and dazzle the world.

ISBN 0-373-22518-0

UNDERCOVER FIANCÉ

Copyright © 1999 by Jaye W. Manus

Visit us at www.romance.net

Printed in U.S.A.

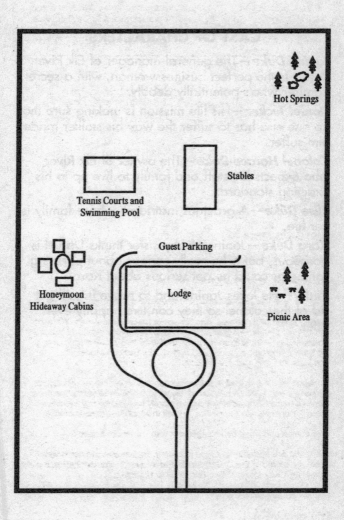

Hot Springs

Stables

Tennis Courts and
Swimming Pool

Guest Parking

Honeymoon
Hideaway Cabins

Lodge

Picnic Area

CAST OF CHARACTERS

Janine Duke — The general manager of Elk River Resort is the perfect businesswoman, with a secret admirer who's potentially deadly.

Daniel Tucker — His life mission is making sure that no one else has to suffer the way his stalker made him suffer.

Colonel Horace Duke — The owner of Elk River, who expects his staff and family to live up to his exacting standards.

Elise Duke — A gracious matriarch whose family is her life.

Kara Duke — Janine's baby sister thinks Daniel is gorgeous, but is he really serious about pursuing Janine or could he get serious about Kara?

Pinky — He loves Janine and to prove it he'll get rid of the colonel so they can live happily ever after.

Chapter One

Concentrate, focus. Daniel Tucker envisioned concentric circles of red, yellow and black surrounding a bright red bull's-eye. Easy now, picture the dart sailing in a perfect arc. Two thoughts intruded: This is stupid. He was bored.

Scowling, he fingered the dart, testing the point against the ball of his thumb. A potential client should be arriving in a few minutes—his only client in more than a month. Antistalking laws were growing teeth. He felt like a soldier in the final days of a war—bored. The more battles his side won, the more obsolete he became.

He craved a useful purpose—and something else, too. He hadn't figured out yet what that something else might be, though.

Shaking off the gloomy thoughts, he again conjured the image of the bull's-eye. He drew back his arm, joints loose, wrist relaxed, the crimson sweet spot glowing like a beacon. And tossed the dart.

A high-pitched squeal shattered the silence. Daniel tore off the blindfold.

There she stood, the most beautiful woman he'd ever seen. The yellow fletch on the dart quivered in the doorjamb, scant inches from her face.

The face of an angel with wide blue eyes and a full, soft mouth. Luxurious chestnut curls fell in soft waves to her shoulders. A wine-red jacket hugged her lush bosom and narrow waist and flared over graceful hips. Visions of dart boards shrank and disappeared, replaced by an image of this goddess rising naked from the sea, riding a seashell, while cherubs—

"Are you nuts?" She looked between him and the dart. "You almost put out my eye."

Her dulcet contralto vibrated within his heart. Daniel snapped his mouth shut. He tossed the blindfold on the desk and straightened the knot of his tie with a jerk. A glance at his watch showed four o'clock on the dot. The goddess must have accepted the "Please Come In" invitation posted on the office door.

"Some people think so," he said and rose. "You must be Janine." She was so stunning, he had to keep checking to make sure her perfection wasn't an illusion.

A small frown formed between her eyebrows. "Yes, I'm *Ms. Duke*." She clutched a large paper shopping bag— Neiman Marcus, he noticed—before her like a shield.

He rolled a hand, gesturing for her to enter. Reality seemed to shift. Women who looked like this only existed on a movie screen or on the airbrushed, expertly lit, artfully arranged pages of glamour magazines. He swept his other darts off the desk and into a drawer. The clattering assured him he was awake and she was for real.

"I'm Daniel Tucker."

She eyed the dart in the woodwork warily.

He moved around the desk and held a chair for her. "Man, J.T. said you were a knockout, but as usual he understated."

"Pardon?" She clutched the bag to her chest.

Those fabulous eyes glared up at him as if he were a bug in need of exterminating. He caught a whiff of light floral perfume with a note of vanilla. He wanted to bury his nose in her hair and snuffle like a horse.

"J.T. said you're beautiful. I bet you hear that all the time." He closed the office door and offered coffee.

She lifted that perfect chin. "I did not come here to be judged like a show dog, Mr. Tucker." She frowned at the dart board hanging on the back of the door. "Or to have my eyeballs skewered."

"Sorry about that, ma'am. I'm learning how to throw blindfolded."

"Whatever for?"

Because the living was so damned easy he wondered why he even bothered getting out of bed in the morning. He lifted his shoulders. "New Year's resolution. Sure you don't want some coffee? Special blend, made fresh. Tea? Soda?" *My heart, bank accounts, car?*

"No, thank you." She set the shopping bag on the floor at her feet. "I'd like to discuss business. Did J.T. tell you about my...problem?"

"Only that you have one."

"I need confidentiality. This is a personal problem. I want it solved without involving my family."

"Confidentiality is my specialty." He leaned back on the chair, but stopped himself before throwing his feet up on the desk. Her posture would make a finishing-school teacher proud; his should at least rise above slovenly. He opened a drawer and swept beanbag animals, puzzles and a miniature croquet set off the desk and out of sight. "What exactly is your problem?"

"I seem to have acquired a stalker."

That dampened his good humor. He leaned forward and rested his forearms on the desk. "Go on."

She looked around the office. The room was spacious, but cluttered with a jungle of plants and two computers. The screen-savers on both computers had words scrolling across the monitors. One said, "Vote for Dan Tucker, Emperor of the Universe." The other said, "Smile, you're gonna die anyway."

The frown line appeared between her eyebrows again.

Daniel tried to guess her age. Her complexion was as smooth as polished marble. From what he could see, she didn't sag or bag anywhere. Late twenties, he guessed. No wedding ring.

"What exactly do you do, Mr. Tucker?" She peered at his duck-decoy telephone as if it might offer information. "J.T. didn't elaborate. Are you a private investigator? A security specialist?"

Lately he hadn't been doing much of anything. "You might say I'm a professional problem solver."

"And your credentials? References?"

"Confidential. My specialty is helping abused women escape their abusers. My clients come by referral only, and I don't keep their names on file. Not even the CIA could trace anyone through me."

"I see."

"I also own some martial arts studios. J.T. runs them for me. His wife, Frankie, is your cousin, right?"

"Yes." The frown line deepened. "I haven't been in an abusive relationship. A man insists we're in love, but we don't have a relationship, and he won't leave me alone. I don't know if you can help me."

The old, ever-present knot in his belly gave a little tug, reminding him that no matter how much time passed he'd never be completely, 100 percent free. "I know more about stalkers than most people care to know. Firsthand experience. I used to have one."

Interest brightened her eyes, and her shoulders relaxed. She leaned forward.

"It started when I won the lottery."

Those elegant eyebrows rose like wings.

"Do you buy Lotto tickets, ma'am?"

"No."

"Don't start. Imagining being a winner is a hoot, but actually doing it is a royal pain in the butt. I hit a jackpot for thirty-two million.'' He paused; he never tired of seeing people's reaction when the number sank in.

Janine's lovely mouth formed an *O*.

''I get an annuity, and let me tell you, it's a tax nightmare. I'm on a first-name basis with every IRS agent in the state. I also made the mistake of getting a big head and letting them put my picture in the newspaper and on television. *Big* mistake. Some folks make careers out of begging for money.''

''Your stalker is one of them?''

''No. At the time, I taught a karate class at the YMCA. She was one of my students. Kind of flaky, I thought, but a nice kid. After I went nuts with a new car, fancy condo, presents for everybody, I made some donations.'' He stroked his thumbs under imaginary lapels. ''The big-shot philanthropist. I paid for an annual YMCA membership for each of my students. She took it as a sign that I loved her.''

''Why?''

''It's what she wanted to believe. If I've learned nothing else, it's this—there's no arguing with a delusion.''

''Does she have mental problems?''

''All stalkers have mental problems. My stalker was borderline schizophrenic, plus she had a disorder called erotomania. If that sounds sexy, trust me, it isn't. It's got nothing to do with sex or anything erotic. It's a delusion about being in love.''

Janine lowered her gaze to the bag at her feet. She twisted a hank of hair around her fingers.

''Strike a nerve?''

''He insists what we have is true love.''

Daniel grunted. Erotomanic stalkers were the absolute worst. ''My stalker called me dozens of times a day. I'd change my number, she'd find it. She broke into my home numerous times. When I called the cops, she told them she was my wife. One time she convinced them to arrest me for domestic abuse.'' He shook his head at the memory.

"I moved out of state, but it only took her three months to find me. She intercepted my mail. She threatened the women I dated. I tried being nice. I tried reason. I got restraining orders. I took her to court. I had her arrested, but she convinced her parents and her attorneys that I was stringing her along. They always bailed her out of trouble."

"How did you make her stop?"

The knot in his belly jerked tighter. "She stopped herself. She committed suicide."

"Oh, my God," Janine whispered.

He blew a long breath in a vain attempt to erase the sourness of old horrors from the back of his throat. "She hung herself off my bedroom balcony. She used a sheet from my bed as a noose." He forcibly relaxed his hands. "That totally, completely sucked. I still have nightmares. But one good thing came out of it. I found my life's calling. I don't want anybody going through what I went through. I stop stalkers any way I can."

Her slender throat worked, and the hair twisting increased. He recognized fear. Perfect hair, makeup and clothing aside, this woman suffered, and his heart went out to her.

"Before we continue with your problem, I want you to understand something about me. I fight dirty."

She stopped twisting her hair. Her eyebrows lifted. He could spend a lifetime studying her incredible face. He'd give his left leg to see her smile.

"People who stalk are not reasonable. Some of them have serious personality disorders. Some are mentally ill. All of them are obsessed. Colorado has an antistalking statute. It's fairly new, though, and not always well implemented. Unless violence is involved, the courts tend to give stalkers probation with a stipulation of counseling. Repeated arrests often do more harm than good. The stalker goes through the court system and comes out feeling stronger for the experience. So I fight dirty."

"You use violence?"

"On occasion. Most of the stalkers I deal with are angry men. Bullies who beat up women and children. I'm a tenth-degree black belt, and I'm qualified with weapons you've probably never heard of." He waggled his eyebrows. "Bullies don't like the taste of their own medicine."

"My stalker isn't violent."

"Stalking *is* violence. You must realize that on some level."

Her slender throat worked with a hard swallow.

"Being nice does not work. Being polite but firm does not work. I have discovered, in many cases, that the judicious use of mayhem does work."

"I see." The softly hesitant words held volumes of skepticism.

"Have you gone to the police?"

"No."

"Have you confronted your stalker?"

"I haven't a clue as to who he is."

He straightened on the chair, and the wheels squeaked. He'd wanted a challenge, and a doozy landed in his lap. He'd never dealt with an anonymous stalker before. They usually targeted celebrities or politicians.

"I don't want anybody killed, Mr. Tucker."

"I haven't killed anybody." He curled the corners of his mouth in a tight smile. "Yet."

She lowered her gaze to the shopping bag as if it contained the secrets of the universe. Perhaps it did. "He's threatened my family," she said quietly. "I want him stopped." She stroked the bag. Her hands were slim with long fingers. Clear polish on her nails had been buffed to a high shine.

Her vanity intrigued him. She knew damned well how gorgeous she was. He felt a connection. He was vain as hell, too.

"I'm at a loss. If I knew who he was, I'd talk to him.

But he could walk into this room right now, and I wouldn't have a clue as to his identity.''

''Anonymous stalkers need control as much as they need love. Anonymity helps maintain the control. You can't reject him if you don't know who he is. How has he threatened your family?''

She reached into the bag and rustled amongst papers. She brought out a pink envelope and placed it on the desk. ''This came in the mail the day before yesterday. It's why I called J.T. I didn't know what else to do.''

''You did right to call him. Stalkers don't go away by themselves.'' He shook a folded sheet of paper from the envelope. He noticed the envelope bore no postmark. A bad sign. It could mean the envelope missed the marking machine in the postal service, or it could mean the envelope had been personally delivered. The letter consisted of three short paragraphs. The first two paragraphs extolled Janine's virtue. The third paragraph chilled his blood.

It isn't fair for him to keep us apart. He works you to death, taking up all your time, and now he is ruining the most romantic day of the year! Valentine's Day is our day! I'll help you, love. Your father is a tyrant. Death to all tyrants! I will make him go away. Then you and I can live together in the mountains forever, happily ever after.

It was signed, ''Love you gobs and gobs and gobs, Pinky.''

''Am I paranoid?'' she asked. ''Or is he threatening my father?''

''Sounds like a threat to me. I always take threats seriously.''

Color drained from her cheeks.

''What's the deal with Valentine's Day?''

''It's my parents' wedding anniversary. Did J.T. tell you about Elk River Resort?''

"He said you're the general manager. I looked it up on the Internet. Nice web site. Did you create it?"

A trace of pride shone in her eyes. "Actually, my sister does our on-line advertising. She's very artistic. Elk River is a family operation. I cannot leave my job. My family depends on me. Not to mention I'm hosting a party for my parents. We'll have guests from all over the world. It's their fortieth anniversary."

"Forty years of marriage, huh? My parents can't make it to seven years no matter how many times they try." In answer to her puzzled look, he added, "My mother gave up after five marriages. Dad is working on wife number six." He laughed—making jokes beat feeling bitterness over his screwed-up family. "I ought to be in the *Guinness Book of World Records* for greatest number of stepparents."

"I'm...sorry," she said.

He waved a hand in dismissal. "But back to you. When did the stalking start?"

She lifted the shopping bag onto the desk and gestured for him to look inside. "A year ago. I was having lunch with a friend here in Colorado Springs. Pinky stole my Day-Timer."

He peeked inside the bag. It contained envelopes, most of them pink, plus cassette tapes and bundles of cards in all shapes and sizes. An impressive collection for only a year's time. "I take it you're the type of lady who carries her life in a book?"

Her eyes narrowed and her full lips thinned. Her expressiveness startled him, enchanted him. No glamour magazine cutout she, but a living, breathing mortal.

"No offense intended. But some people are organizers and some aren't. What was in the Day-Timer?"

"Everything." A faint blush blossomed on her cheeks.

Daniel suppressed a sigh.

"Names, addresses, my schedule. It was right before

Christmas, so it contained information about my entire year. The first letter arrived a week later. He sent a box of chocolates, too. I threw them away. The letters and gifts kept coming. When I realized he wouldn't stop, I began saving them. I keep looking for clues. He knows all about me, but I know nothing about him.''

''What about the cassette tapes? You're taping phone calls?''

She twisted a hank of hair around her fingers. ''He's never called me. The tapes are recordings of love songs, religious sermons and radio commercials. It's a jumble of nonsense. I don't know why he sends them.''

''Maybe he's hearing messages from you. He's letting you know he's receiving them.''

''Please…''

''I'm serious. One stalker was convinced his victim sent him daily messages via the Geraldo Rivera show. He spent hours transcribing every word so he didn't miss any messages.''

''That's insane.''

''That's delusion at work.''

She rolled her eyes. ''At first I was angry because I was certain he stole my Day-Timer. Then I thought he would grow bored and give up. But the letters have grown increasingly personal. It's as if he knows everything about my life. He knows everything I do.'' She closed her eyes for a moment and sat perfectly still. When she looked at him, her expression held a tremulous plea that touched him deeply. ''Very little frightens me, but Pinky scares me to death. I don't like it. I won't tolerate it. Can you help me, Mr. Tucker?''

''I'll do my best.'' He began emptying the bag, sorting the contents into stacks of letters, cards and cassette tapes. ''You haven't told anybody about Pinky? Your parents? Friends?''

''No, and I have no intention of doing so. My father is

seventy-seven years old. He doesn't need the stress. I want this problem solved with the least amount of fuss as possible."

He suspected her need for privacy went much deeper than concern about her father's age. He'd talk with her about it later.

"The party I'm giving for my parents is very important. We're hosting a family reunion, plus, friends we haven't seen in years will be attending. I can't cancel the party just to make Pinky happy."

"You're right about that. It would only encourage him. Let me sort through this mess. I'll see what I can pick up, maybe come up with a profile about his character. Then we'll discuss strategy."

A trace of a smile curved her luscious mouth. She opened her slim handbag and withdrew a leather-bound checkbook. "About your fee—"

"I don't have a fee."

"Pardon?"

He adored the way she said that. All snooty and refined, like a princess momentarily ruffled by the riffraff. "I have more money than I know what to do with."

"I pay for whatever services I receive."

"I don't take cash from stalking victims." He cocked his head, studying the gentle contours of her oval face and the sculpted lines of her cheekbones. He resisted examining her shoulders and breasts, but awareness of her alluring body heated his blood. He'd like to have her in his debt.

He'd really like to have her in his bed. Thaw the ice, rev her engine, goad her into calling him *darling*—and mean it. He pushed his tongue against his palate and kept his mouth shut. Now would definitely be a bad time to let her know what he was thinking. Especially since the frigid glare she gave him said she suspected exactly what he was thinking.

"How about a trade?"

She tilted her head to one side. "A trade?"

"I get rid of Pinky, you give me a honeymoon."

"Pardon?" Her voice had risen slightly, and the corners of her mouth twitched.

Seeing her fight a smile convinced him that heat pulsed beneath her icy veneer. "You've got the Honeymoon Hideaway, right? Fancy cabins, room service, moonlight and romance. I could really go for that. Can you set up a honeymoon for me?"

"I could...." She relaxed—Daniel nearly melted into a puddle beneath the desk. "Are you engaged to be married?"

I'm going to marry you.

The thought shocked him. Still, the sheer rightness glowed in his being like a bright, white light. The last time intuition had struck so hard he'd impulsively purchased a lottery ticket and changed his life forever.

"Not yet. We'll just keep it open ended."

She lowered her gaze to the checkbook. "I'm going to have to think about this. Perhaps I haven't explored all my options."

He touched the stacks of pink envelopes and fancy cards. He knew he could help her. He needed to help her. One way or another he had to see her again. "If you give me twenty-four hours to study Pinky, I can outline a plan of attack. Then you can decide if you want my help."

"I'd be more comfortable if this were strictly business."

"Barter is as good as cash. So what do you say?" He extended a hand over the desk.

"Well...J.T. does highly recommend you." She shook hands with him. Her skin was cool and silky. Luckily for Daniel the desk was between them, or he'd have drawn her hand to place over his heart.

"I'll buy you dinner, then. Tomorrow, seven o'clock."

She cast him a cutting glance that might have cowed a lesser man. Daniel was enchanted. Finding the key to unlock her icy heart might prove to be the most enjoyable challenge of his life.

"I doubt your girlfriend would approve."

"Business, Ms. Duke, to discuss Pinky. How about we meet halfway, in Woodland Park? The Alpine, seven o'clock."

Her eyes acquired a gleam as she gave him a long, considering look. With unconscious grace she slid one hand along the edge of her lapel. Those elegant fingers trailed tantalizingly over the rise of her bosom. Daniel's heartbeat thudded heavily in his ears.

"Do you really think you can help me?"

"Yes, ma'am."

"Very well," she said. "Seven o'clock, the Alpine. Don't be late." She glanced at the dart stuck in the door frame. A half smile appeared and stole the remainder of his heart. "Do leave your toys at home." She strolled out the door.

Daniel stared at the tantalizing sway of her hips.

Pumped up by the prospect of becoming a hero in the enchanting Ms. Duke's eyes, he tackled the contents of the Neiman Marcus bag. He didn't know squat about anonymous stalkers, but he was a quick study.

He'd find a way to get rid of Pinky or die trying.

Chapter Two

Keys in hand, Janine studied the parking lot. Despite the bright sun shining over the mountains, the temperature hovered in the thirties. She shivered. Until Pinky entered her life she'd been as safety conscious as any reasonably intelligent woman should be. Nowadays she was downright paranoid.

Daniel Tucker hadn't been what she expected. Her cousin had talked about him, claiming him more like family than an employer. She'd imagined an authority figure with a wall full of credentials and a serious demeanor. An ex-cop or an attorney, perhaps a Raymond Burr look-alike. Instead, Daniel had an impudent air and a smart-aleck mouth. Baskets of toys filled his reception area and his office looked like a big kid's playground, full of desk toys, fancy electronic gadgetry, far too many house plants, and silly posters on the walls.

And handsome! She hadn't expected him to be so ridiculously good-looking. Eye candy, her sister would dub him.

His reaction to her didn't bother her. She was used to men fixating on her body parts. She didn't like being treated like a bimbo, but she was used to it.

Her reaction to him, however...

His staring and open admiration hadn't annoyed her the

way such ogling usually did. She'd indulged in a bit of ogling herself. She'd even flirted; she never did that.

She pulled sunglasses from her handbag and jammed them on her face. Too old for silly flirtations and crushes, she wasn't the least bit interested in him as an attractive man.

She hurried to the Jeep, unlocked the door and jumped inside, pulling the door shut with a slam. She hit the door locks. Windows on the second floor of the office building drew her gaze. In Daniel's cluttered office she'd felt safe.

She'd dreaded the appointment and had almost chickened out. She'd expected a humiliating encounter, with Daniel patronizing her as if she were too stupid to handle Pinky by herself. Instead, she'd felt a kinship, a sense of not being so alone. By being so open about his own stalker, he'd made her feel comfortable enough to share her story. The connection and safety she'd felt accounted for his attractiveness.

She prayed Daniel could help her. She wanted her life back. She craved peace and privacy. If he could help her, let him flirt all he wanted.

SOFT KNOCKING broke Daniel's concentration. When J.T. McKennon walked into the office, Daniel smiled in greeting. J.T. wore his work uniform, a red T-shirt with the Full Circle logo and black trousers. He plopped a briefcase on the desk.

"I saw the lights on when I was driving past. I figured you were still working. When are you going to get a life?"

"After I finish saving the world from evil. Should take me a few more weeks." He glanced at his watch, surprised to see how late it was. No wonder his stomach growled. "Did you work late?"

"Shari has the flu. I took over her self-defense class." He popped the latches on the briefcase. "I brought the payroll."

Daniel used a remote control to turn off the stereo. He'd been listening to the cassette tapes Pinky had given Janine. The lament-filled love ballads and psychobabble commentary were giving him a headache. "You should have canceled the class, man. Frankie doesn't like you working late."

"She took the boy to see her sister. You know how it is when the girls get to talking. I'll probably beat them home." He jutted his chin at the calendar pages and correspondence Daniel had spread out on a worktable. "What's all that?"

The stalker was a prolific writer, sometimes sending three or four letters a week. The majority of letters were five or more pages long. All the letters were dated, and most were notated with the time. Curious as to whether Pinky's interest waxed and waned according to some predictable cycle, Daniel had sorted the correspondence into chronological order.

Using black ink for letters, blue for cassettes and green for greeting cards, he'd filled in a calendar according to when items were received. He circled in red any envelope that didn't bear a postmark.

Cards clustered at mid-month and the end of the month. The cards were embossed and foiled, and many were oversize. All were filled with mushy doggerel that passed for poetry among the sentimental set. The prices printed on the backs of them showed the majority were in the five-dollar range. Pinky might be buying cards when he cashed a biweekly paycheck.

"What did Janine tell you about her problem?"

J.T. paused in the midst of pulling files from the briefcase. "Janine contacted you?"

"Called me, made an appointment and showed up right on time. You're surprised?"

He lifted a shoulder in a rolling shrug. "I'm surprised she asked for help." He chuckled.

"What's funny?"

"Frankie's going to kill me."

"Why?"

"You know how she's been lately. Ever since she got pregnant, she's been playing matchmaker. If she isn't eating, she's plotting how to marry off her single friends. She wanted to have you and Janine over for dinner. Her words—you'd make a cute couple."

"She still can." It flattered him that Frankie thought he was good enough for her lovely cousin.

J.T. swung his head. "Won't be the same. Oh, well. So what's going on? She didn't give me details."

Daniel debated how much to tell. Since hiring J.T. to run the studios, they'd formed a solid friendship. J.T., Frankie and their little boy had become the family Daniel always longed for. He trusted the big man like a brother, but he also respected Janine's privacy. Still, J.T. was her cousin-in-law and he would never gossip. Daniel needed someone to bounce his thoughts off of.

"She's in trouble."

"How much trouble?"

"On a scale of one to ten, about a twenty. An anonymous stalker is making death threats against her father. Look at this."

He pointed out the marked-up calendar pages and envelopes. What bothered him most were the postmarks. The first letters were postmarked from Colorado Springs, then a March letter bore a Cripple Creek postmark. After that the postmarks came from small towns like Woodland Park, Midland and Florrisant—all within easy driving distance of Elk River. None of the letters in June or beyond bore a Colorado Springs postmark. By September half the envelopes lacked a postmark. In December, only two letters bore a postmark. None in January had one.

J.T. grunted. "Hand delivering mail. That's not good."

"According to the maps, the lands surrounding the resort

are either Bureau of Land Management or national forest. I'm betting this joker lives at Elk River.'' Daniel hadn't read all the letters, but what he had read told him Pinky considered Janine his personal property and he was getting frustrated with a one-sided relationship. ''Why is she so insistent about keeping it hush-hush?''

''I couldn't tell you.'' J.T. made a musing noise. ''Except she's the independent type. Frankie calls her Wonder Woman.'' He picked up a pink envelope. ''This has been going on for a year?''

''Yep. I'm putting an end to it, if she'll let me. What's her soft spot?''

''What do you have in mind?''

At the man's suspicious tone, Daniel's grin widened. J.T. was as staunchly loyal as a Buckingham Palace guard, but Janine was his cousin-in-law and he'd die to protect his family. ''Not what you're thinking, my man. My intentions are pure.'' *Sort of.* ''Her situation calls for some serious intervention, but I get the impression she isn't enamored about the way I do business.''

J.T. took his time answering. ''Soft spots and Janine don't mesh.''

Daniel scanned the paragraph that threatened her father. ''How close is she to her old man?''

''The colonel?'' J.T. blew a long breath. ''As far as she's concerned, he can do no wrong. From what I've seen, the feeling is mutual.''

Interesting.

Daniel tossed out ideas about how to handle Pinky. J.T.'s background in personal security and experience as a body-guard made his suggestions sound.

As J.T. was leaving, Daniel asked, ''So, Janine is available?''

The big man turned his head to look over his shoulder. ''If you mean, is she single, then yes. But available, probably not.''

"Meaning?"

"Meaning, she doesn't take crap off anybody." A slow grin brightened his face. "And you, my friend, are full of crap."

BY THE NEXT EVENING, when Daniel parked at the Alpine restaurant in Woodland Park, he knew without a doubt that Janine Duke desperately needed his help. He stepped out of his Tahoe. He inhaled deeply the crisp mountain air. Patches of snow marked the edges of the parking lot. He eyeballed the distance between his vehicle and the car next to it. He'd picked up the Tahoe from the dealer a few days ago, and wanted no dings or scratches on its pristine paint job.

At the restaurant door he glimpsed his reflection in the glass. He stroked a hand over the side of his hair and adjusted his tie. One real benefit of winning the Lotto had been discovering how great he looked in an Armani suit.

Inside, he spotted Janine. Seated at a window table, she stared at the traffic on Highway 24, or perhaps at the mountains beyond.

Janine spotted Daniel's reflection in the window glass. Her breath caught. In a dark gray, double-breasted suit cut to emphasize his broad shoulders and narrow waist, he was even better looking than she remembered, and a fluttery sensation rose in her chest.

A mistake, she thought. She shouldn't be asking for help from a stranger. Pinky hadn't sent a letter today. What was the big deal about letters, anyway? For the most part the letters, cards and gifts were innocuous. As disconcerting as it was to have a secret admirer, she could live with it.

Daniel met her gaze in the window glass. She tried to ignore the fluttering that now touched her belly. "You're late," she said.

"I'm right on time. You're early." He sat and picked up a menu.

Subdued purples and blues in his tie complemented his bronze-on-bronze hair and skin. The sculpted lines of his jaw and neck hinted at a physique in its prime. She raised a menu, blocking the view. Pinky's untoward pursuit of her or her untoward awareness of Daniel Tucker—she couldn't decide which was worse. "Where are my letters?"

"I left the bag in the truck."

An ivory-colored turtleneck sweater set off her rich coloring. Her hair glimmered by candlelight with golds, reds and copper. No way was he going to give in to the natural urge to tell her how gorgeous she looked. Her situation was far too serious.

"Have you ordered yet?" he asked. "Would you care for a drink? They have a nice wine list."

"No, thank you. What did you think of the letters and tapes?"

"Are you aware that Pinky is one of your employees? Or else he's living in the air ducts at the lodge."

She closed her eyes and pressed her fingertips against her forehead. "I knew you were going to say that."

A server interrupted them. She recited the evening specials and asked if they'd like an appetizer. Daniel ordered calamari, consulted briefly with Janine, then ordered the venison scallopini special for them both.

He cocked his head. "You didn't mention the possibility of Pinky living at the resort. Testing me?"

"Certainly not." Her genuinely troubled expression made him contrite. "I had hoped I was wrong."

"You have no idea who he is? No suspicions whatsoever?"

She shook her head. "It must be somebody I hired this year, but that's more than twenty people. I check references though. I haven't hired any criminals."

"Pinky might not be a criminal—yet. But he is unbalanced, and he has a serious grudge against your father." He plucked a bread stick out of a basket and used it to emphasize his point. "Pinky has decided your father is the reason the two of you can't be together. The anniversary party is throwing fuel on the fire."

"I won't cancel the party. It's too important."

"I've come up with a plan to distract him from obsessing about your father and maybe flush him out into the open."

She sipped from a water goblet. Violets, he thought. Her eyes were the exact shade of blue as African violets. Incredible.

"Do you have a significant other?" he asked. He hoped not.

"I have a gentleman friend. Elliot Damsen."

He arched an eyebrow. "*Gentle*man friend?" He was confused. Nothing in Pinky's correspondence indicated he felt threatened by Janine's romantic liaisons. "How friendly?"

"We meet in Colorado Springs whenever our schedules coincide. We share season tickets to the symphony."

"Is he married?"

Violet fire crackled in her glare. "No, he isn't married. Not that it's any of your business, but Elliot and I have dated casually for years."

"How can anybody date casually for years?"

"It's a comfortable relationship. And none of your business."

Casual, comfortable—neither fit Janine Duke. Elliot must be a world-class wuss. "So Pinky doesn't know about Elliot?"

"Unless he follows me when I leave the resort, then I don't see how Pinky could know."

He refrained from grinning in triumph. "Good. We'll leave comfy old Elliot out of the picture altogether. As of now, I'm your boyfriend. And nothing casual, either."

"Pardon?"

He *loved* the way she said that. "I'm the love of your

life now. When Pinky realizes I'm the real threat, he'll forget about your father. He should reveal himself.''

She blinked slowly, several times. When she'd asked for Daniel's help, she hadn't the faintest idea what kind of plan he might come up with. She'd imagined he'd stake out the mailbox or interview people, or perhaps produce some magical bit of modern technology designed to ferret out secret admirers. ''You'll pose as my boyfriend,'' she said slowly. ''And I pretend I'm in love with you?'' The absurdity tickled her. ''That isn't the sort of plan I can pull off.''

She expected laughter, not the burning intensity he focused on her eyes. Her throat went dry.

''You don't have much choice, ma'am. If you haven't figured out who Pinky is by now, you probably never will. At least, not until he attacks your father. Or you. We need to flush him out of the woodwork. We better do it before the party pushes him over the edge.''

''I don't merely live at the resort, I work there. I can't…''

''You can't what?''

Have people gossiping. Laughing behind her back. Pointing. Snickering about her private life. ''I'm hiring you as a professional. I expect a professional solution.''

''You expect a simple solution. I wish I had one for you.''

His sincerity shone through. As much as she hated his idea, she recognized its merits. Suffering some minor embarrassment meant little in comparison to protecting her father from harm. ''You honestly think Pinky is dangerous?''

''He seems to believe you know who he is and you're conspiring with him to keep the love affair secret. He's growing frustrated. He wants to bring the relationship out in the open, but he doesn't know how. So he's using your dad as a scapegoat. That kind of thinking is extremely dangerous.''

She took a sip of water and her hand trembled. Water drops spread on the tablecloth. ''Is that why your stalker committed suicide? Frustration?''

''She wanted to make sure she was always in my thoughts.'' He made a facial shrug. ''She got her wish.''

The server brought the appetizer. The smell of top-quality olive oil and the sight of perfectly fried batter glistening on the calamari distracted Janine. She worked hard to maintain her weight, but the calamari tempted her. She slipped a single piece onto her bread plate.

''Your plan will take Pinky's attention off my father?''

''A real lover is far more threatening to a would-be lover than a father.''

Lover. Imagining Daniel as a lover was much too easy. ''He'll reveal himself?''

''There, I'm not so positive. He's deeply invested in his anonymous act.''

She nibbled the calamari. It tasted as good as it looked. No amount of ignoring Pinky or wishful thinking was making him go away. Besides, how much damage could a pretend boyfriend do? ''Very well, Mr. Tucker. We'll try your plan.''

''Good. I'm looking forward to that Honeymoon Hideaway cabin. That will include champagne, right?''

''You get rid of Pinky, and I'll supply enough champagne for you to bathe in every night.''

WOW, DANIEL THOUGHT as he entered the lobby of the Elk River lodge. He enjoyed skiing and had spent a lot of time in fancy resort towns like Vail, Aspen and Breckenridge. He liked the ambiance of ski lodges: crackling fires, healthy people, lots of talk. But this place, despite its size, felt like a home. It radiated a warmth that spoke of family and togetherness and happy times.

Employees moving throughout the lobby and lounge were easy to spot by their white sweaters, black trousers and brass name tags. Daniel doubted Pinky had direct contact with the public. His letters showed he was intelligent and reasonably well-read, but he'd be underemployed so he could concentrate on Janine. He probably worked in maintenance or housekeeping.

He ambled across the lobby. At the registration desk two young women inputted information into computers. Both raised their heads to watch his approach.

He leaned an arm on the counter. "Hi."

A perky blonde, her name tag read Debbi, patted her hair and adjusted the neck of her sweater. "Welcome to Elk River. May I help you?"

"I sure hope so."

Her eyelashes lowered coquettishly. "Do you have a reservation?"

"I'm here to see someone. Janine Duke. Do you know where I might find her?"

The other young woman swiveled her head like a deer going on alert. She was taller, younger and thinner than Janine, but he didn't need to read "Kara" on her name tag to know this was Janine's younger sister.

"Do you have a business appointment?" Kara asked.

"Actually, Kara," he said and leaned both arms on the counter. "She and I have a date."

"A date?" She sounded shocked. Next to her, Debbi cocked her head and blinked rapidly.

He glanced at a huge clock mounted on a far wall. It was framed by an impressive rack of elk antlers. He was three minutes early. "Didn't she tell you about me? She told me about you."

Kara patted her hair. "Good things, I hope?"

"She somehow failed to mention how pretty you are. You don't think she's jealous, do you?"

Blushing, she giggled behind her hand.

He stepped back and placed a hand over his heart. "Seeing you almost makes me sorry I'm madly in love with your sister. Ah well, such is fate. Maybe in our next lifetime—"

He caught a movement out of the corner of his eye. Janine stood under an open doorway leading to the east wing. Arms crossed, she glared at the scene taking place at the desk. She did not appear amused.

JANINE DIDN'T FEEL the slightest amusement. She resented having to ask for Daniel Tucker's help. To have a lovesick moron stalking her from the shadows, mocking her attempts to roust him into the open and forcing her to plead for help as if she were some helpless maiden, stuck in her craw.

Watching Daniel flirt outrageously with her sister annoyed her.

Daniel swung away from the counter and held his arms wide. "Cupcake!"

Seeing his intention to hug her, she tensed for a major rebuff. Reason returned in the nick of time. Her parents' anniversary was in ten days. Ten short days in which she had to stop Pinky from harming her father. Only Daniel Tucker could help her.

She really hated that.

He enfolded her in an exuberant embrace. He wore a heavy coat lined with sheepskin, but the power in his lean body reached her. He wasn't overly tall, but neither was she, and he engulfed her. The scent of soap, shaving cream and masculine warmth surrounded her and stole her breath. When he released her, she huffed a sigh of relief.

He had brown eyes, like polished pennies, and they danced with good humor. "You look fabulous, cupcake. As usual."

She didn't recall stupid pet names being part of the plan. She noticed Debbi and Kara drinking in the scene as if they watched a sappy movie. "I'm glad to see you, too, Daniel. Did you have problems finding the place?"

"You give great directions. It's a nice drive. I enjoyed myself." He draped an arm over her shoulders.

The impulse to ram her elbow into his gut nearly overwhelmed her. Smiling made her jaws ache. She could do this. She had to do this. Her father's safety depended on it.

"I see you've met Kara and Debbi. Ladies, this is Daniel Tucker. He'll be my guest for a day or two." Light sensations tickled her ear and neck, raising gooseflesh along her back. He was playing with her hair! She stepped away and grabbed his hand. The size of his hand took her aback. As much as his overacting ticked her off, his powerful hands reassured her.

Kara and Debbi repeated Daniel's name. They sounded like cooing doves. Janine refrained from rolling her eyes in disgust. "I'm putting him in the east wing. Room 202."

"That's too small." Kara typed rapidly on the computer keyboard. "You ought to give him a room over on the third floor. It's nicer—"

"I've made the arrangements," Janine interrupted. "Come along, dear. I'll give you that tour I promised. Kara will take care of your luggage." She urged him to follow her into the east wing. As soon as they were out of earshot of the registration desk she stopped and turned on him. "I don't think I made myself clear, Mr. Tucker."

His coat hung open, revealing an ecru-colored, cable-knit sweater. Hand knit and expensive, she noticed. The attention he paid to his clothing irked her. The attention she paid irked her even more. She had neither the time nor inclination to moon over a handsome man.

"I'm not given to public displays of affection. And I don't appreciate being called *cupcake*. No one will buy that lovey-dovey stuff. So put a cork in it."

He managed an expression of almost childlike innocence. "In order to flush out Pinky we have to go over the top."

He spoke reasonably, even sounded businesslike. "We can't give him any reason to explain me away. You have to convince him that you're madly in love with me."

"Anyone who knows me is well aware that I don't *madly* do anything."

"Pinky doesn't know you. Not you, the person. He only knows you, the object of his obsession. He has created, entirely in his own mind, the you he loves. Normal rules don't apply. You have to shatter the image he's created in a way he can't justify. I thought I explained all this."

Subdued, she rubbed her fingertips over the headache forming in her temples. He had explained it. He acted exactly the way he'd promised. She, however, hadn't realized how embarrassing it would be. Her ears burned as she imagined Kara and Debbi telling everyone within earshot that Janine had finally snagged herself a cute boyfriend.

"Pinky thinks you're a goddess. Remote, unattainable, untouchable. A woman worthy of worship. I get a sense that something happened in the past few weeks. Something that threatened his image of you. He's trying to put you back up on the pedestal. He blames your father for whatever happened."

Metal rattled as a young man wheeled a cart laden with table linens out of a storeroom. Startled, Janine suddenly felt small and vulnerable. She imagined watching eyes wherever she went. She'd been sleeping poorly, overly alert for any suspicious noise in the night. Every pink envelope she received made her want to vomit. Stress headaches plagued her. Relationships with resort employees were growing strained as she wondered which one of them had invaded her privacy and threatened her father's life.

"Let's go to my office," she said. "I don't want to talk out here."

She unlocked her office door. As she turned the key, fresh resentment built. She feared Pinky had been snooping around in her desk and files. Recently she'd been locking the door, even if she was only going across the hall to the kitchen for a cup of coffee.

"I know you're scared," Daniel said.

She almost said, *You have no idea.* Except, he did. The experience with his stalker still haunted him.

She handed over the latest missive she'd received from Pinky. "It was in my message box this morning. No envelope."

He unfolded the sheet of lined notebook paper. His expression darkened. He made a soft, growly noise. "'Cut him to pieces and scatter his body for the crows to eat.' Humph, nice imagery." He turned the paper over and checked the blank backside. "So he's giving up pretending to mail letters. Bad sign. Where is your father right now?"

"He and Mom went to Denver yesterday. They're meeting with suppliers. They won't be back until tomorrow. I called him this morning right after I found that. He's okay. No problems."

As he looked around the office, he seemed to approve of what he saw. "So tell me, what happened a few weeks ago? What set Pinky off?"

Clueless, she shook her head. She busied her hands with straightening papers on her desk. "I have no idea what you mean."

"Think about it."

His commanding tone caught her off guard. So did the sudden blazing intensity in his eyes.

"You have a serious situation here. Pinky has graduated from puppy love to full-blown rage." He rattled the note. "He wants a response from you. If he doesn't get it, he'll escalate."

Even before the first threat to her father, she'd been noticing a shift in the tone of Pinky's letters. *Rage.* Daniel pinpointed exactly what her instincts had been warning her about.

"Think back to around the second week of January. Something unusual happened."

She swiveled her chair so she could see a wall calendar. "It's been a snowy winter. We've caught a lot of overflow from the ski resorts. Everybody has been working really hard, but we've had no problems with the staff. By the second week of January we were catching our breath." She turned back to her desk and flipped through an appointment book. A notation caught her attention.

"What is it?" Daniel asked.

"Les Shuemaker." A frisson tickled her spine—this man was downright spooky in his ability to pinpoint problems. "The second week of January. The colonel and I argued about Les Shuemaker."

"Is Shuemaker an employee?"

"He owns Wild and High Outfitters. It's a retail chain that sells camping and skiing equipment. He'd like to open a concession here at Elk River. My father is for it. I'm against it."

"And?"

Even remembering the incident embarrassed her. "It wasn't the business I objected to. We've been discussing concessions for some time. People on vacation spend a lot of money on impulse buys and souvenirs. I, however, didn't like Les Shuemaker."

"Why is that?"

She sighed. He wouldn't rest until he knew everything. "He's a lecher. He implied that I could wrangle an extra half percentage point of his gross sales if only I were extra nice to him. He offended me. Of course he was a perfect gentleman whenever the colonel was around. That especially offended me. He began pressuring the colonel to make an agreement on the spot and I...I lost my temper."

"In public?"

"In the restaurant." She closed her eyes. "The colonel had no idea why I was so angry with the man, so he was upset with me. Then Shuemaker said something idiotic and I dumped a bowl of soup on his lap.''

Daniel's smile showed million-dollar teeth. His eyes sparkled.

''It isn't funny. It's humiliating.'' He kept grinning, though, and his was an infectious smile. To her horror her cheeks began twitching with the urge to laugh. Some of the tightness eased in her chest. ''The colonel was very angry.''

''He yelled at you?''

''We were both yelling.'' She tried to banish the image of Les Shuemaker's calf-eyed surprise when she'd hit him where it hurt with steamy soup. ''I'm a professional. So is my father. We generally conduct our tussles behind closed doors.''

''What kind of soup?''

''Pardon?''

''What kind of soup did you dump on the lecher's lap?''

A laugh burst free and she clapped a hand over her mouth. Daniel Tucker, she decided, had a twisted sense of humor. ''Winter squash,'' she said between her fingers. ''Chef's specialty.''

He nodded. ''So your dad yells and the goddess lifts her skirt to show off feet of clay. No wonder Pinky is ticked off.''

''I was yelling, too,'' she reminded him.

''That's worse. Yelling is much too human. Do you see what I'm getting at?''

She saw his point. As long as she was perfect, Pinky contented himself with anonymous notes. ''I never would have connected the incident with Pinky's attitude. I suppose you do know what you're doing.''

''I've done my homework.'' He steepled his fingers over his chest. ''That's why you need to step out of character. Even if it means public displays of affection.''

She never fraternized with employees. She kept her personal life 100 percent private. Having Daniel hanging all over her, hamming it up and pretending he loved her would cause gossip and speculation.

"Why is this so hard for you?" he asked.

His question bothered her in ways she couldn't define. "You wouldn't understand. Not that it matters. I've already conceded I need your help."

The corners of his eyes crinkled with his smile. "Tough girl, huh."

"Not tough enough to make Pinky leave my father alone." She reached for her coat. "We'll begin with a tour of the grounds."

He opened the office door. "Just remember to giggle at my jokes."

Chapter Three

Shaken by Pinky's latest missive, Janine had trouble maintaining a pleasant demeanor. Pinky had threatened outright murder. No amount of denial or putting a spin on it made it anything less than a death threat. Arm in arm she strolled with Daniel through the lobby. She forced a smile even though it made her face ache. Her head throbbed. She introduced him to employees and guests she knew by name. Each time she said *boyfriend,* her throat choked.

Young or old, beautiful or plain, women turned their heads to watch him walk by. He moved with the easy grace of a natural-born athlete. His penny-bright eyes appeared to miss nothing. He exuded self-confidence, intelligence and goodwill—he radiated *attitude.*

They walked outside onto the huge deck behind the lodge. In fair weather it sported tables and umbrellas for alfresco dining. A few hardy souls garbed in ski togs braved the biting cold. The smell of hot cocoa and buttered rum rose like perfume. Daniel commented on the view. Strategically planted trees blocked the sight of the parking lot, but not the forest and mountains gleaming pearly white.

A bus lumbered up the graveled drive and parked below the deck. Daniel and Janine stepped aside to make way for a group of people dressed for skiing. Laughing and talking, their boots making the wooden deck rumble and shake, the people carried skis, poles and snowboards onto the bus. Daniel kept an arm wrapped firmly around Janine's waist.

"Is the shuttle driver your employee?" he asked.

"No. We contract with the bus company. Why?"

"He's staring at you."

She sneaked a peek and recognized the driver. He'd been working for the shuttle company for as long as the Dukes had owned Elk River Resort. "He isn't Pinky."

"You're sure?"

She chuckled at the idea of the shuttle driver being a deranged stalker. "Positive. He and my father are friends." She waved to prove her point. The driver waved back, then shut the bus doors and shoved the transmission into gear. The bus rolled into the parking lot to make the turnaround.

Janine walked down the steps. "I've hired twenty new employees this year. Of those, twelve were hired specifically for the holiday season, mid-November through the end of February. Four of the seasonal employees worked for us last year."

"You have sixty people on staff, right? How many of them live at the resort?"

"At the moment, eighteen. We offer room and board as part of the employment package. It can be a tough commute in the winter."

"Where do they live?"

She pointed toward a fence nearly concealed by juniper trees. A green-painted roof was visible beyond the foliage. "The dormitory can house thirty people. The managerial staff have rooms inside the lodge in the east wing."

She gave him the grand tour. Daniel listened attentively as she pointed out various buildings. Warmed with pride, she stopped having to force a smile.

Even in the midst of winter, the resort grounds sparkled. All the outbuildings were clean and painted white with green trim. The parking lots were graded and cleared of ice and snow. Evergreen hedges and trees concealed areas with less-than-aesthetic features.

"I can see why you love it here," he said. He breathed deeply. "Wood smoke and snow. Ought to bottle it."

His charm was getting under her skin. She was beginning to relax, even to enjoy herself. "You're quite the romantic."

"Hopelessly." A light breeze tousled his hair. Cold turned his cheeks ruddy. He playfully flipped at her furry coat collar. "Aren't you?"

She reminded herself he was an employee with a specific task to accomplish. No flirtations. No silliness. "No. I'm a businesswoman."

"Nine-to-five and nothing else? I don't believe it. What do you do for fun?"

"Balance spreadsheets."

He threw back his head and laughed.

They walked past the tennis courts and picnic grounds. She pointed out the stables. From a distance a faint jingling of bells said guests were enjoying a horse-drawn wagon ride.

A discordant noise caught her attention. She followed the source and spotted puffs of black smoke rising toward the jewel-like sky. She headed toward it.

"What's going on?" Daniel asked.

"I'm about to find out." She reached a garage. Off by itself, tucked behind the dormitory and equipment storage sheds, her father used it to store his antique Jeep. The maintenance people used it to repair mechanical equipment. She considered it an eyesore.

In the graveled yard two men worked on a tractor outfitted with a grading blade. The vehicle sputtered and its engine ground as if in pain. Every few seconds black smoke belched from the exhaust pipe.

The head of maintenance, wearing coveralls and a

greasy, billed cap, grinned at her. "Howdy, Ms. Duke. I told the colonel I could get this old girl running."

Janine swept her gaze over the yard. Tools, gasoline jugs, engine parts and a barrel of grease littered the ground. Discomfited by the junkyard appearance, she glanced at Daniel. He seemed interested in the tractor.

"I appreciate you getting it running again, Juan," she said. She swept out a hand. "But you can't leave the yard looking like this."

The man seated inside the cab shouted over the engine noise. "We gotta get those trails scraped, ma'am. The colonel wants it done today. With the old tractor running we don't have to hire Kendricks. He's a robber. Charges an arm and a leg."

Wiping his hands on a rag, Juan said, "Randy is right, ma'am. We got to work those trails. Don't be worrying none. We'll set this place right before sunset."

The garage wasn't visible from the lodge, and guests had no reason to come back here. If she hadn't been so boastful about showing off the grounds, she wouldn't mind the mess.

"The engine sounds terrible," she said. "Are you sure it'll make it up the hills?"

Juan laughed. "She's a real monster, ma'am. Now that she's running, she'll go anywhere. Especially with me riding shotgun for Randy." He turned his toothy smile on Daniel. Questions sparkled in his eyes.

As if in answer, Daniel hugged her waist and pressed his cheek briefly against hers. "It sounds great to me, cupcake." He thrust out his right hand. "Daniel Tucker. Janine is showing me the place. I'm impressed. You're the man who maintains the grounds for my little sweetie here?"

"Juan Hernandez." He pumped Daniel's hand. His cheeks reddened as if he were about to burst into laughter. "I keep the machines running. Nice meeting you." Juan turned for the tractor. His coveralls sagged with the weight of tools in every pocket. He climbed into the cab with Randy.

Janine watched the vehicle lumber out of the yard. Realizing Daniel had left her she turned around. He peered inside the garage. "Over-the-top is one thing," she said. "But is calling me goofy names truly necessary?"

He flashed her a boyish smile. He gestured excitedly inside the garage. "Is that what I think it is?"

Men, she thought wearily. Did they never outgrow their delight with ridiculous toys? Even her father, a man in his seventies, collected firearms, golf clubs and military memorabilia as avidly as a six-year-old collected action figures. She followed Daniel into the garage.

Her nose wrinkled in distaste. The place smelled of mice, motor oil and rotting wood. The narrow windows set high near the ceiling held ancient glass coated with dust, grease and spiderwebs. For years she'd been begging her father to tear down this building and replace it with a proper maintenance garage. For years he'd been telling her he'd get around to it. She was beginning to believe he secretly reveled in this small corner of disorder in his otherwise highly structured world.

Daniel rubbed both hands over the flat hood of the colonel's Jeep.

"It's from World War II," she explained. "The colonel is restoring it. He's been hauling it around for more years than I can remember."

He climbed behind the steering wheel. "This is cool. I love old cars."

She had a distinct feeling the colonel was going to adore Daniel. The idea scratched her already-raw nerves. Elliot wanted to meet her family, but she kept finding excuses to put him off. She knew the colonel would dismiss Elliot, a patent attorney, as a paper pusher. She doubted if Elliot would like her father, either. As quirky as Elliot was, he was rather intolerant of the quirks of others.

Even in the wan light Daniel's face glowed as he examined the dashboard and stick shift. He made engine noises. The colonel would definitely like him.

"Mr. Tucker."

He paused in his exploration. His grin was pure evil. "It really turns me on when you say my name like that."

She leveled on him her iciest glare. "Is that supposed to reduce me to giggles?"

"Only if you think it's funny."

"I don't."

He turned on the seat so his feet rested on the running board. "What do you find funny? Is Elliot funny?"

Startled by his mention of Elliot, she drew warily aside. She didn't like the inane idea that Daniel could read her mind. "This has nothing to do with Elliot. This has to do with your disrespectful attitude toward me."

He sat straighter and frowned. "I don't mean disrespect. It's just that a beautiful woman like you—"

She thrust up a hand, her palm rigid. "Stop right there. I didn't take this face out of a drawer and put it on just so you can get your jollies."

He shrugged. It might have been a sheepish gesture, except his expression was anything but contrite. He looked at her the way a soldier eyed an enemy bunker—he saw a challenge. Her scalp tightened.

He leaned forward with his elbows on his knees, putting them nearly nose to nose. His nearness disturbed her. His alluring scent was even worse. Males didn't affect her— she didn't allow them to affect her.

Daniel Tucker affected her. She wanted to touch his face and explore the texture of his sensual mouth. An absurd impulse rose to plant her hands on his knees just to see how he'd react.

"Explain to me how it is you can date a guy for years and keep it casual."

The air grew heavy and close. She wanted to peel out of

her heavy coat. A funny tingle began at the backs of her knees, creeping upward. She ordered herself to think about something else. Elliot—she couldn't even remember what he looked like at the moment. Pinky. That broke her spell. She lifted her chin. "I don't owe you any explanations."

"How serious are you about him?"

She saw it now. He thought he could bed her. Even worse, naughty little speculations about his sexual prowess popped uninvited, and unwanted, into her head.

He is not desirable, she told herself firmly. He was not sexy. He was a caricature, a conceited ass—a playboy who traded on his good looks. A jerk who thought she should be flattered he deigned to hit on her. He was probably a lousy lover, too.

"I can see I've made a mistake. I'll take care of the problem by myself. Send me a bill for your travel expenses. I'll pay it promptly." She turned for the door.

Daniel had her by the arm before she even realized he'd moved. She stiffened.

"You need me," he said.

"I most certainly do not."

"What did I do wrong?"

She jerked her arm from his grasp. "Making passes at me is not part of the plan. I won't tolerate it."

"Okay, okay. I'm guilty of finding you fascinating and beautiful. But that's no crime. You make it sound crude."

"It is crude *and* offensive. Now go home. You're fired."

The door slammed shut, pitching the garage into darkness. "Oh, for Pete's sake," she muttered, then louder, "Hey! There's somebody in here."

She headed for the door. A loud snap stopped her midstep. That could not have been the lock in the hasp. Yelling again, she rushed to the door. It refused to budge no matter how hard she pushed on the handle. She slammed her fist against the door. The metal clanged dully.

Daniel shoved his shoulder against the door, but the steel

door and hinges didn't budge. She yelled at whomever had locked the door to unlock it. She heard shoes crunching gravel outside, but he or she refused to answer her cries.

Daniel strained to lift the huge tracked door.

"It's locked," she said. "You'll never budge it." Either the person outside was completely deaf or else he'd deliberately locked them inside the garage. She pounded on the door until her fists ached.

A splashing noise made her stop pounding. She lowered her gaze to her shoes where liquid seeped beneath the door. The sick-sweet stench of gasoline made her gag. Daniel must have smelled it, too, because he grabbed her arm and dragged her backward.

"Open that door!" she screamed. "Open it right now!"

A dull whoosh answered. Stunned she stared as fingers of bluish flame flickered under the door. Smoke seeped through the cracks in the wooden wall.

"Well, cupcake," Daniel said, his voice eerily calm. "Looks like you actually do need me."

Dried out by winter winds the wooden garage caught fire with astonishing speed. Thick black smoke filled the interior. Coughing and gagging, she pulled the collar of her coat over her mouth and nose.

"Is there another way out?" He grabbed her arm and dragged her across the floor. They stumbled over cans, boxes and tools. She stubbed her toes and banged her shins in her haste to escape the flames.

She pointed at windows she could barely see through the smoke. "They're too small. We're trapped!"

The horrendous noise was as frightening as the increasing heat and smoke. Rushing and crackling, the flames sounded like a ravenous beast gnawing through the wooden walls. Outside, people were shouting. Something clanged against the tracked garage door. Janine screamed to let them know she and Daniel were trapped. Her throat and lungs burned.

Daniel practically jerked her off her feet. He grabbed a box that sat against a wall and tossed it aside. He was a shadow creature tearing through debris. Without knowing why he acted as he did she relied on instinct and helped toss aside boxes and cans. Smoke blacked out the light from the windows and flames. She couldn't breathe. Her lungs were afire. Tears streamed from her burning eyes. She lost all sense of direction. A box slipped from her weakening fingers and dropped on her foot. She barely acknowledged the pain. She wanted out. Away from the flames and the smoke and the horrible noise.

"Watch out!" Daniel yelled. He caught her arm and shook her. "Don't move."

She sensed more than saw him whirl. He kicked the wooden wall. Wood snapped with a resounding crack. He kicked it again and then a third time. Daylight glimmered beyond the smoke. He shoved a broken plank, twisting it until the fastening nails gave way.

He shoved her into the hole. Her coat caught. Wood squeezed her shoulders and hips and a protruding nail caught her scalp. She wriggled and squirmed, aided by Daniel pushing her from behind.

She popped free and went sprawling onto her hands and knees. She choked and gagged. Her tortured throat felt as if sandpaper scraped it raw. Hands helped her off the gravel. Excited voices swirled around her. She tried to tell people Daniel was still inside, but only a croak emerged.

People dragged her out of the yard, away from the garage which was now burning out of control. Sparks and cinders and ash drifted like hot snow. People used hoses and buckets of water to fight the flames. She struggled to rise, but hands held her down on a patch of frozen grass. Unable to see more than a blur of faces and bodies she gulped sweet, fresh air into her aching lungs.

"Hey, cupcake." Daniel dropped onto the grass beside her.

With a cry, she hugged him. He pulled her onto his lap and held her as if he never meant to let her go. He stank of smoke. His arms felt wonderful. Grateful he'd survived, she buried her face against his neck and sobbed in relief.

By the time the volunteer fire department trucks arrived, the garage had burned nearly to the ground. Resort employees had managed to prevent the fire from spreading to nearby trees and buildings, but the garage and its contents were a complete loss. A pall of dark smoke hovered over the resort. The stench of burned rubber and chemicals filled the air.

"Janine!" Kara dropped to her knees and hugged both Janine and Daniel.

"I'm okay," Janine croaked. It hurt to talk. She coughed. "We're okay."

Soot blackened Daniel's face. His eyes glittered like burnished flint. She knew what he was thinking, because she was thinking the same thing herself. Pinky would pay for this.

It was nearly midnight before Janine finished with the paramedics and the sheriff. The paramedics had wanted to transport her to a hospital. Along with smoke inhalation she had a gash in her forehead from a rusty nail. She'd allowed them to bandage the cut and to treat her with a few whiffs of oxygen to clear her lungs, but refused to leave the resort. She told the sheriff about the stalker. He kept asking whether she was sure she didn't know who Pinky was, as though if he asked enough times she would suddenly know. His attitude said there was something wrong with her. A few of his questions made her think he blamed her for goading Pinky into setting the fire.

She retreated to her bedroom. She immediately jumped into the shower as much to rid herself of humiliation as to wash away the stench of smoke.

She'd hated Pinky before. She absolutely, with all her heart and soul, detested him now.

A knock on the door made her freeze. Her heart seemed to rattle in her chest. She clutched her robe at her throat. "Who is it?"

"Daniel."

She opened the door. Smiling, he hoisted the tray he carried. He'd showered and changed his clothing, looking none the worse for their ordeal. A leather carryall was slung over his shoulder. Glad for a friendly face, she invited him inside.

"Your sister made us some food. Sandwiches, salad. Chocolate cake." He winked. "Bourbon. I could use a drink. How about you?"

She usually didn't drink more than an occasional glass of wine. At the moment she wouldn't overly object to getting good and sloshy drunk. "How are you?"

"Still tasting smoke, but I'm okay." He dropped the bag on the floor, set the tray on a table and poured generous quantities of bourbon into a pair of crystal tumblers. "Take it neat, tough girl?"

"Not that tough. Ice and water, please." She fiddled with the neckline of her robe. Made of heavy satin it covered her from neck to toes, but she was all too aware of her nakedness underneath. Her skin was still warm and damp from the long shower she'd taken, and the fabric clung to her hips. She watched his hands while he mixed the drinks and uncovered the food and snapped out linen napkins.

He'd saved her life. He'd risked having the roof fall on his head while making sure she'd gotten out of the garage first. Her throat choked up.

He handed her a drink. "Nice room. Looks like you."

She wondered what he meant by that. Years as an army brat had turned her into a minimalist as far as possessions were concerned. She had little interest in knickknacks. The room was rather plain, with mauve-painted walls enlivened by framed fine-art prints. The furniture was functional; her only concessions to luxury were the designer linens on the bed. She caught him peering at a stack of paperback novels. She loved sexy historical romances, gory horror stories and trashy Hollywood glitzy sagas. His interest discomfited her.

She sipped the bourbon and water. The alcohol burned her throat, but warmed her belly. He was the first man, other than a relative, who'd ever been inside her private room.

A man who'd risked his life to save hers. "I owe you an apology."

"For what?"

She picked up a sandwich. It was too late to eat, but her stomach gurgled indelicately. "Back in the garage. When I fired you."

"I'm fired?" His sunny good humor teased a smile from her.

She should fire him. He was obnoxious...he'd saved her life. "I don't appreciate men making passes at me. Especially when I have a job to do."

He regarded her. "I stepped out of line."

"You did."

"Can I plead temporary insanity?"

She bit into the sandwich before he caught her smiling.

"Sorry about your head." His fingertips grazed the bandage. Even that light touch made her wince. "I didn't have time to check for nails."

"I'm thankful you figured out how to get us out. I was starting to panic. I never would have thought of breaking through the wall."

"Breaking boards is my specialty." He flashed a cocky grin. "It drives the chicks wild."

A laugh burst free before she could stop it. She quickly gained control. "Sit down and eat."

"How did the cops do with the interviews?"

Good humor fled. "The sheriff doesn't believe me about Pinky. He acted as if I'm deliberately concealing Pinky's identity. Or that it's somehow my fault the garage burned down.''

''Humph. I should have warned you. Cops have a bad habit of forgetting who the victim is. Did I tell you my stalker had me arrested?''

''You mentioned it.'' Appetite gone, she set the sandwich on the plate. She eyed her drink, seriously considering the oblivion alcohol offered.

''Buck up. We'll catch him. He'll get tagged with attempted murder and arson.''

She didn't see how. Nobody claimed to have seen anyone hanging around the garage before the fire. Nobody confessed to setting the blaze. Anger washed through her. ''I gave Pinky's letters and cards to the sheriff. He probably thinks they're cute. Like mash notes from a teenager.''

He chewed thoughtfully on a steak and cheese sandwich. He toyed with a pickle spear. ''One good thing. Pinky isn't worried about your father anymore. My plan is working out great.''

''I am so relieved,'' she said dryly. The fire today was going to seem like a picnic compared to how the colonel was going to react when he found out she'd been concealing her problem with Pinky. ''What if he decides to set the lodge on fire?''

He ate half the sandwich before he wiped his mouth with a napkin and replied. ''I doubt it. Yeah, he lost it at the garage, but there was a lot of temptation. Gas cans sitting around. You and me alone in a private place. I have a feeling he reacted before he realized he could hurt you.''

The door drew her gaze. As a precaution the sheriff had assigned a deputy to patrol the resort. She wished for an occupying army. ''What if he knows you're in here right now?''

''No gas cans sitting in the hallway.''

''Don't be flippant. He tried to murder us.''

He reached across the small table and placed a hand over

hers. Her breath caught in her throat. When he joked around and acted like a chauvinistic clown, she found him easy to dismiss as just another conceited, too-big-for-his-britches playboy. With his eyes gazing steadily into hers he appeared somehow dangerous. And sexy. Her belly did a little flip-flop.

"I won't let anything happen to you, Janine." He squeezed her fingers.

"Who will make sure nothing happens to you?"

His smile caught her off guard. "Why, cupcake, I do believe you care." Chuckling, he returned his attention to the food. "Don't you worry about me."

It bothered her deeply that she was doing exactly that. "In any case, you've done your job. I thank you with all my heart. But it is time for you to leave."

"I haven't finished my sandwich."

"I was thinking about in the morning."

He made a dismissive sound. "I thought I wasn't fired."

"The police are involved now. They'll find Pinky. It's too dangerous for you to stay here."

"If Pinky runs me off, then he'll get the idea that violence is the answer to his problems."

"He wouldn't dare."

"Don't count on it. Since he attacked in broad daylight he doesn't care about witnesses. It's plain dumb luck nobody saw him."

She clamped her arms over her bosom and focused on him her most frigid glare.

"Look at this situation from his point of view. You're his goddess, the love of his life. He needs an excuse to justify his own cowardice. Who do you want him to blame, me or your dad?"

"But the police—"

"He may very well be a sociopath and capable of lying convincingly to the police." He freshened her drink with a splash of bourbon. "We can't let him think for a second that he can control you with violence."

Sickening visions of Pinky murdering her father turned her shaky inside.

"You can't placate these nuts. You can't let them take control. You have to push back, fight back. No amount of wishing makes them go away."

"How am I supposed to fight back when I don't even know who he is?"

"Don't let him run me off."

If it were only her own safety at risk, she would argue. She would accept the protection offered by the police and suffer Pinky's harassment. But if Pinky could so blithely attempt to burn her to death, who knew what he'd do to her father. "I'm scared if we make him mad he'll hurt the colonel."

"I'll keep him so busy he won't even think about your dad. I promise." He yawned mightily and covered his mouth with his hand. "Sorry."

"You must be exhausted. I'll show you to your room. It's just down the hall."

"I'm staying here." He jerked a thumb at the door. "Rustle me up a blanket and share a few pillows. I'll be fine on the floor."

Awareness of her nakedness under the robe warmed her blood. She wished Daniel did look like Raymond Burr, preferably grossly overweight. "Is that necessary?"

"It is until we know for certain Pinky doesn't have access to room keys." He shifted on the chair and reached to his side. A fastener snapped. He placed a handgun on the table.

Her eyebrows raised. The colonel had taught all his children weapons safety and how to shoot. Still, the sight of such compact deadliness dismayed her. "A Luger 9 mm. Nice. Do you have a concealed carry permit?"

His sudden smile dazzled her. For a scant second she

forgot Pinky and the handgun. Nothing mattered except the powerful warmth of his smile. If only he weren't such a conceited jackass....

"The lady knows peashooters. I think I'm in love. And yes, I have a concealed carry permit. Who other than you has a key to this room?"

"My mother."

"Is there a master key?"

She winced. "Yes."

"Prepare a pallet then, woman. I'm your guard dog tonight."

Chapter Four

At 5:00 a.m. on the dot Janine awakened. She glared at the clock. Around three in the morning she'd snapped wide awake. It had finally hit her—Pinky had tried to murder her. Shaking with chills despite the sweat suit she wore to bed, she'd spent the rest of the night hugging a pillow and listening for the beastly roar of flames. She'd finally drifted back to sleep, but habit awakened her. No amount of exhaustion would allow her to go back to sleep now.

Groggy and irritable, she tiptoed around in the dark so as not to disturb Daniel. By feel she selected slacks, a sweater and a blazer and carried them into the bathroom. She glumly studied her face in the mirror. The scratch on her head was reddened and inflamed. It hurt to touch it. No way would she consider putting makeup atop the wound. "Not so gorgeous now," she muttered. She hoped Pinky got a good look at her "perfect" face today and felt bad about it.

After she showered, dried her hair and dressed, she opened the door a crack and peered out. She couldn't see Daniel in the darkness. She wanted to let him sleep, but she had a resort to run.

"Too late to awaken me with a kiss."

She choked back a scream. He turned on the table lamp. Seated with a foot on his knee and his hands clasped behind his neck, he grinned at her.

Despite heavy beard shadow and messy hair, he looked as if he'd enjoyed the sleep of innocents. Her grouchy mood darkened further. "I thought you were still asleep."

"With you stomping around? For such a petite woman you sure do make a lot of noise. I could swear you don't weigh more than one-twenty, but I guess you're packing a lot more than that under your clothes."

She chuffed a harsh breath. "I will have you know—" She shut her mouth, too late realizing he teased her.

He dropped his foot to the floor and leaned forward with his elbows on his knees. "We're both early risers. We have a lot in common."

"We have nothing in common." She looked pointedly at her watch. "I have work to do. If you're going to play bodyguard, you have exactly fifteen minutes to grab a shower."

He snatched up his bag and scooted into the bathroom. She gathered the blankets and pillows off the floor. She pressed a pillow to her nose. It smelled of soap and shampoo, and it roused memories of sex. She groaned and tossed the pillow onto the bed. Celibate for years, she usually didn't think about sex. She especially didn't want to think about sex in conjunction with Daniel Tucker.

He was ready to go in ten minutes.

Downstairs the resort staff had already swung into high gear for another busy day. Clanging, banging, rattling and Chef's temperamental shouting emerged from the kitchen along with the aroma of baking bread and roasting meats. Housekeepers loaded up carts with cleaning supplies. Janine wondered which one of them had tried to burn her to death in a stinky old garage. Everyone looked guilty.

She stopped in the kitchen to fill a carafe with coffee before she and Daniel went to her office. Her phone began ringing before she had a chance to sit down. Maintenance wanted her approval to begin cleaning up the burn site. A reporter wanted details about the fire. Guest services needed advice about what to tell guests who were upset about the rumors of arson. Between calls she logged invoices into the computer. Daniel sat quietly on a small sofa, moving only to refill her coffee cup. She appreciated his silence.

A knock startled her. Hot coffee splashed her hand and she cursed under her breath. She noticed Daniel sliding a hand over the bulge of the holster on his hip. She called, "Come in."

A man showed a badge and introduced himself as Walt Helmsley, an investigator with the state police. Another man materialized in the doorway behind the investigator. Glad to see the sheriff's department uniform and a friendly face, Janine smiled in welcome.

"Daniel Tucker," she said, "Mr. Helmsley and Sergeant Mike Downes." She diverted her telephone calls to voice mail. "Gentleman, I've hired Mr. Tucker to help me find the stalker. I can't recall everyone I talked to yesterday. Do you know about Pinky?"

"The sheriff briefed us," Mike said. His expression radiated concern. As an old friend of the family, the deputy sheriff had a personal stake in what happened at Elk River. "I want to hear it from you. Start over from the beginning." He and the state police investigator brought out pens and notebooks.

She began with losing her organizer book and ended with why she had hired Daniel. She thought repeated telling should get easier. It did not. The story sounded stupid. She felt stupid.

Mike's forehead knit as if he felt angry as well as concerned. He glanced at Daniel then back to her. "Why didn't you come to me, Janine? I take threats against the colonel seriously."

Relieved he didn't follow the sheriff's lead in blaming her for Pinky, she said, "I didn't want the police involved."

"I'm a friend, too." He sounded hurt.

Catching herself pulling her hair, she dropped her hand onto the desk. She toyed with a paper clip. "I didn't want the colonel to know. He doesn't need the stress. It's a private problem. *Was* a private problem."

"Colonel?" Helmsley asked.

"My father, Colonel Horace Duke. I thought I could handle this on my own."

"You could have been killed." Mike turned a heated glare on Daniel. "Your little plan is stupid, sir. And dangerous."

Daniel arched an eyebrow. His expression remained otherwise neutral. "Seems to me my plan is working out exactly the way I intended. What do you know about erotomania, Sergeant?"

Mike and the investigator exchanged a puzzled look.

"It's a mental disorder," Daniel explained. "A delusional fixation on another person as a love object. Read love letters written by thirteen-year-olds and you'll get a glimpse into the kind of thought processes we're dealing with. Except this guy is an adult and he's willing to act out his fantasies. If you guys intend to catch Pinky, you need to get educated."

"Are you a shrink?" Mike was openly hostile now.

"Just a regular guy who's devoted the past five years of his life to stopping stalkers." He grinned at the investigator. "And no, you guys haven't heard of me. I keep a low profile. No press, no advertising. If you want to check me out, contact Gail Porter with the El Paso County district attorney's office. She's referred several clients to me."

"I don't know if you're qualified or not," Mike said. "I know for darned sure you're endangering your life. Not to mention Janine's life!"

"I'm doing nothing illegal."

"Interfering with an investigation and obstructing justice are illegal."

Daniel showed both palms. "I'm not doing either of those. You guys have my blessing to arrest Pinky. You won't hear a peep out of me."

"Mike," Janine said. "Mr. Helmsley. Mr. Tucker is not

the problem. Pinky is. I apologize for not calling you, Mike. In hindsight, you're absolutely correct. But, I suggest we focus on the matter at hand and worry about who is right or wrong later.''

"Ma'am, Mr. Tucker," Helmsley said, "stalking is against Colorado law. No offense, but civilians aren't qualified to handle these matters.''

"No offense," Daniel said smoothly, "neither are the cops. Pinky isn't your run-of-the-mill firebug. He's seriously disturbed, but he's smart." He jerked a thumb at Janine. "Here's an intelligent woman. She deals with a large staff. She knows people. But Pinky sat in this office, interviewed for a job and fooled her completely. He'll fool you, too.''

Helmsley smiled, close-lipped. "Obviously you've never sat across the interrogation table from me, sir.''

Daniel chuckled. "Obviously you've never dealt with an erotomanic stalker harboring sociopathic tendencies who uses anonymity as a weapon. Pinky isn't scared of the cops. You'll never rattle him.''

Janine massaged her aching temples. An island, she thought. She'd buy an island and post a huge sign saying No Testosterone Allowed. "Gentlemen! Stop the bickering. It's going nowhere. I and everyone at Elk River will cooperate fully with the police investigation.''

She found a list she'd created yesterday. She handed it over the desk to the investigator. "Here are the names of the people I've hired in the past six months. Mr. Tucker assures me that Pinky began working here during that time. As for Mr. Tucker, he's staying.''

Seeing Mike forming a protest, she held up a hand and shook her head firmly. "Your goal is to arrest Pinky. Mine is to protect my father. I fail to see where our goals are incompatible.''

Mike cast an unhappy glance at Daniel. "Provoking Pinky is a mistake, Janine.''

"He's already provoked. If Mr. Tucker is dumb enough

to set himself up as a target, then I will let him continue for as long as it keeps the colonel safe.''

"Dumb?" Daniel mouthed silently. He made a face at her.

"I also ask that you gentlemen cooperate with me. As far as anyone else is concerned, Mr. Tucker is my boyfriend. Nothing more.''

She ended the interview. After she saw them out of the office, she pawed through her desk drawers in search of aspirin.

"So you think I'm dumb, huh?" Daniel asked, grinning.

"I hold serious doubts about the intelligence of anyone who paints a target on his forehead. I wish you wouldn't fight with the police, either. Especially Mike. He's an old friend." She swallowed two aspirin then chased them with a slug of coffee.

"Your *friend* doesn't know what he's dealing with."

"He's an experienced law officer." She stared glumly at her telephone. The message indicator flashed.

"As long as they don't get in my way."

The door opened and Kara poked her head inside.

"Knock first," Janine snapped. She pressed a fist over her pounding heart.

"Sorry. Are you okay?" She flashed an adoring smile at Daniel.

"I'm busy right now. What do you want?"

Kara made a hissy noise through her teeth. "You don't need to bite my head off. I just wanted to tell you breakfast is ready. Chef made those caramel rolls you like so much."

Janine laid her head on her folded arms. Frazzled nerves or not, she had no right to take it out on her sister.

"I'm sorry," she called, but Kara was already gone. Rolling her eyes in self-disgust, she rose. Daniel's too-bland face annoyed her. "In case you were wondering, the answer is Yes, I'm always a grump. Especially in the morning.''

"I wasn't wondering. But thanks for the warning."

"Are you always this chipper and perky?"

"Without fail."

In the family dining room the heady aroma of freshly baked bread filled the air. The comfortable room and mouth-watering scents soothed her frazzled nerves. Her appetite roared to life. Seeing Kara acting extra careful, her shame deepened. She hated her hot temper and tendency toward snappishness. She worked hard at allowing petty annoyances to roll off her back, she longed for sweet serenity, but those seemed like impossible goals to reach. "I'm sorry for yelling. You didn't deserve it."

Kara passed off the apology with a careless wave. "No problem." She faced Daniel. "And you!" She wrapped her arms around his neck and hugged him. "You saved Ninny's life. I'm so glad you're here!"

A trace of color appeared on his cheekbones. He hovered a hand over Kara's back then patted between her shoulder blades. His sheepish expression fascinated Janine. He couldn't possibly be embarrassed.

Janine glanced at the doorway then lowered her voice. "Listen," she told Kara, "there's something you need to know."

"Yeah, no kidding. Why didn't you tell me you had a stalker? I never knew your life was in danger. How long has this been going on?"

Janine indicated the sideboard. Serving bowls and covered hot trays held the food. "Help yourself, Daniel."

"Well?" Kara asked. She selected the biggest caramel roll and plopped it onto Daniel's plate.

Janine hesitated. Many of Kara's best friends were staff members—any of whom could be Pinky. "You have to swear that what I tell you doesn't go beyond this room."

"What about Ross and Megan?"

At the mention of her brother and other sister Janine winced. She envisioned the entire family swarming in to do battle. "You didn't call them, did you?"

Kara lifted a shoulder. "I did, but Ross is out of town and Megan is helping Tristan feed cows."

"No more calls." Keeping an eye on the doorway, Janine told her tale. Telling it still wasn't easy. Kara's show of horror made it worse. By the time she finished, Daniel had refilled his plate and Kara had eaten her breakfast. Janine managed to choke down some fruit, oatmeal and part of a caramel roll.

"Erotomania?" Kara whispered. "Is he a rapist? A pervert?"

Daniel answered. "It's a love fixation, not sexual desire. If Pinky was a pervert, Janine would know it by now. I dealt with one—"

"Please," Janine interrupted. "I've heard enough stories to give me nightmares for a year. Take his word for it, Kara."

Kara wagged a finger between her sister and Daniel. "So you guys aren't really dating. It's all a trick to get this Pinky guy to show himself?"

"Right."

The young woman popped a piece of roll in her mouth and chewed, her expression thoughtful. "Wait a minute! I know who you are. You're J.T.'s boss. You own the karate studios. Frankie told me about you."

"The studios are a sideline. Stopping stalkers is what I do."

Janine recognized the gleam in Kara's eyes. Kara loved people without discrimination. She especially loved good-looking men. No doubt she was, at this very moment, figuring out a way to date Daniel. Seated side by side at the table, they made a stunning couple. Janine cleared her throat, loudly.

"He has a job to do. I need your cooperation."

"I'm happy to do anything you need." She directed the words toward Daniel.

I bet you are, Janine thought.

Kara sobered. "The colonel won't like this, Ninny."

Well aware of how her father would react, Janine said nothing.

A knock caused all three to look toward the doorway. Janine recognized a maintenance worker. "Yes, Jason, what can I do for you?"

"I'm sorry to bother you, ma'am." Hands shoved in his pockets, he lingered under the doorway. "Mr. Hernandez asked me to find you. A guy showed up at the garage. Says he's from the EPA."

The Environmental Protection Agency, Janine thought with an inner groan. Bureau of Land Management property and national forest surrounded the resort. The EPA kept a close eye on any potential contaminants or environmental hazards. They were going to demand an accounting of every single chemical burned inside the garage.

"Tell Juan to send the gentleman to my office."

Jason nodded and scooted away.

"How long has Jason worked here?" Daniel asked.

"I hired him in November." Janine smiled. "But he isn't Pinky."

Kara's laughter echoed the sentiment.

"Why not?"

"For one thing, he's only a kid. For another, he's a very sweet boy. He works hard and Juan likes him. He says Jason is a mechanical wizard."

"We'll see." Daniel filled his cup with fresh coffee.

Janine didn't like his tone of voice. Her own paranoia about her staff was bad enough—to have two of them peering suspiciously at people who were doing their jobs was too much.

An unmistakable voice rang in the hall, approaching the dining room. Janine stiffened. Breakfast felt like a brick in her belly. No time to argue with Daniel now. She had other problems. Her father was home.

Relegated to the background, Daniel observed the Dukes. His first impression was that Colonel Horace Duke didn't look as if he were seventy-seven years old. His hair was silver, but he had a lot of it. Ruddy-faced, lean and muscular, he stood well over six feet tall and carried himself as if steel instead of bone formed his spine. He had a big, booming voice. His pale blue eyes radiated fearsome light. He appeared as hale and hearty as he did in the numerous photographs covering the dining room wall above the sideboard.

Elise Duke hugged her daughters and inquired about their health. Sleek and ageless, she didn't look motherly, but her demeanor certainly was. She used both hands to grasp Daniel's hand in greeting and he fell headfirst into her aura of charm. A funny pang centered below his breast bone. As a kid, he'd spent many hours fantasizing about having a mother exactly like Elise.

"Sit down, Colonel," Janine said. She stood nearly nose to nose with her father, but twisted a hank of hair so hard Daniel was surprised she didn't have a bald spot. "I can't think with you trying to bully me into a corner."

Elise touched her husband's arm. "She's right, dear. We're all upset about the fire, but it's time to speak rationally. And peacefully. Do sit down."

The colonel blustered, but he sat. Kara filled his coffee cup and served him breakfast while Janine told her tale. Daniel admired her delivery. She spoke calmly and clearly, pausing whenever her father interrupted, but then continued without breaking her line of logic. He figured if they ever got Pinky into a courtroom, his defense lawyers would drive themselves crazy trying to rattle Janine.

"I wondered about those pink envelopes," Elise said. "Why didn't you tell us, dear?"

"I thought he was a pest, nothing more. He wasn't a problem until he threatened the colonel. I didn't know he'd burn down the garage."

"This is unacceptable," the colonel said. "Communication is the key to any successful operation. You failed in your duty."

"I did not!" She jabbed a finger in Daniel's direction.

"I hired Mr. Tucker because he's an expert. I'm taking care of things. Besides, this is a personal problem."

"A personal problem inside my resort!"

"Don't shout, dear," Elise said. "But your father is correct, Janine. This is a family problem now. The first thing we have to do is cancel the anniversary party."

"No!" Janine jumped to her feet. "I'm not giving in to that little creep's wishes. I refuse. It's your fortieth anniversary."

"Mom is right," Kara said. "We can have a party anytime. The guests will understand."

"We'll do more than that." The colonel slapped the table with a meaty hand. "I'm shutting down the resort until that miscreant is arrested. You're certain this Pinky person is a viper in our nest? Then we'll take no chances. We'll lay off the entire staff."

Janine paced furiously, eyes blazing violet fire. Her heels clicked-clacked on the wooden floor. "We can't lay off the entire staff. Some of them have been with us since we opened."

"I will issue my orders by close of business today."

"Like hell you will!" Janine shouted.

"I will not tolerate insubordination."

"I won't tolerate idiocy!"

Daniel swung his head back and forth to track the action. If this was similar to what Pinky had witnessed, no wonder he'd gone off the deep end. The colonel looked ready to strangle his daughter. Janine looked angry enough to bite iron nails in half. Elise's serenity said these types of shouting matches were common.

When Janine and the colonel ran out of steam, they glared at each other across the dining table. Kara raised a hand and waved hesitantly. "What if you leave, Janine?"

"I'm not going anywhere."

"She may have a point," Elise said. "You haven't taken a vacation in years. Perhaps you should go down to Mexico for a few weeks. Or take a cruise. The police will surely catch this man while you are out of harm's way."

"I'm not leaving."

"A sound strategy," the Colonel said. "I'm ordering you to commence leave beginning today."

Seeing Janine building up for another round of shouting, Daniel rapped a spoon against a coffee cup. The tinkling caught everyone's attention. He glanced at the wall decorated with a saber, photographs, plaques, framed certificates and mounted guide-ons, a tribute to the old man's military career.

"Sir," Daniel said. "Under normal circumstances your strategy would be ideal. Unfortunately, we aren't facing a normal enemy. Pinky doesn't conduct himself honorably or predictably."

"You advocate my daughter remains on the front line?"

"If there was a front line, I'd be the first to send her to the rear. This is guerrilla warfare. You probably know more than most about the problems of dealing with a terrorist."

The colonel rested a forearm on the tabletop. "Explain, sir."

"Suppose Janine takes a month-long vacation. If the police find evidence leading to Pinky's arrest, then the problem is solved. That's a big *if*. Arson is a notoriously difficult crime to solve. Plus, all we have are suspicions that Pinky set the fire. A possibility exists that it could be someone else. A disgruntled employee or even a guest who's a firebug."

He paused to give the colonel time to consider. "If Pinky isn't arrested, then when Janine returns he'll pick up where he left off. As an extreme solution Janine could completely change her identity and relocate. That would mean she'd never again have any contact with you, nor you with her."

"Oh, my, no," Elise said.

"I can help her change her identity, relocate, begin a new life. The only way it will work is if she completely and irrevocably severs all past ties. But I don't think you want that.''

''Your recommendation is what then?'' the colonel asked.

''We don't allow Pinky to choose the battlegrounds. We have to force him into the open.'' He slid a look toward Janine. She wore a funny smile, half admiring, half skeptical. ''Pinky has deluded himself into thinking you, sir, are the reason he and Janine can't be together. Should you cancel the party you reinforce his delusion and increase his sense of control.''

''I see,'' the colonel said, nodding.

''Closing the resort won't solve the problem, either. We can't underestimate his determination.''

''It seems to me your strategy is a dangerous one. To yourself and to my daughter.''

''I have experience, training and resources. I apologize for the garage. I was remiss in failing to consider such swift retaliation. But Pinky's revealed his weakness. We can turn it against him.''

''And that weakness is?''

''Rage. It makes him reckless.''

The colonel faced Janine. Love shone beneath his fierce expression. Fear lurked there, too.

''First and foremost I will protect Janine, sir.''

''Have you military experience, young man?''

The widening of Janine's eyes seemed to tell him, *You backed yourself into a corner now, wise guy.*

Daniel heaved a sigh. ''Unfortunately, no. I was too young for Vietnam and the Gulf War was over before I had a chance to join up. If they wouldn't let me fight, I didn't want to join. I'm no paper pusher.''

''I know the feeling,'' the colonel muttered. ''You appear well versed in battle strategy though.''

''I've studied for years under martial arts masters. The basic philosophy of my instruction is the art of war in the pursuit of peace. More than that, I understand stalkers. I can stop Pinky. All I ask is your cooperation.''

Elise folded her slim hand over the colonel's gnarled, thick fingers and said, "It would be a catastrophe to shut down the resort. To put sixty people out of work because of one criminal is criminal in itself. What kind of cooperation do you need, Mr. Tucker?"

He wanted to request that there be no more shouting matches, but doubted if Janine and the colonel were capable of restraining themselves. "First and foremost, you have to keep my true role a secret. The police are aware I'm a professional, but no one else can know."

Janine, the colonel and Elise faced Kara. The girl widened her eyes and held up her hands. "I can keep a secret," she protested. She made a zippering motion across her closed mouth.

Daniel doubted if Kara had a malicious bone in her body. The family's reaction, however, said she was a weak link. He had no choice except to work around her tendency to talk too much. "You all need to trust me to protect Janine. I'll take every precaution to not place her in a position where Pinky can retaliate directly against her. I need all of you to do the same."

"What do you mean?" Elise asked.

"I intend to keep him focused on me. But anyone, any of you, who gives Janine a hard time risks Pinky's rage. We need to keep stress levels at a minimum."

Elise leveled a look on her husband. The colonel didn't meet her gaze, but the way he darted his eyes at his wife said he got the message.

The colonel muttered into his coffee cup. He glowered at his eldest daughter. "You should have gone to the police the first time this miscreant—"

Daniel interrupted. "She's done nothing to encourage him. She isn't responsible for the way he feels or the way he acts. If she'd known his identity in the beginning a quick intervention by the authorities or someone like me might have made a difference. *Maybe*. Janine is blameless.''

''I'm not blaming her,'' the colonel said.

''We're dealing with a person whose fantasy life is more real to him than reality. We can't let his delusions affect our esprit de corps.''

''I stand behind my daughter.''

''Yes, sir.'' He patted Janine's hand. ''The best thing you can do is help her understand she's done nothing to encourage Pinky. She has nothing to feel guilty about.''

Color pinkened her cheeks, and she withdrew her hand.

''Why Janine?'' Elise asked. ''Why would a perfect stranger choose to stalk her?''

''Good question, ma'am. Unfortunately, delusions only make sense to the deluded. He thinks she's the epitome of perfect womanhood. He's created an image that she happens to fit. He could have just as easily fixated on a model he saw in a magazine, or an actor he watched in a movie.''

''That sounds insane, Mr. Tucker.''

''Call me Daniel, ma'am.'' He wanted to call her Mom. ''Pinky isn't insane. He is deluded, though, and dangerous.''

''Is he dangerous to our guests?''

''He's dangerous to anyone he believes stands between him and Janine. That's where I come in.'' He caught Janine's eye and winked. ''Trust me, I'm paid well to put myself in the line of fire.''

Chapter Five

Deep in thought, Janine headed for her office. Anger tensed
her up inside, made worse because she couldn't figure out
why. The party would commence; her father wouldn't shut
down the resort or fire anyone without cause. She had what
she wanted.

Perhaps it was the sense she got from her father that he'd
discovered a soul mate in Daniel. Perhaps it was the adoring smiles her mother and sister had focused on him. Or
perhaps she plain hated admitting she had a problem she
couldn't solve herself. A nagging inner voice called her
jealous that Daniel had so smoothly coaxed her family over
to his side.

The official from the EPA stood in front of her office.
She apologized for making him wait. A thin, sour-looking
man, he snorted brusquely. He had a stack of forms for her
to fill out. Acting as if she set the fire for the express purpose of polluting the environment, he gave her the option
of hiring a private expert to test the soil around the burn
site for contaminants, or the EPA would conduct the testing
and bill her for the service.

Another black mark against Pinky. Like a volcano he'd
exploded and now the tsunamis struck in the aftermath.

After the EPA official left her office, Daniel said, "When

bureaucrats die do you think they're reincarnated as locusts or as hyenas?''

"I'm not in the mood for jokes."

"That was a serious question."

"I have a million things to do."

He leaned back on the sofa and hooked his arms behind his neck. "I like your family."

"Yeah, yeah, and they just adore you." She placed her hand on the phone to call the insurance company. "You're a regular chameleon, aren't you?"

"What does that mean?"

"All that crap about battle strategies and guerrilla warfare?" She fluttered her eyelashes and placed a hand over her heart. "'They wouldn't let me fight, so I just refused to join up to be a paper pusher.' 'I'm a student in the art of war.' *Gag!* I needed a manure shovel in there!"

His rich laughter filled the office, tempting her to escape her bad mood. "It's called empathy. It's a lot more effective than growling like a tiger guarding a kill."

She sneered. "It sounded phony to me."

"Nothing phony about getting a point across. I always try to understand the other person's point of view." He wagged an admonishing finger. "If you want to score points with your dad then quit trying to outshout him. Do what your mom does. Get calm and get quiet."

"I don't need lectures from you." Especially when he was right and she was wrong. A mind reader, she decided, intuiting her deepest longings to be serene and gracious. He probably thought she was a bad-tempered idiot. She felt like a bad-tempered idiot.

The laugh lines deepened in his cheeks and around his eyes. "Unless you actually enjoy shouting. You do, don't you?"

"I do not." The words were as weak as her conviction.

"Do, too."

"Stop making fun of me." She snatched up the telephone and punched numbers on the keypad.

While she spoke to the insurance company about paying for an environmental inspection, Daniel scribbled on a sticky note. He stuck it on the telephone.

The note read: "Sorry—not making fun." She tossed the note in the wastebasket. He wrote another: "Strength comes in many forms—shout if you want to." Envisioning her desk covered with sticky notes, she grabbed the notepad off the desk and dropped it in a drawer. She finished the phone call then faced Daniel. "Apology accepted. Please drop it."

"Fine by me. Can I see your employee records now?"

She pulled the folders from the filing cabinet and handed them over.

"You're still angry with me," he said. "Why?"

Sighing, she slumped over the desk. Fatigue made her eyes scratchy. "If you had an ounce of sense you'd be angry, too. Pinky tried to murder us."

"Is that it?"

"It's enough."

He hummed a skeptical note and shook his head. "Nope, that's not it. You're mad at me."

"I am not." She wished she could throw him out of the office—out of her life.

"Hey, have I told you I'm psychic?" He pressed the pads of his index fingers against his temples and scowled in exaggerated concentration. "Ooh, the Great Tucker sees it all now."

She caught herself holding her breath, waiting for him to continue. Unable to stand the suspense, she cried, "What? What do you see?"

"You're angry because you got what you wanted. *But,* you needed me to get it." He waggled his eyebrows.

"I am not jealous of you."

"Did I say anything about jealousy? But now that you mention it, are you jealous?''

She hated the acid arcs cutting through her midsection. She hated herself for the anger, too. She should be gracious and grateful. "You don't understand. I have to work so hard for everything. Then you waltz in there, and in thirty seconds my parents are looking at you as if you're an angel descending on a light beam."

He nodded.

"I know I'm...abrasive sometimes. But you would be, too, if you were part of this family."

"Seems like a nice family to me."

"That's the problem. All of them are wonderful. My brother, Ross, is brilliant. He breezed through school, making straight As without even cracking a book. And you think you're smooth? He invented the concept of charisma."

"Okay..."

"Then there's Kara. Everybody is her best friend, plus she's artistic and creative. My other sister, Megan, well, whatever she wants, she gets." She snapped her fingers. "Just like that. She's married to a guy who thinks she walks on water."

She tried to shut up, she truly did, but the words spilled as if a balloon had burst inside her. "Trying to keep up with my father is impossible. He's super smart and he knows everybody. He never gets tired. His standards are so high, I have to be Superwoman all the time." She swept out a hand. "And then Mom. Oh, hell, you met her. She's just plain perfect."

Feeling very sorry for herself, she caught herself pouting. She never pouted in public, but in a twisted sort of way, the complaining felt good. "Then there's me."

"I'm having trouble following what exactly is wrong with being you."

"This." She tapped herself on the nose. "I look like a

bimbo. I've always looked like a bimbo. And nobody takes a bimbo seriously. I have to work twice as hard and get twice the results before anyone realizes I have a brain.''

"I take you seriously."

"No, you don't. You've been flirting with me since we met."

"What's wrong with that? I'm not being thick. Honest. But how come I can't flirt and still respect you?"

She opened her mouth for a snippy retort, but his question intrigued her. She'd never considered flirtation and respect as compatible.

"I respect you. I take you seriously." He cocked his head. "I also think you're beautiful. No contradictions as far as I'm concerned."

"I hate being treated like a cardboard cutout." Looking at him proved impossible. She doodled on a scratch pad. "I get sick of men treating me like a Barbie doll. Of women feeling threatened. I've never stolen a boyfriend or husband, but that's what they think. People think I'm either a man-hungry bimbo or stuck-up."

Unhappy memories swamped her. Her father's Army career had meant changing schools often while she grew up. Always the new girl, having to walk down halls while girls clustered in hostile cliques, making catty remarks and starting vile rumors. Popular boys thinking she was easy; not-so-popular boys too intimidated to ask her out on dates. Teachers who treated her like a bubble-head. Her fairy-tale marriage to Eric complete with a tragic ending.

"First impressions only last until second impressions kick in," Daniel pointed out gently.

She laughed in spite of herself. "That's the dumbest thing I've heard all day."

"But it's true. First impressions are always about appearance. That's human nature. You can't take it personally." He craned his neck as if trying to peer behind her desk. "Besides, the way you dress. You like looking good."

He had her there. She loved beautiful clothes. She enjoyed cosmetics and fixing her hair.

"How about a deal," he said. "I'll stop calling you gorgeous, and you stop being mad at me."

The genuine sweetness in his face and voice were difficult to resist. "I get the distinct feeling you enjoy arguments."

"Debating champ in college. I've got the medals to prove it. So what do you say?"

"You have a plan," she said with a sigh. "I've agreed to the plan. Call me anything you want."

LAW OFFICIALS wrapped up their investigations by the end of the day. After sifting through the debris for evidence and finding nothing, and interviewing dozens of people without discovering a single eye witness or strong suspect, the law officials could do nothing further at Elk River. It would take weeks for crime analysts to compile reports concerning physical evidence found at the scene.

The colonel made arrangements to hire Sergeant Mike Downes and another deputy in their off-duty hours. The deputies would patrol the resort and keep an eye out for trouble. Janine spent the day assuring the managerial staff that while an arsonist was in their midst, resort operations were to continue as normal, and she assured guests the garage fire was an accident despite any rumors to the contrary.

By eight o'clock she was so exhausted she nearly fell asleep at her desk. Daniel wanted to have dinner in the restaurant. Didn't he ever wear out? She refused to heed his arguments. They retired to her room.

"I'll arrange for a cot," she said.

"If you bring in a cot somebody is going to gossip about your boyfriend not sleeping in your bed."

"You aren't sleeping in my bed."

He pointed to the couch. It was short, with only two cushions, but it would be more comfortable than the floor. "Your virtue is safe with me. Pretend I'm a German shepherd."

"Fine, whatever." She sought sanctuary in the bathroom. She didn't have pajamas since she'd always slept in the nude. She resigned herself to wearing a sweat suit to bed for the next few days.

When she came out of the bathroom the sight of Daniel stopped her short. He'd made up a bed on the couch and now lounged atop the covers as he studied an employee file. He wore a pair of purple boxer shorts and nothing else.

All her life she'd been surrounded by attractive men. Most women agreed her father and brother were exceptionally handsome. Her father's troops had been young, virile and in good physical condition. Her ex-husband had looked like a Nordic god. But Daniel Tucker...

His body was lean and perfectly proportioned, with muscles so chiseled and well defined he appeared to be carved from golden marble. Intrigued by the thick, yet graceful lines of his neck and the depth of muscle on his arms, she stared. Heaviness filled her midsection. Her breasts tingled and ached. Her mouth went dry.

Visions of sex invaded her brain. Wild, romping, passionate sex. Noisy, sweaty, knock-the-mattress-off-the-bed sex. Touching every inch of his bronzed skin. Those big, powerful hands working magic on every inch of her skin. The sheer shock of desire startled her, dismayed her... excited her.

He looked up. Heat bloomed on her cheeks.

"Yes?" he asked.

"You're in your...your...underwear."

"No jammies," he said. He resumed studying the file. "I'm not spending another night in my jeans. We're grown-ups, so no offense, right?"

She glanced down at her heavy sweatshirt and long fleece pants. She ought to prance around in panties and see how he liked that.

"Don't you—" She bit her lower lip. She would not, no matter how provoked, act like a silly girl. At thirty-five, a grown woman in full control of her faculties, she refused to lust after any man. She forced a smile. "The bathroom is yours, Mr. Tucker. Good night."

"Mind if I do some reading?"

"I don't care if you practice the bass drum in a marching band."

She crawled under the covers and pulled a pillow over her head. No matter how tightly she squeezed her eyelids shut she kept seeing those damned purple boxer shorts... and that lean, muscular, incredible body.

"WE CAN ELIMINATE these four, too," Daniel said. He tossed employee files on Janine's desk. "Too old."

Janine slipped the folders back into the filing cabinet. She slid a weary glance at her desk. Her rule was, handle each piece of paper only once. Receive it, act upon it, then either file it or throw it away. Normally by day's end her desk was clean. At the moment her In box overflowed. After spending hours with insurance adjustors plus handling the usual resort business, plus jumping at every shadow and looking over her shoulder for another attack by Pinky, it had been a long, stressful day. Having Daniel Tucker clinging to her like a burr hadn't helped matters any.

She'd introduced him to many of the employees. No one could have guessed his intentions by his smiles and interested questions.

While in public he insisted on holding her hand. She couldn't even recall the last time she'd walked hand in hand with a man. Though ridged with calluses, his hands were surprisingly graceful. She kept reminding herself his displays of affection meant nothing personal. She made herself think about Elliot. Nice, reliable Elliot who made no demands and never shook up her life. Sweet Elliot about whom she'd never suffered a single sexual fantasy.

"What has age got to do with anything?" she asked.

"The kind of personality disorders that lead to stalking show up at a young age. Nobody decides to suddenly start stalking on his thirtieth birthday. Antisocial behavior leads to problems with the law. Since nobody has a criminal record I think we can safely assume Pinky is fairly young."

She pointed with her chin at the folders he'd retained. "You can eliminate the women, too."

"Not yet."

"Pardon?"

He chuckled. "This isn't about sexual desire. Pinky's letters lack sexual overtones even when he writes about your appearance and how you dress. It could be he's put you on such a high pedestal that sex would be profane. Or, we could be dealing with a woman who is identifying with you. Sort of the way little girls fall in love with fashion dolls and supermodels."

"Oh." A shudder rippled along her spine. A male secret admirer was creepy enough. Imagining a woman lusting after her life put a sour taste in her mouth.

"On the other hand, Pinky's powerful reaction to me says he's probably a guy." He divided the folders into two stacks. He placed a hand atop the taller stack. "These employees deal with the public on a regular basis. It's possible he functions well enough to make customers happy and still keep an eye on you, but I doubt it."

He shifted his hand to the short stack. "These people are more likely. Four in maintenance, four in housekeeping, a wrangler and a kitchen helper."

She interrupted with a laugh. "Are you talking about Devon Hightower?"

"He's the one."

"If he's obsessed with anything, it's horses. I don't think

he's spoken five words to me since he started working here.''

He regarded the stack of folders through narrowed eyes. ''Have you noticed how he acts around other women?''

''I notice he does his job. The head wrangler doesn't complain. Cody's very picky about the people who work with the horses.'' The idea of shy, skinny, horse-happy Devon Hightower living a double life made her laugh again.

''I like your laugh.''

The gentle inquisitiveness in his bright eyes caused a pang in her chest. At the moment he looked so sweet part of her melted inside.

''Wish I was a stand-up comic. I could listen to you laugh all day.''

A snippy reply eluded her. She fussed blindly with a stack of order forms. ''Find Pinky and I'll have more to laugh about.'' She began sorting through the day's mail. No pink envelopes today. Realizing she'd been holding her breath, she released air in a long sigh.

''I want to search the dormitory.''

''No.''

''No what?''

''No, you cannot search the dormitory.'' She slit open an envelope and dumped out its contents.

''What's the big deal? It's your property. You have a right to inspect it.''

''I like to think I'd use any means at my disposal to catch that creep. But there are lines I can't cross. Searching the dorm is one of them.''

''Why?''

''My employees aren't soldiers living in army barracks and I'm not the Gestapo. If you can pinpoint one person as being Pinky and give me hard evidence to back it up, then I'll say yes. Not until then. I have no more right to search the dorm on a whim than anyone has a right to search my room."

He huffed and made faces. She continued opening mail. He finally stopped grumbling.

"This is a special circumstance."

"Not special enough to violate the privacy of innocent people. A search would be akin to breaking and entering. We'd be no better than burglars."

"No one has to know."

"I would know." She leveled on him an admonishing gaze. "You don't fight *that* dirty...lowering yourself to a criminal's level, do you?"

He looked away. He crossed and then uncrossed his legs. He shifted on the sofa.

A life-long association with the military had introduced her to many people who believed the ends justified the means. That kind of thinking was responsible for much of the evil in the world. Daniel's inability to meet her eyes said he possessed scruples and a conscience, along with enough integrity to feel shame.

"I didn't think so. So I'm sure you'll come up with a better plan."

"Yeah, yeah, I always do." He glanced at his watch. "Can we eat now?"

The lateness of the hour astonished her. Also astonishing was Daniel's appetite. At breakfast and again at lunch he'd eaten enough to satisfy a high school football team. She doubted if he carried more than one hundred and seventy pounds on his muscular frame. How he ate so much and stayed so lean boggled her mind. She had to count every calorie or risk ending up fluffy as a bunny.

"I'll order a meal sent up to my room."

"We need to stay in the public eye."

"I'm tired."

"You went to bed early last night."

Where she tossed and turned, so restless with frustrated

lust that she'd awakened this morning feeling as if she'd run a marathon. Damn those purple boxer shorts—boxers weren't supposed to be sexy!

"I hardly ever eat in the restaurant. People will think it's unusual."

"It's supposed to be unusual. We're lovebirds, remember? Besides, Pinky didn't send any messages today. He might be hoping I'll leave. We need to dissuade him of the notion I scare easy."

"We may have a long wait for a table."

"You're the boss lady. Pull rank."

"Paying customers always come first," she said sweetly. "Employees, like *us,* have to wait our turn."

He opened the door for her. As she passed he said, "I know you like me. Go on, say it."

She refused to let him bait her.

As she predicted, the restaurant was crowded with diners, and they faced a wait. The maître d' offered to put her at the top of the waiting list, but she coolly informed him that she and Daniel would take their turn. They sat in the lounge and ordered drinks.

She relaxed on a comfortable sofa and sipped from a glass of wine. People milled about in the lounge, many of them sunburned from a day on the ski slopes. She envied their carefree attitudes. Daniel made small talk, asking about the many places she'd lived all over the world. After a while she grew aware of him mimicking her actions. When she drank, he drank. When she fiddled with the neckline of her sweater, he tugged at the collar of his. She uncrossed her legs and crossed them in the other direction. A few seconds later he did the same.

The mimicry had a curiously erotic effect and she found herself leaning closer to him to better hear his voice. A fire burned in the huge central fireplace. Light from the flickering flames danced against his shiny brown hair. He made a silly observation about a man who was wearing chartreuse ski pants. She laughed.

He leaned so close she could smell him. A ticklish shiver rippled across her skin as his clean, earthy, masculine scent assaulted her senses. She swallowed the sudden thickness in her throat.

"Not only that," he lowered his voice, "I think he's wearing a girdle."

She covered a snicker with a hand. The man did have a suspicious-looking panty line under his too-tight clothing. "Stop making cracks about the guests."

She drew back far enough to clearly see his eyes. She was overdue for an eye exam and probably needed reading glasses. The reminder that she was nearing middle-age bothered her. The sheer beauty of his eyes came into focus. The color wasn't merely brown, but a lively mixture of copper and bronze, highlighted by a dark ring around the pupil. His lashes were lush enough to film a mascara commercial.

He moved in again. His breath caressed her ear and goose bumps prickled her back. "The girl bussing tables. She keeps looking this way. Don't stare."

She lowered her face and pretended he merely whispered sweet nothings in her ear. His denim-clad thigh drew her attention. The wear-softened fabric molded over the sharp sculpting of his knee. An image of his perfectly proportioned, golden tanned legs filled her head.

She sipped hastily from her wineglass. The tangy Chardonnay brought her back to the present. *Grow up,* she told herself. She didn't deny he was gorgeous. She couldn't even deny how he affected her. But she wasn't some giddy teenager bowled over by any cute guy who walked past. She absolutely refused to consider what kissing him might feel like. Or how his smooth skin would feel pressing hotly against hers.

She leaned over to place the wineglass on a table and

peeked at the employee. Short and dark-haired, with a stocky, almost boyish figure, the girl moved unobtrusively through the lounge. She carried a sack into which she placed used napkins, paper drinking straw covers and other trash. The girl was a new hire, assigned to housekeeping. Janine blanked on her name.

Daniel snuggled up close to her. "She doesn't seem very friendly," he whispered in her ear.

"Maybe she's having a bad day," she whispered back. Then she remembered. "Marie. Uh, Marie Padillo."

"She's on my shortlist. Has she ever done anything or said anything that made you uncomfortable?"

Suspicion slithered through her brain. Had Marie ever done anything untoward? She let hair fall over her face so she could watch Marie unobtrusively. The girl worked efficiently, but made no effort to chat with guests or even to acknowledge them. If someone got in her way, she stepped back and waited silently for the person to move.

"Hey, you guys!"

Janine jumped at the sound of her sister's voice. She turned on the sofa and faced Kara.

Kara had exchanged her uniform for a fuzzy green sweater and skintight leggings. Sequins sparkled on the sweater. Earrings in the shape of miniature, mirrored disco balls shimmered through her poufed-up hair. She leaned on the back of the sofa and smiled dreamily at Daniel.

Jealousy ripped through Janine's midsection.

"What are you doing?" Kara asked.

"Waiting for a table," Daniel said. He looked her up and down. "Cute outfit. Got a date?"

"I'm free as a bird. Cody and the guys are letting me sing with them tonight." She pointed at the wide, double doors leading to the ballroom. "The band starts at nine. Music, storytelling, dancing. Do you like country music, Daniel? And line dancing? Cody puts on a great show."

Kara loved attention. Especially the attention of good-looking males willing to assure her she was the cutest little thing this side of the Mississippi. Daniel played right into her hands.

That it didn't matter one little bit if Kara flirted with Daniel, and it didn't matter if he flirted back, made sense in Janine's head.

The rest of her hated it.

She struggled to maintain a pleasant expression. She made herself stop twisting her hair.

"Sounds like fun. I'd love to hear you sing." Daniel turned an ingenuous smile on Janine. She wanted to slap him. "What about you? Are you up for dancing? I do a pretty good two-step."

"It's been a long day." She winced at her grumpy tone. "You and I still have work to do." To emphasize the point she looked for Marie. The girl had disappeared.

With both arms resting on the sofa back, Kara swayed her backside as if to music only she could hear. A passing gentleman stared so hard he nearly walked into a plant. The woman accompanying him gave his arm a jerk. "Ninny's always a big old party pooper. Come by yourself, Daniel. Trust me, you'll find plenty of dance partners."

"I'll see if I can talk her into sitting in for a set."

Brows arched into a snooty expression, the young woman challenged Janine with a half smile. "Good luck talking her into anything."

Party pooper? Because she wasn't a shameless little hussy who teased every male who came along? Because she didn't wear flashy earrings and skintight clothes? Because she was nearing middle age and she hadn't had sex in years, and she had so many responsibilities it felt as if the world rested on her shoulders? If Daniel wanted Kara, good luck!

"Our table is ready, Daniel. That is, if you still want to eat." She stalked away.

Chapter Six

Daniel studied Janine's stiff back. The vibes he picked up were very interesting. She couldn't be jealous, but the possibility intrigued him. Not so interesting were the open stares following her through the lounge. Every man in the place stood taller to watch her pass by. Many ogled her graceful hips. Daniel tossed back the remains of his drink. His fingers squeaked against the condensation on the glass.

"Oh, geez, I'm not supposed to provoke her, am I?" Kara whispered. She straightened the hem of her sweater with little jerks.

With a battalion of half siblings and stepsiblings, he knew full well that one of life's greatest pleasures lay in tormenting one's brothers and sisters. He suspected Kara rarely passed up an opportunity to light a match between her older sister's toes. "She's under a lot of stress."

"You still don't know who Pinky is?"

"Not yet. Have you heard anything?"

"Other than everyone talking about you snagging Miss High and Mighty?" She giggled. "No."

"Then the rumor mill is in high gear. Good."

Sobering, she plucked at a loose thread on the couch back. "When you say it like that... A lot of people think she's stuck-up, but she isn't, not really. She's always fair and she takes care of people. Most of the staff don't even realize how much she does for them. She lets the colonel take credit for all the benefits.'' She walked her fingers along the sofa cushion. ''You must think I'm pretty mean.''

''Nah.''

''Really?'' Her big eyes shone with hopefulness.

''You're okay in my book.''

''You want to know the truth?'' She peered at her sister who now spoke to the maître d'. ''Sometimes I am mean. I can't help it. She—she intimidates me. She's so smart and organized. I always feel like a little kid around her.'' She wrinkled her nose. ''I'm a ditz.''

''A charming ditz.''

''Oh, yeah?'' She picked a piece of lint off his shoulder. ''So when you aren't working, what's your preference? Perfection or ditziness?''

He trod dangerous waters here. Rousting Pinky was challenging enough without getting embroiled in a war between sisters. ''You know what they say about opposites attracting.''

She pushed upright and smoothed a hand over her mane of hair. He imagined any man she seriously set her sights on was a goner. ''All right, I get it. Good luck, then.''

''You don't think I stand a chance with Janine?''

''It'll be fun finding out.''

He agreed. ''So does anyone seem upset about me and Janine?''

Mischievousness lit up her eyes. ''Cody.''

''The head wrangler?''

''He's been trying to work up the nerve to ask her out for years. He's acting pretty grouchy today.''

It was unlikely that a man in his forties, well acquainted with Janine, would begin stalking her. But stranger things had happened. He mustered an image of the tough-looking cowboy with the waxed handlebar mustache. He'd seemed friendly enough when Janine introduced him earlier today. ''What did he say?''

She lifted a shoulder in a coy shrug. "Something about you being a worthless city boy."

"I've been called worse. What about Marie Padillo?"

"What about her?"

"Has she ever said anything to you about Janine?"

She laughed and clapped a hand over her mouth. "You think Pinky is a woman? No way! Besides, Marie is madly in love with Steve Woods, even though they fight all the time."

"Were they fighting today?"

"Probably. Her roommate said Marie didn't leave the dorm today. That usually means they're fighting." She searched his eyes. "Is Pinky a woman?"

"We don't know."

She shuddered. "Gross."

"I better go. Keep your ears open." He stuck his hands in his pockets and strolled over to where Janine waited. He slid an arm around her waist and felt her stiffen.

The maître d' led them to a table next to the wide expanse of windows that offered a view of the deck and the forest beyond. Tiny white lights strung in trees complemented the clear night sky. The view enchanted him. Living here, away from the city, surrounded by nature, would be heaven.

"You and Kara seem to have hit it off." Her clenched fists rested atop her unopened menu.

"She's a cute kid. What do you recommend?"

"I recommend you remember you have a job to do, and it doesn't include slobbering all over my sister!"

He bit down hard on his lower lip. When the urge to bray laughter passed he smiled gently. "I meant, what do you recommend for dinner?"

Her face reddened. Not even the scratch on her forehead detracted from her incredible beauty. He imagined that even if she were to wear goatskins and plaster herself with mud, she'd still be beautiful. "The trout is excellent," she said quietly.

The table was small enough that it was no stretch for him to place a hand over hers. In his peripheral vision he noted the attention servers paid them. "Tell me about your head wrangler."

"Cody?" She sounded bewildered. "What about him?"

"Kara says he's none too happy about me being here. He doesn't like me horning in."

"Don't be absurd. He's been working for us since we bought the resort. Besides, you said Pinky is young. Cody is forty-five." She canted her head, a sweetly appealing gesture.

His heart did a flip-flop. He wished they were sharing an intimate dinner in her room.

"You were talking to Kara about Pinky?"

"She seems to know everything going on around here. She's a good source."

"She tends to exaggerate. There is nothing going on between me and Cody. I've never dated a staff member, and I never will."

"Do you ask the staff not to fraternize with each other?"

"That's impossible."

"I gathered that. We can pull Marie off the shortlist. She's involved in a relationship with Steve Woods."

Her raised eyebrows said it was news to her. It occurred to him Janine might be lonely. By discouraging intrusions into her private life, she discouraged intimacies.

During dinner—the trout was excellent, as she promised—she seemed distracted. She answered when he asked questions, but did nothing to encourage a conversation. He studied employees. The window glass did a good job of reflecting the activity behind him. He pretended to admire the view while he observed servers and busboys, who all seemed to be too busy to pay much attention to him.

When they left the restaurant, he heard music in the ballroom. Over the sound of people talking and moving around on the wooden floor he discerned the twang of an acoustic guitar, the mellower notes of a bass guitar and the sing-song wail of a fiddle.

"Dancing will really drive Pinky crazy," he said. Holding her close would drive him crazy. He'd like to sit by the fireplace and coax her into laughing again.

"I'm tired and I still have paperwork to finish." Her lips curled in a tight smile. "But if you really want to hear Kara sing, go ahead. I'll be perfectly fine on my own for an hour or so."

His inner radar pinged. She was definitely jealous of her little sister.

On the way to her room she stopped in her office to pick up paperwork. He gathered the files for the employees he had put on the shortlist. She also entered a storeroom and fetched a fat bundle of white terry cloth. When they reached her room she gave him the bundle.

"In case you get cold," she said.

He shook out a robe emblazoned with the Elk River logo. "I hardly ever get cold," he said. "But thanks. Mind if I use your phone? I have some business to take care of."

"Help yourself." She disappeared into the bathroom and shut the door.

He took advantage of her absence to shuck his boots, sweater and jeans. She'd allotted him a space in her closet. While he hung up his clothes he couldn't help admiring her belongings. Sleek suits in natural linen, wool, silk and cotton. Soft blouses. Tailored trousers. She preferred warm reds and golds and yellows. Many of the suits were red. Her taste ran to classic lines and exquisite tailoring. He wondered what she'd look like in a slinky little dress and high heels.

Or just high heels and pearls. Now there was an image guaranteed to keep him up all night.

He pulled on the robe. Heavy and warm, it felt as soft

as lambswool against his skin. He called his assistant. She filled him in on what had happened at the office in the past few days, which was mostly nothing. He gave her the names and social security numbers of the people on the shortlist and asked her to run a thorough background check on each one. Janine had checked references and criminal records, but he possessed the means to delve more deeply into personal lives.

Janine came out of the bathroom while he was on the phone and shot him a disapproving glare. The robe had fallen open, revealing red silk boxer shorts. He suppressed a grin. The boxers covered more skin than most bathing suits. He suspected the real reason for her disapproval had something to do with the fleece sweat suit she insisted on wearing to bed.

She said nothing, however, as she worked at a computer. He studied files until his vision blurred and he was yawning. He made up a bed on the couch, assured her the light wouldn't bother him and peeled off the robe. He stretched out the kinks in his muscles. He was used to at least two hours of hard exercise a day. He'd go for a long run tomorrow and maybe make use of the lodge's small workout room.

Feeling eyes upon him, he turned around. Janine wore a peculiar, possibly dangerous expression. She shut down the computer, then rummaged in a dresser drawer.

Wondering what he'd done wrong this time, he said, "Good night."

She stomped into the bathroom.

He'd settled under the covers when she came out of the bathroom. She wore a pair of emerald satin tap pants and a matching camisole. The flimsy material ruffled with her every movement, caressing her curves like a flow of jeweled water. The tap pants were cut so high on the sides that when she leaned over the table to turn off the lamp he glimpsed the bewitching curve of her derriere. When she pulled back the bedcovers, her full breasts swayed, unfettered and tempting, the points of her nipples poking against the satin.

"Good night, Mr. Tucker. Sleep well." She turned out the bedside lamp.

Though robbed of the view, her image was burned on his retinas. Heat flooded his groin and even the baggy boxers were suddenly, uncomfortably, much too tight.

If Pinky were to kill him right now, it could only be considered an act of mercy.

VOICES AWAKENED DANIEL. Snapped to alertness, he slid a hand beneath the pillow and folded his fingers around the grip of the 9 mm. Eyes wide, he stared toward the source and realized the door was open. Pale light from the hallway formed a shining corona around Janine's hair.

"...let me put some clothes on." She spoke in a whisper.

A man replied, but his voice was too soft for Daniel to discern exactly what he said. Adrenaline charged his senses. Pistol in hand he sat up on the sofa. He'd spent much of the night tossing and turning in a vain attempt to relax despite the torment of thwarted sexual desire. Still, he cursed himself for not hearing the knock on the door that had roused Janine.

"He's sleeping," she said, then chuckled. "On the couch, Colonel. Don't get all ferocious because of him. We have a strictly business relationship."

Daniel relaxed and lowered the pistol. He groped on the floor next to him, found the fluffy robe and worked it over his arms.

The words didn't come through, but their affection for each other did. Daniel initiated all calls and visits to his father, but only rarely, since his father had no true interest in his children. Eavesdropping on such a loving bond gave Daniel an ache like an empty tooth socket.

"I'm awake," he called. He turned on a nearby lamp.

Janine stepped aside and her father entered the room. The colonel was dressed in crisply pressed wool trousers and a ribbed British army sweater.

"I didn't mean to wake you." She clutched the lapels of her satin robe closed over her throat.

"Don't worry about me." Daniel swung his legs off the sofa, but made sure the robe covered him adequately before he stood up. Despite the early hour the colonel looked as crisp and fresh as his clothing, with every hair in place, his face clean shaven and his eyes alert. Daniel jerked a knot into the robe's tie. "Good morning, sir. Is there a problem?"

For a few seconds the old man stared at the sofa. "I do not approve of this arrangement."

Daniel bit back a smart-aleck reply about how he himself didn't approve of sleeping on the couch when he'd rather be sleeping with Janine. When he was certain nothing stupid would emerge, he said, "I understand your concern, sir, but this is a necessary tactic."

"The troops are gossiping. It's affecting morale."

Janine tossed Daniel a warning look, and he clamped his mouth shut. She placed a hand on her father's arm. "It's not affecting job performance."

The colonel stared at a spot above and beyond his daughter's head. "Your mother is concerned. She didn't sleep well last night."

Daniel lowered his face to hide a grin. The old man wouldn't, or perhaps couldn't, come out and say he was afraid for Janine. He didn't seem like the affectionate type, and perhaps didn't know how to say he loved his children. His love for her shone through, anyway. This family had peculiar dynamics. They appeared to respect each other's privacy, but they were close. He couldn't help comparing it to his own family, where narcissism was the rule rather than the exception.

"I'll talk to Mom."

"Mr. Tucker is the reason I'm here."

"Oh?" He wondered if he was about to get canned. He hoped not. If he left now Pinky's self-confidence would soar, and God only knew what kind of nastiness he'd pull to get rid of the colonel.

"Do you own a new Chevy Tahoe? Silver in color?"

New was an understatement. The Tahoe still carried temporary tags. A sick sensation settled in his belly. "Yes, sir. What about it?"

"Mike discovered some vandalism in the parking lot."

"What kind of vandalism?"

"The full extent of the damage is difficult to note in the darkness. Mike claims the tires are slashed. There might be some damage to the paint as well."

Muttering cusswords under his breath, Daniel grabbed clothing. He rushed into the bathroom to dress. When he came out the colonel had left. Janine's face skewed in apology. Seeing her twisting her hair in agitation, his anger faded. If this was Pinky's doing, then Pinky deserved his wrath.

He playfully ruffled her tousled hair. "It's just a truck. Don't sweat it. Get dressed. I'll wait for you."

Mike Downes waited for them in the lobby. Having received special permission from the sheriff to make an authority presence while working off duty, he wore a uniform. He handed a nine-volt flashlight to Daniel and asked for the tag number of his Tahoe. When Daniel told him, the deputy nodded in confirmation. Before the man turned away, Daniel caught a grim smile. The deputy probably thought Daniel got exactly what he deserved.

Outside, the air seemed to freeze in Daniel's throat. Great plumes of steamy breath marked each exhalation. Cold crept beneath his heavy coat and prickled his jeans-clad legs. Tall lamps illuminated the parking lot, but pitched the shadows into utter blackness. Daniel followed a flashlight beam around the Tahoe. All four tires were as flat as deflated balloons. He crouched by a rear wheel. The rubber gaped, showing shredded steel belting, as if it had been attacked by an ax. Small chunks of tire rubber littered the ground.

"I'm so sorry." Janine ran her fingertips over scratches on the paint.

Somebody—Pinky—had used a piece of sharp metal to mar the silver paint. Long scratches ran the length of the body. The windshield and windows were smashed and spiderwebbed with cracks. Even the side mirrors had been destroyed.

"Hey," Mike called. He aimed a flashlight on the Tahoe's hood. "Look at this."

Gouged into the paint so deeply that bits of metal curled from the wounds were the words: "I will kill you."

"When did you find this?" Daniel asked as irony pinged him. He'd wanted a challenge. He couldn't think of anything more challenging than a sneaky, vicious, truck-trashing nut. Anger crawled through his guts. He stared at the crudely etched message; he could practically smell the rage behind the death threat. Pinky needed only to take a baby step to wreak this kind of damage against a human being.

He suddenly wanted Janine away from here. He knew she'd never leave.

"The colonel ran the plate number. When it didn't belong to a registered guest, I figured it might be yours." Mike whistled appreciatively.

"You're quite the junior detective," Daniel muttered, earning a scowl from the deputy. "So how did Pinky figure out this was my truck? Print out a list of registered guests and prowl through the lot until he found a car not on the list?" He turned a slow circle, shining the flashlight on other vehicles. A cursory inspection didn't reveal any untoward damage to nearby tires, windshields or paint jobs.

Janine hugged herself and shivered. "He must have seen you. You got something from the truck yesterday."

"Oh, yeah, my sunglasses." A spot began to itch between his shoulder blades. The itch climbed his neck and tightened his scalp. He imagined Pinky hiding nearby, enjoying the reaction to his handiwork. If the little creep wanted a show, he was about to get one. He spun on Janine. "This is a brand-new truck!"

She jumped as if he'd poked her with a stick.

He flung his hands in the air and stomped in a furious circle. He slammed a hand against the hood. The clang echoed in the still air. "It's got less than a thousand miles on it!"

"Cut it out," Mike said. "This isn't Janine's fault."

"Who's fault is it, then?" He kept stomping and pounding the truck. "I've got a five-hundred-dollar insurance deductible! Who's gonna pay for that?" He poked at her chest with a rigid finger. "You said it would be just fine parked out here. What kind of a two-bit operation are you running, anyway?"

Mike grabbed Daniel's arm. He'd been expecting it, but the deputy's strength surprised him. Mike's fingers were like steel clamps, biting into his biceps. Daniel allowed the deputy to drag him away from Janine.

"If I wanted my truck trashed, I could have left it in the city."

"One more word and I'm cuffing you." Even in the deceptive light offered by the parking lot lights there was no mistaking the genuinely ferocious anger on the deputy's face.

Janine chuffed harshly. Frozen breath swirled before her face. Without a word she turned and stalked away.

Daniel could have groaned. He'd expected her to realize what he was doing and play along. He whispered, "Get a clue, Sergeant."

Mike growled an obscenity and shook Daniel's arm.

Daniel offered no resistance, but went with the flow and

let the deputy's shaking tug him in close. Again he whispered. "Pinky's watching. Say something official."

The deputy stopped shaking him. "Huh?"

"Pinky is watching." He spoke slowly, making certain to enunciate every syllable.

Mike dropped his hold.

"I'm going to hit you," Daniel whispered. "Lock me down against the truck. Just do it." He waited until he sensed the deputy understood. "You stupid hick cop! Aren't you even smart enough to guard a parking lot?" He shoved Mike's shoulder.

Daniel had time for a lone thought—*don't need to play so rough*—before Mike had him by the coat, spun about and slammed against the Tahoe's hood. A burly forearm pressed down hard on the back of his neck. His cheek burned against the frozen metal. If it looked as real as it felt, then Pinky should be impressed.

"Do you see someone?" Mike asked against Daniel's ear.

"No, but I bet he's watching." The gear on the deputy's Sam Browne belt dug painfully into Daniel's backside. The deputy played his role with obvious relish. "Give me a warning, then head for your car. See if anyone follows me."

"Got it." In a louder voice, Mike said, "I ought to haul you in for assaulting an officer. Seeing how you're Janine's friend, I'll let you off with a warning."

"Yeah, yeah, get off me." The pressure eased on his neck and Daniel staggered upright.

Mike had his nightstick out. He used it to gesture threateningly at Daniel's belly. "You remember who you're talking to, boy. When you cool off, call me. I'll take the report about your truck."

"Whatever you say. *Sir.*" He stomped across the parking lot, his boots crunching gravel. The sensation of being watched grew stronger. Pinky could be hiding anywhere—

maybe holding the ax, knife or metal shard he'd used on the truck. He slipped a hand inside his coat and fingered the Luger.

The heat of the lobby struck him as soon as he stepped inside. So did the quiet. He could hear people inside the restaurant preparing the dining room for another day, but the lobby and lounge were empty, and the registration desk was deserted. He resisted looking behind him. He prayed Mike spotted Pinky lurking in the parking lot.

Daniel found Janine in her office. The door stood wide open, and she sat behind her desk. As soon as he walked in, she stood and thrust a slip of paper at him.

Something other than anger burned in her violet eyes— hurt. He shut the door. He noted she handed him a personal check, with her name printed on it, made out to him in the amount of five hundred dollars. "What's this?"

"Your deductible."

No amount of warning helped. He laughed. She dropped onto her chair as if her legs were cut from beneath her. He made himself cough to kill the laughter, and swung his head from side to side.

"Do you think this is funny? Humiliating me in front of Mike like that?" She pointed at the door. "Go laugh somewhere else."

"I should have warned you," he said. "I like to improvise."

"Pardon?"

"I don't give a rat's behind about the truck." Not exactly true. He'd been salivating over owning the big, four-wheel-drive sport utility vehicle ever since the model first appeared on the market. He'd waited four months for the custom-outfitted truck and had picked it up from the dealer only a week ago. "I was yelling for Pinky's benefit. I think he was watching us."

Comprehension dawned, and her mouth went slack. "I thought you were angry."

"Not at you." He touched fingers to the still-burning flesh on the back of his neck. "If it's any consolation, your buddy roughed me up pretty good. So why didn't you yell back?"

She toyed with a pen, practically bending it in half. "I thought you were acting unreasonable."

Insight into her conflicted personality struck him. By nature she was hotheaded and passionate, but she wanted to be calm, cool and collected. Public scenes revealing her true nature pained her. "I assumed you knew I was pretending. Sorry."

That charming, becoming blush appeared on her cheekbones. Even in jeans and a sweatshirt, with messy hair and not a trace of makeup, she was so beautiful it hurt his heart. He envisioned her wearing emerald silk under her jeans. He longed to kiss and make up with her.

She'd probably slug him if he tried.

"Mike is watching the lot now to see if anyone followed me into the lodge." He leaned both hands on the desk. "I absolutely do not blame you for Pinky trashing my truck." He tossed the check in her direction. "And don't worry about the deductible. It's covered."

The telephone rang. Janine answered. She nodded then handed the phone to Daniel. "It's Mike. He's calling from his car."

Daniel put the phone to his ear. "See anything?"

"Nobody followed you into the lodge. I've driven four times through the lot and around front, too, but I didn't see anybody."

"I could swear he was watching us. Is there any activity at all?"

"Over by the stables, but there's no one hanging around just doing nothing. I repeat, Mr. Tucker, what you're doing is idiotic. This Pinky fellow means business. You'll end up with a bullet in your back and never know what hit you."

Despite the harsh words, the deputy didn't sound as hostile as before.

"If you have a better idea, I'm willing to listen. Just remember, if Pinky chases me out of here, he'll go right back to obsessing about the colonel."

"You might be right. I'll put in a call and send another deputy out to take a report on the truck damage. Got to warn you, without a witness the chances of proving Pinky did this are about zero."

"Don't I know it." He knew more than most people how difficult it was to connect property vandalism to a specific perpetrator. Stalkers generally knew it, too. Which was why they often vented their rage against their victims' personal belongings. His stalker had periodically trashed his home. When she couldn't get inside, she threw rocks through windows and vandalized his garden. Once, she'd used red paint to scrawl obscenities on his car.

"I'm going to tell the state cops about this," Mike continued. "They might find something to tie in with the arson. Not much chance of that happening, either, but they've got the equipment to pursue it."

"Anything that works."

"Do the Dukes a favor and get your truck towed out of the lot ASAP. No need to upset guests with Pinky's love note."

"I'll get right on it. Here's Janine." Daniel handed her the telephone.

Janine's side of the conversation consisted of monosyllables. Judging by her expression, the deputy upset her. After she hung up, she said, "Mike spent the whole night patrolling the resort. He kept an eye on the dorm. He didn't see anything out of the ordinary."

"He's only one man and this is a big resort. Pinky knows you hired off-duty cops. Don't ever think he's stupid."

"He's treating us like we're stupid."

"That's his problem."

"Mike says you're a screwball."

He gave the comment a moment of consideration. "Some people think so. I prefer *unconventional*."

The corners of her mouth twitched, and her eyes softened. "And a hotdogger."

"Guilty as charged."

A real smile appeared on her lovely face, and Daniel wanted to sigh. He resisted voicing a seductive comment.

"He says I'm crazy for allowing you to do what you're doing."

"That's up to you to decide."

Her gaze turned inward. Her slender fingers tip-tapped on the desk. The smile faded. Mauve shadows marred the tender flesh beneath her eyes, and the scratch stood out like a paint smear on her pale forehead. "I've wasted a year denying the effect Pinky has had on me. I used to enjoy getting mail, but now I dread it. I've always trusted people to do their jobs. Going around scared and suspicious all the time is killing me."

He intuited rising self-blame. He knew the pain of the myriad what-ifs and if-onlys. "Pinky isn't your fault. You did nothing to encourage him."

"If I'd done something when he sent the first letter—"

"Like what? Erect a billboard telling him to leave you alone? Buy spots on the radio? He set it up so there isn't anything you can do."

"If we make him too angry, won't he go after my father anyway?"

Her primary concern was always for her father. All his life he'd wished for someone who cared that much about him. He wanted this fierce, complex, vulnerable woman to care about him. "Your father is safe as long as Pinky is worrying about me."

"Does it count if I worry about you?"

He patted the center of his chest. "I happen to think I'm pretty tough. Nobody is chewing up my hide without a fight."

Chapter Seven

"No, no, Mrs. Rowe," Janine said into the telephone. "Family is more important than the job. We'll miss Phil, but we'll survive. He needs to be with you right now."

Daniel pretended not to listen to her conversation. Her kind tone drew him. No tough girl now, but a compassionate employer concerned about her employee.

She chuckled softly. "I know he's worried about leaving us shorthanded. Tell him to call his supervisor in a few days. Don't worry about his paycheck or his job. I understand about emergencies. You take care of yourself, all right? I hope your husband gets to feeling better soon."

She hung up and sighed. "We can eliminate Phil Rowe as a suspect. His father had a heart attack. He left the resort yesterday evening. Hand me his file, please." She opened the folder and made another call. She ordered flowers sent to his parents' address.

"That's two down." She made a frustrated noise and eyed him expectantly.

Another suspect, a housekeeper, had twisted her ankle last night while dancing. Her supervisor had taken her to the emergency room. Unless she'd somehow managed to vandalize the Tahoe while hobbling on crutches and doped-up on painkillers, Daniel felt satisfied she wasn't Pinky. He wished he could narrow the suspect list further.

Daniel joined the family in the private dining room for lunch. The meal consisted of leek soup, turkey salad and crusty whole-grain rolls still warm from the oven. As Daniel ate the delicious food he warned himself to watch out or he'd gain twenty pounds during his stay at Elk River. He still hadn't taken his run or worked out in the gym.

Elise and Kara fussed over him, expressing their fear about the death threat carved into the Tahoe's paint job. The colonel assured him that the resort would pay for the damage. Daniel liked the attention; he liked this family. He especially liked the way Janine planted herself between him and her sister.

"I'll include the damages in my final bill to Janine." He smiled blandly at her. When she ignored him he guessed she hadn't informed her family about their barter deal. He savored the idea of vacationing in the Honeymoon Hideaway—with Janine wearing jewel-colored lingerie while bathing him in champagne.

Keeping an eye on the open doorway, he lowered his voice. "I've narrowed the list of suspects to seven." The family leaned toward him, listening intently. "Brian Cadwell, Devon Hightower, Jill Pruett, Ellen Schulberg, Lanny Lewis, Craig Johnson and Jason Bulshe. Any comments?"

Elise looked confused. "Can you explain why you believe they are suspects? They're all pleasant, hardworking young people. We haven't had a speck of trouble from any of them."

"Yeah." Kara wrinkled her nose. "That's a weird list."

"First off, understand these are the most *likely* suspects. Pinky could prove to be an exception."

"Why these particular people?" Elise asked.

"First, they are all new hires. All of them are single—"

"Jill isn't," Kara said. "I mean, she isn't married, but she is engaged. She's got a ring and everything. Her boyfriend has visited a couple times. I've met him. He works in Cripple Creek."

"Good, we're down to six." He crossed Jill Pruett's name off the list. "Anyone else?" When everyone remained silent, he continued. "All of them list Colorado Springs addresses before working here. All of them are under twenty-five years old."

"Isn't that rather discriminatory, Daniel?" Elise chided gently. "Young people have such a bad reputation these days. I believe it is undeserved."

"Pinky definitely suffers from an antisocial personality disorder. He could be a full-blown sociopath. The behavior shows up early. He may have stalked another victim, or committed other crimes. He may have a drug or alcohol abuse problem. That none of your employees has a criminal record tells me he isn't old enough to have been caught. Unfortunately, I don't know a legal way to check juvenile records. The authorities may or may not find a sympathetic judge to unseal the records. We can't depend on that happening."

He waited for other questions or objections. "All the suspects hold unskilled jobs that require minimum contact with the public. The people in maintenance and housekeeping have free run of the lodge. Devon Hightower, in the stable, and Brian Cadwell, in the kitchen, are more restricted. I included them because they're new and so probably spend a lot of time running errands and fetching supplies."

"Have you given this list of suspects to the police?" Elise asked.

"I have."

"None of them are crazy," Kara said.

"Understand, personality disorders, even sociopathy, don't make people insane. That Pinky managed to get hired and conceal his identity tells me he's extremely high-functioning. He may have so compartmentalized his life that he's totally unfazed by the cops. If he's a sociopath then he understands he'll get in trouble if he's caught, but he doesn't believe his actions are wrong. He's an effective liar.''

"Based upon what you're telling us," the colonel said, "is there enough evidence to muster out this group of people?"

"We can't even consider that, dear," Elise said. "It would be unwarranted and unfair for all of them to suffer for the actions of one."

Janine nodded in agreement. "It wouldn't solve the problem, anyway." She glanced at Daniel and he urged her to continue. "Losing his job might slow him down, but it won't stop him. Plus, it'll give him that much more reason to hate you, Colonel."

"Then he might burn down the lodge." Kara darted nervous glances at the door. "But, Daniel, it can't be anyone on your list. They're all so...normal. They're nice. Well, except for Devon." She made a disgusted face. "I can't understand him when he talks. He's so shy it's pathetic."

Daniel made a note of her comment. "What I want is for Janine to hold a meeting with these employees."

"Will Pinky confess?" Kara asked.

"I doubt it," Daniel replied. "I want to see their reactions. Pick up some clues."

Janine shook her head as if chasing flies. "I can't hold a staff meeting with you present. It's unprofessional."

He quirked an eyebrow.

The colonel cleared his throat. "We have a specific SOP, Daniel."

"What's that?"

"Standard operating procedure," Elise translated. "This is an exception, dear. It falls outside our policy manuals."

"Way outside." Daniel touched the side of Janine's hand with the tip of his little finger. He tried to tell her with his eyes that he understood her reluctance to make her personal life public. And he was sorry. "We'll put the onus on me. I'll play the bad guy. Maybe I can provoke a reaction."

"How do I justify accusing these six?"

He leaned his chin on a fist and mulled over what would really drive Pinky crazy. The stalker knew he'd broken the law and could go to jail. He wished he had Pinky's correspondence back from the police. As cagey as the stalker was about concealing his identity, he revealed pieces of himself in his writing. Rage was the key, but there was something else, too.

"Well?" Janine freshened his coffee cup. "What's your big plan?"

It hit him. Pinky believed Janine knew his identity. In his deluded state, he thought they shared a secret. Shattering the illusion should rattle Pinky's cage.

"I'll do the accusing. I'll play the jerk boyfriend and you play the eager-to-please cupcake trying to make me happy at Pinky's expense. It'll drive him nuts."

"It'll never work," Janine said. "All you'll accomplish is offending valuable, *innocent* employees. And if you think finding good workers willing to live so far from the city is easy, think again. We're understaffed as it is."

"They'll be offended by me, not you. You have to do something else. You have to make it clear you do not know who Pinky is."

"But I don't know."

"He thinks otherwise. If I had the letters, I could show you what I mean. I have a hunch that by double-teaming him, we can make him angry enough to reveal himself. You have to convince him you aren't on his side."

"That won't be difficult."

The colonel stirred his coffee so hard that the spoon rattled the cup. "I do not approve of this tactic."

"I don't, either," Elise said. She held up a hand as if to ward off interruptions. "But I understand where Daniel is going with this." Her calm gaze touched each person before settling on Daniel. "Will he attack you? Or attack Janine?"

A stalker's greatest weapon: fear of making him angry. Stalking and harassment were as much mental and emotional crimes as they were physical. He understood the family's reluctance. They were nice people who played by the rules. They couldn't comprehend the stalker's mental processes. "I'm prepared for that eventuality, ma'am. If he gets physical, I will stop him."

The colonel harrumphed louder and more grumpily than before. Before he could object, Janine spoke. "All right. You know what you're doing, Daniel, so I have to trust you. I'll set up the meeting."

Feeling good about the possibility of forcing Pinky into tipping his hand, Daniel strolled out of the dining room. He slid an arm around Janine's waist. She shoved his arm away. She walked quickly, her heels snapping like gun shots. He lengthened his stride to keep up with her.

"You just love the sound of your own voice, don't you?"

He lifted an eyebrow at her non sequitur. "Doesn't everybody?"

"No."

He caught her arm. She half stumbled before catching her balance, but he maintained his hold. "You're mad at me again."

She averted her gaze. Her lower lip pushed out, very young and very kissable. He wished he could take her away from here. Someplace with a beach and fruity drinks and glorious sunsets.

"I'm not mad at you." She spoke softly, for his ears only. "I'm just...angry."

"Pinky's really screwing up your life. I understand."

The anger seemed to drain from her face and body, leaving her with slumped shoulders. Moisture shone in her eyes and her chin trembled. He guided her toward her office. Without a word she unlocked the door and entered. She went to the watercooler, but made no move to fill a cup.

Instead she stood with her back to Daniel, her head lowered, her body perfectly still.

He wanted to comfort her, but instinct said she needed privacy to pull herself together.

Finally she sighed and turned around. "How did you stand it when you were stalked? How did you cope? I'm finding it harder and harder to leave my room. I have nightmares. I want to scream at people. Everyone looks guilty."

He perched on the corner of her desk. Her office was too utilitarian, he decided. She needed some toys to liven the place up. Or a nice philodendron in a colorful pot. "My problem was the opposite of yours. My life's an open book. If you want to know something, just ask. When she started stalking me I talked to her, but attention reinforced her delusion. My family blamed me for encouraging her. So did my friends. The cops showed more hostility toward me than toward her. Everyone was a critic. I'm too friendly, I flirt too much, I lead women on. I send mixed signals."

"I bet that hurt."

"What hurt the most was the guilt. I began second-guessing everything I did or said. I felt isolated. Trapped. I didn't know who my friends were. When she committed suicide, I blamed myself. It took me a long time to get angry over the way she manipulated me. Mental illness aside, she knew exactly what she was doing. She had no right."

"Is that why you keep reminding my father how Pinky isn't my fault?"

"I'm reminding *you*. Stalkers get away with their crimes because it's so hard for people to realize who the real victim is." He held out a hand. As if tugged by a string she approached and laid her slender hand on his palm. He folded his fingers over hers. "I don't want anybody to suffer the way I suffered. Nobody should ever feel that alone, or that helpless."

"I am glad you're helping me." She lifted her gaze. Her

violet eyes were sad. "You're not an easy man to work with."

He stroked her fine skin with his thumb. Visions of her wearing green satin lingerie filled his imagination, then faded behind more vivid images of her smiling and happy and glad to be alive. Images he yearned to make reality. "I'm a nice guy."

"With an ulterior motive."

He nodded earnestly. "As soon as I get rid of Pinky, I'm going to work on you."

She jerked her hand away from his.

"I'm not making a pass." He showed his palms in a gesture of innocence. "I'm not being crude. But if you'll take the time to get to know me, you'll like me."

"Like you?"

"And more." He waggled his eyebrows. "Pardon the cliché, but this could be the start of a beautiful friendship."

Her luscious mouth curved in a tight, dangerous smile. She moved around the desk, each action deliberately taunting him. He followed the sway of her hips and the movements of her hands. She settled daintily on the chair and stroked a finger against a stray curl, brushing it away from her cheek. "You're wasting your time. I am not interested. My life is full. I have everything I want."

Maybe she didn't want to admit it, but she was definitely interested. He rested on an elbow, putting them at eye level. "Not interested at all?"

"Not in the slightest. You aren't my type." She reached past him. Her hand brushed his arm. He felt her heat through his sweater. His skin tingled.

"What is your type?"

"Not you." She pulled a stack of papers from the In-box. "Get off my desk."

"Tell me what your type is."

She plucked a pen from a holder and began reading an order form. She kept her gaze firmly on the paper, but Daniel knew she was aware of him. Faint color had appeared on her cheeks, and she exhaled loudly.

"You know I'm your type," he whispered. "You've been waiting for me all your life."

"Don't be absurd."

He pushed off the desk and sauntered to the couch. He flopped on the cushions and hooked his hands behind his neck. "You're thinking about me right now. I can tell."

"Of course I'm thinking about you. You will not shut up. So, please, be quiet."

With a prissy expression on her face, she wrote on the order form, folded it, inserted it in an envelope and sealed it. Her daintily flicking tongue turned him hot and cold inside. She affixed a stamp and a return address label. She began writing on the next sheet of paper, then frowned and scribbled on a scratch pad. Still prissy, she stuck the pen in the electric pencil sharpener.

Anguished grinding made her jerk the pen out of the sharpener.

"Good thing you aren't thinking about me," Daniel mused. "Might do something dumb."

JANINE SWALLOWED two aspirin neat. She suspected they wouldn't help. Curing her apprehension about the upcoming confrontation would take a lot more than over-the-counter analgesics. She downed the requisite glass of water and shifted on the chair. Paperwork spread out on the conference table demanded her attention, but her concentration was shot.

Not that she feared confrontations. Running Elk River smoothly and seeing to the comfort of occasionally difficult guests meant daily confrontations of some type or another. Over the years she'd grown adept at handling conflicts in a cool, even-handed manner. Business conflicts. Impersonal conflicts.

She checked her watch. The six employees on Daniel's suspect list would be arriving soon. Her temples throbbed.

Despite Daniel's arguments to the contrary, she did blame herself. If only she hadn't carelessly lost her Day-Timer...if only she'd aggressively ferreted out Pinky's identity when he first began sending letters and tapes...if only she had somehow recognized him before she hired him...if only she'd controlled her temper despite Les Shuemaker's provocation...if only she hadn't agreed to Daniel's crazy plan and angered Pinky so much that he'd burned down the garage.

Her bumbling threatened her father's life and her family's livelihood. How could she not feel guilty?

She especially hated being cornered into putting her private life on display. Within hours after this meeting everyone on staff would know about Pinky. She'd be the subject of gossip. Behind her back people would laugh and point fingers and delight in how Little Miss Perfect got her comeuppance.

She looked around the room. The lodge had three conference rooms; this was the smallest. With only one table and eight chairs, bare walls and every bank of fluorescent lights turned on, it looked rather forbidding. The flat carpeting did little to dampen noise. The sound of her breathing seemed to echo off the high ceiling.

"Head hurt?" Daniel asked.

Impotent anger and fear were giving her chronic headaches and perhaps an ulcer. She couldn't remember what feeling good felt like. "I'm okay."

She shuffled papers aimlessly. The anniversary party loomed, and she still had a zillion details to tend to. She needed to track down the cases of champagne she'd ordered, but which hadn't been delivered yet. The decorations weren't ready.

Throw Daniel Tucker with his sexy smiles and piercing copper eyes into the mix and her life was shot.

Damn him.

She did not like him. No way, no how. She didn't like pretty men. She didn't like flirts. She didn't like being pursued. She knew what he really wanted, a one-night stand. A hot, heavy, temporary tryst. Fun and games. After suffering nights of fantasizing about him in his fancy boxer shorts, he tempted her far more than she'd ever admit to anyone.

Double damn him.

As if he hadn't a care in the world, he lounged on a chair with his feet kicked up on a table. He played with a small wooden puzzle, twisting and turning the pieces in an attempt to shape it into a ball.

"All those aspirin will eat holes in your stomach," he said. "Do you get migraines?"

"No. It's probably my eyes. I think I need reading glasses."

He chuckled. "I had to get reading glasses last year, but they make me look like a nerd. I'm thinking about laser surgery."

His vanity bemused her. He treated his conceit like a joke.

The door opened and Jason Bulshe poked his head into the conference room. *Pinky?* Janine wondered as she beckoned for him to enter. In her nightmares Pinky looked like a lizard, dark and sly, never blinking, slithering through the shadows. Craig Johnson, Ellen Schulberg and Brian Cadwell followed Jason into the room. Jason and Craig looked like typical Colorado ski bums with their longish hair, sunburned faces, baggy jeans and cock-of-the-walk athleticism. Brian was dark, short and pudgy as if he freely sampled the goodies he helped create in the kitchen. Ellen, still wearing her housekeeping uniform, nervously tucked strands of lank brown hair behind her ears.

All of them looked guilty. If one were Pinky and this

meeting enraged him, what kind of stunt would he pull to top arson and vandalism?

"Where is Lanny?" Janine asked. She glanced at her watch. "And Devon?"

"Lanny will be here in a sec, Ms. Duke," Craig said. "He's cleaning up."

"And Devon?"

The employees looked at one another. None offered an explanation for the wrangler's tardiness. Janine encouraged them to sit. She and Daniel had arranged it so the six would be seated directly across the table from her. Lanny Lewis hurried into the room. Tall and gangly, he stumbled on the carpet and blushed. His hands were damp and raw. Mumbling apologies, he sat at the table.

"We'll wait for Devon," Janine said.

Daniel dropped his feet to the floor, but he continued playing with the puzzle. The five young people fidgeted on the chairs. They looked as if they wanted to whisper to each other but didn't dare.

Devon arrived. Gaze fixed on the floor, hat in hand, he shuffled into the room. Skinny and long-legged, he wore tight jeans and square-toed boots crusted with mud. A clumsy, dirty-looking bandage bound his left hand. After he sat down, Janine asked about his hand.

He mumbled something and she caught the words ...*bit me.*

"Pardon?"

His cheeks turned crimson. His Adam's apple bobbed in his throat as he tucked his wounded hand beneath the table. "Got bit."

"A horse bit you?" Janine asked. She wanted to grab his collar and shake him.

The blush touched his ears.

"Let me see." Ellen reached for his hand. Devon nearly fell off the chair. The other young men laughed.

"That's enough," Janine said. Pity mingled with suspicion. "You make sure Cody sees that, Devon. If it needs medical attention, you get it."

He sank on the chair. A few more inches and he'd be under the table.

"Got bit, huh?" Daniel slammed the puzzle on the table. Pieces scattered. "Or maybe you cut it when you slashed my tires."

All heads swiveled toward Daniel. Even though Janine had known this was coming, Daniel's outburst shocked her, anyway. The man had missed his true calling. With his looks and his acting skills, he could be a major movie star.

"Yeah, you, cowboy. I'm talking to you. I'm talking to all of you. One of you creeps trashed my brand-new truck and I'm—"

"Daniel." Janine placed a hand on his arm. "Please, dear, I told you I would get to the bottom of this."

All the young men, with the exception of Devon who looked ready to crawl under the table, glared at Daniel. Ellen pressed a hand over her mouth.

"You better handle it, cupcake." He clamped his arms over his chest. His thin sweater strained over his powerfully muscled arms.

"This is my friend, Daniel Tucker—"

"Boyfriend," he interrupted. Mr. Charm had disappeared, replaced by an irritable oaf with a petulant scowl. "And *guest*."

She forced herself to speak. "As you may be aware, an employee is stalking me. He calls himself Pinky. For the past year he's been sending me letters and gifts. None of which I want or encourage. This person is responsible for setting the garage on fire and for vandalizing Daniel's truck. He's making threats. While he has deluded himself into believing I am flattered by the attention, I most assuredly am not. I think it's sick and disgusting. I want it to stop."

Brian Cadwell grasped the table edge with both hands. He blinked owlishly. "You think it's one of us?"

"*I* think it's one of you." Daniel jumped to his feet. His chair flew backward, and the table bucked with the force of his hands. "And once I get my hands on Pinky, I'm going to rip out his lungs. *After* he pays for the damages."

Like school kids facing a teacher throwing a temper tantrum, all six cringed wide-eyed and silent on their chairs.

Ellen fingered her brass name tag. "I don't even know what you're talking about."

"Is that so?" Daniel was poised as if about to leap over the table. "I want to know which one of you is sending my girlfriend love notes. Who cut the *love* note into my truck? Huh? Is it you, cowboy? Think you're cute?"

Devon's head quivered in what might be either a negative reply or sheer terror. Janine's heart ached with sympathy. Pain thudded like hoofbeats inside her skull.

"Now, Daniel," she said. "We aren't exactly accusing anybody. Please calm down, dear."

"I'll calm down when the little sneak shows some guts." His eyes flashed with coppery fire. He pointed at Jason. "Is it you, kid? I saw the way you were looking at Janine the other day."

Jason's mouth thinned to a white line.

Daniel swung his accusatory finger toward Craig. "Or you? Did you trash my truck? Are you harassing my girl?"

Time to play the good cop, she thought grimly. Janine caught Daniel's hand. His muscles flexed. "I told you I'd ask the questions. We can get to the bottom of this without a lot of shouting or making wild accusations."

"Fine. If some guy wants to play sixth-grader and send you mushy notes, I don't care. But trashing my truck? I want to know who did it." He righted the fallen chair and sat hard.

"You keep saying guy," Ellen said. She darted timid glances at Daniel. "Why am I here?"

"I saw a girl sneaking around in the parking lot the other morning. It looked like you." Daniel glared at the young woman. "*Just* like you."

Ellen shook her head hard. "It wasn't me, Ms. Duke! Honest! You can ask my roommate. I start shift at five o'clock in the morning. I was in my room all night."

"I was in my room, too," Brian exclaimed. "At least until three in the morning. That's when I start mixing bread dough. This isn't fair! You can't accuse us just because your boyfriend says so."

Lanny Lewis spoke up. "This is like being back in high school."

"Scraping up a truck is a high school thing to do," Daniel said. "Did you think keying cars is funny, kid?"

Lanny hugged his elbows and glared daggers at Daniel.

All of them were angry. Except for Devon Hightower. He stared at his boots, his expression mortified. "Okay, okay." She rapped the tabletop with her knuckles. "You're right, this isn't fair. But it is very serious. We're talking about crimes. Arson. The truck sustained thousands of dollars worth of damages. Do any of you know who might have done this? Have you heard anything?"

Daniel snorted disparagingly. "Why bother, cupcake? Pinky's a punk. He doesn't have the guts to step forward."

"We're not punks," Craig said. Hot spots of color flared on his cheeks and forehead. He rested his clenched fists on the table. "*I'm* not a punk."

"So what do you know?" Daniel shot back.

"Nothing!"

Ellen cleared her throat. "We can ask around. See if anybody knows who Pinky is. Right, guys? I mean, we're kind of like family here, right?" Her chin trembled and her voice turned watery. "You aren't going to fire anybody, are you?"

Craig snorted and flipped hair out of his face. "If you want to know something, Ms. Duke, you should just ask."

"I am asking. Do any of you know anything about Pinky?"

"No, ma'am."

"Uh-uh."

"No way."

"Not a clue."

"Nope."

Devon Hightower shook his head.

Janine looked to Daniel for guidance. Other than causing major embarrassment for everyone concerned, she didn't see how they were accomplishing anything.

Daniel draped an arm over her shoulders. "All I know is, somebody trashed my truck. I'm not going anywhere until I find out who did it. So if you know who Pinky is, tell him this for me. When I catch him I'm going to use his little pinhead to buff out every scratch on my Tahoe."

"Uh." Brian shifted on the chair. "How do you know Pinky even works here?" He slid a glance at Jason who sat next to him. "We got a lot of guests who are freaks. Snowboarders. They get kind of crazy."

"Hey!" Craig leaned over to see the chef's assistant. "Snowboarders aren't freaks. Fat mama's boys are the freaks."

Janine rapped on the table. "Be quiet. I know for a fact that Pinky works here. He, uh, he sends very personal letters. He acts as if we're well acquainted despite the fact that I have no idea who he is."

Daniel nudged her knee with his.

Continuing tore her up inside. It sounded so stupid. She sounded stupid. "I have never knowingly had any contact with him. I haven't the slightest interest in him on any level. I don't know why he is stalking me. I want it to end."

"He's pretty damned pathetic," Daniel said in aside. He hugged Janine so tightly she nearly slid off the chair. "I come here for a nice vacation, to spend some time with the woman I love, and what do I find? Some loser who doesn't even have the guts to look me in the face.''

"I'm really sorry,'' Ellen said. "About your truck and everything. But none of us did it. I didn't do it.''

"It doesn't make me happy to have to question you like this.'' Janine met the eyes of each employee in turn. Except for Devon. He refused to lift his head. His shyness was getting on her nerves. "I can't tolerate having a criminal on staff. It's reached a point where if there's another incident like the garage fire, we'll have to follow police recommendations and close the resort. Everyone could lose their jobs.''

"The cops want you to close Elk River?'' Brian looked stunned.

Is it you, Brian? she asked with her eyes. "It's for the safety of the guests.''

"I say shut the joint down, cupcake.'' He squeezed her shoulders. "You can come live with me. I'll take you on that cruise through the Greek islands you've always wanted.''

Craig relaxed, but rebellion glinted in his eyes. "Maybe some crime victims get what they deserve.''

"You got a problem with me, stud?'' Daniel sounded dangerous.

"I get paid to crank wrenches, not to listen to some rich dude whine about scratches on his fancy truck.''

"Got the hots for my girlfriend? Want to talk about it?''

"I ain't talking to you, man.'' Craig stood. "I don't get paid enough to take this crap off nobody.'' He stalked to the door and jerked it open. He paused as if waiting to be called back.

Janine opened her mouth, but Daniel nudged her knee again. She remained silent. Craig slammed the door behind him. The remaining employees shuffled and squirmed. Lanny cracked his knuckles, each pop like a tiny firecracker.

Brian raised his hand. The childish action made Lanny snicker. Ellen hid a grin behind her hand. Brian snatched his hand onto his lap.

"Yes, Brian?"

He leaned far over the table as if separating himself from the group. "Craig's a freak," he whispered. "He smokes dope when he goes snowboarding. Him and his room—"

Lanny punched Brian's shoulder. "Shut up, you little suck-up!"

"It's true!" Brian cried. He rubbed his shoulder. "I hear those guys talking all the time."

"That is enough," Janine said. Pinky or no Pinky, watching this bunch revert to sophomoric name calling and tattling was too much. "Unless one of you has some useful information, you may go."

Chapter Eight

Janine shoved Daniel's arm off her shoulders and dropped her forehead to the table. Imagined whispers rippled through the now quiet conference room: *Ms. Duke is crazy. Her boyfriend is crazy. She's mean and unfair and out of control.*

"That went well," Daniel said.

She turned her head enough to see him. "If you're the Marquis de Sade."

He patted her back. "We can eliminate Craig."

"Huh? I thought he'd be at the top of your list. I'm ready to fire him just for being rude."

"The kid's got an attitude problem, but he isn't Pinky."

She began gathering paperwork. The headache encircled her skull, squeezing her brain. Maybe it was a migraine. Maybe she had a brain tumor. Maybe an aneurysm bulged in her brain, soon to explode. "He looked like he was ready to start punching you. For all I know he's waiting for you right now."

"Pinky has only one hobby. That's you. Craig's a snowboarder. I bet if you talk to his friends they'll tell you he hits the slopes every chance he gets. Besides, Pinky isn't going to do anything he believes will make him look bad. No way would he walk out or threaten to quit."

"Oh." She hugged a fat manilla folder to her chest. "So I may have lost a perfectly good mechanic for nothing."

"I'll apologize to him." He smiled sweetly. "That is, if you want a dope-smoking freak on staff."

"You will apologize." It relieved her to have eliminated one person off the list of suspects. She made a mental note to talk to Juan about Craig's alleged marijuana smoking. She had a zero-tolerance policy regarding illegal drug usage. "So, O Great and Wise Daniel, what do your psychic powers tell you? Which one of them is Pinky?"

"I don't know."

Not the answer she wanted. "What about Devon?"

His eyebrows lifted in a facial shrug. "He's definitely got some problems, but the vibes felt wrong. He seemed blanked out. Not listening. Pinky would be paying more attention."

"I never see him hanging around inside the lodge. He doesn't eat with the other employees, or attend any of the activities. I don't think I've ever seen him in the east wing. Somebody would notice if they saw him sticking notes in my box."

"Devon makes a good suspect." He snorted. "But that Brian's a little weasel."

She pressed the back of a hand to her forehead. "No," she groaned. "You've met Chef. He's like a third-world dictator. Finding people willing to put up with his tantrums is next to impossible."

"Pinky would put up with a dictator in order to stay close to you. Has Brian ever approached you? Done or said anything that made you uncomfortable?"

"Never."

"Have any of them volunteered for extra duty? Offered to help you with a special project? Tried to be friends?"

"No." Realizing she sounded as if she operated out of an ivory tower, she made a sheepish face. "I don't encourage apple polishers. Except for Devon they all seem so normal. Even Craig.''

"Did you notice, Jason never said a word. Think he has something to hide?"

"At the moment everybody seems to be hiding something. But Jason?" She wrinkled her nose. "He's so cute. I bet he has dozens of girlfriends. He doesn't need to stalk me."

Daniel sat on the edge of the table and folded his arms. He cocked his head. His slight smile bugged her.

"What?"

"He's *cute?*"

"He's a very attractive boy. What's the matter, you don't like the competition?"

"Ha! This from a lady who hates being judged on her appearance. Kind of shallow, don't you think?"

She tapped her fingers against the folder. "I do not judge people by their appearance. And you're one to talk about being shallow. You've been judging me ever since we met."

"*Au contraire,* my charming Ms. Duke. Granted, I happen to think you're the most beautiful woman I've ever seen."

"Stop it." Whether she was speaking to him or warning herself not to respond she wasn't sure.

"And on a biological level, the attraction is powerful. But judge your character?" He shook his head. His eyes danced with coppery lights. "Not even close. Do you want to know what I think about your character?"

"No."

"Liar. You're dying to know."

"I am not. And I warn you, if you persist, then you're going to find out exactly what I think about your character."

His shoulders shook with silent laughter. "I know what

you think about me.'' He tapped himself on the nose. "What's the equivalent of a male bimbo? A him-bo?"

While it wasn't what she thought of him, it was what she *wanted* to think. She wanted to dismiss him as just a pretty face with nothing beneath the surface. She wanted to deny her attraction to him. Her own superficiality stung like a barb.

"I don't get women...if they don't think they're pretty, they wish they were pretty. If they are pretty, they want to be prettier. If they know they're pretty, they run around scared that no one takes them seriously because they're too pretty. Why not accept your looks and enjoy it? So what if the dummies don't take you seriously? What about all the people who do?"

"Our society objectifies women. TV, movies, magazines. Women only have worth when they fit societal standards of attractiveness."

"Bull."

"I've been subject to that kind of objectification all my life."

"Now you're a victim of society?"

His question made her feel like an idiot. She despised whiners who blamed everyone else—who blamed society— for their bad behavior. Seething with frustration, she squeezed "No" through her teeth.

"Your problem isn't the way you look. Your problem is attitude. And that chip you're lugging around on your shoulder makes me itch to knock it off."

"I don't need you analyzing me. And I am in no way challenging you. I hired you to solve a specific problem. I will thank you very much to stick to that problem and leave me alone."

"I thought you liked to argue."

"Not when my head is about to explode!" She turned abruptly, tripped over a chair leg and dropped the folder. Papers scattered. Eyes closed, head down, she stood with her arms locked at her sides and her fists clenched. Worse than sounding like an idiot, she acted like one.

Daniel gently grasped her shoulders and guided her onto a chair. Too weary to fight, she sat. He urged her to lower her chin to her chest. She made a small sound of protest.

"Relax." He began massaging the base of her skull. He worked his thumbs in small, slow circles. He used the pads of his fingers to firmly rub her scalp, but concentrated most of the pressure in his thumbs. He worked his way down her neck. As he probed the knots in her muscles, she couldn't help a groan. It hurt so good.

The knots loosened, and her skin warmed. He worked his hands behind her ears and over her scalp. Heaven. When he reached her temples she leaned her head back. The throbbing pain melted beneath his fingers. With a touch so light it almost tickled he massaged her eyebrows and the outer corners of her eyes.

"Feel good?" he asked.

"Umm-hmm."

"How's your headache?"

"Bearable." Along with being a movie star, he could also be a massage therapist. "Where did you learn how to do this?"

"Here and there. You ought to try my foot massages. Pure bliss."

She opened her eyes and found him looming over her. Such a lovely mouth with a full lower lip. Such lovely eyes.

While using his nails to lightly scratch her scalp he eased around her. He maintained eye contact, and though her eyelids lowered in pure pleasure, she watched him, too. Fullness seeped into her belly. His fingers slid over her ears. He cupped her face in both hands. He lowered his face to hers, but paused. Slight trembling reverberated through his palms.

She wanted him to kiss her. He wanted to kiss her. He

hovered so close she smelled him. That he awaited her permission left her giddy with strange power.

Reason said rebuff him. Reason said he was just like every other horny male who treated her like a toy.

Reason and Daniel Tucker failed to compute. "Are you going to stand there like an idiot?" she asked. "Or kiss me?"

"And have you thinking I'm crude?" He straightened, withdrawing his hands, slowly, agonizingly over her cheeks. He picked up fallen papers.

With her mouth hanging open, she watched him acting as if their little interlude hadn't meant a thing. She wanted to slap him. But that would mean rising from the chair, and she didn't trust her knees to support her. He tucked the papers into the folder and handed it to her. She took it automatically.

Arguments formed, but all sounded stupid in her head.

"Something wrong?" he asked.

Only everything. She couldn't believe she asked him to kiss her—she couldn't believe he refused! "Did we accomplish anything today?"

He frowned thoughtfully. "I now know you're a sucker for a good massage."

Paper crunched in her fingers. His grin widened. Arrogant tease, she thought. He enjoyed her discomfiture far too much.

"Our suspect list is down to five. Pinky is on notice that if he tries any more vandalism he could lose his job and you. Plus, he knows who his real enemy is. Me." He winked. "Nice touch about me taking you to Greece, eh?"

"Lovely." His comment spooked her. In all her world travels, she'd never visited the Greek islands. Visiting Greece was her dream vacation. Either he'd made a lucky guess, or he actually was psychic.

She rose and took a moment to straighten her blazer and

regain her composure. Looking directly at him proved impossible. "What do we do now?"

"Pinky needs some time to digest this. Telling him he really is anonymous should knock him off balance. He's going to have to come up with some way to convince you otherwise." He sobered and placed a hand on her upper arm. "You have to be careful."

Prickles ran up and down her spine. "I am."

"I mean, really careful. I'm not willing to bet your life that I can predict Pinky's behavior."

She wished he was teasing her again. The headache returned, gallumphing back and forth through her skull like an out-of-control billiard ball.

"The best I can do is speculate. There's no way to know for sure what he's thinking. Until we catch him, we can't know for sure he's one of our suspects. He could be anybody. Even someone you've known for years. Cody. Or your crazy chef. Your buddy the cop. I believe in my heart one of those five kids is Pinky, but we aren't risking your safety. Got it?"

This was not what she wanted to hear. "I get it."

"You stick with me. Allow no one, for any reason, to get you alone. Don't answer doors. Let me do it."

Gooseflesh broke out on her arms. She shivered. "Isn't it dangerous for you to answer doors?"

"Better me than you."

"I'm not paying you enough to risk your life."

His eyebrows rose and his eyes gleamed. A compelling, sexual gleam that struck her squarely in the belly. She wanted to grab him by the sweater and kiss him. Ravish him. See if he remained so cool and cocky after that!

"Want to renegotiate?" he asked, his voice so silky she almost sighed.

She needed to muster indignation regarding his seductive tone. Knowing and doing were worlds apart. Right at this moment, she wanted to taste his lips, press her nose against his skin, run his fingers through his hair....

The door burst open and both of them jumped. Daniel conjured the Luger before Janine realized he'd moved. She'd have screamed, but the lump in her throat prevented it.

Kara flung out a hand. "There you are! I've been looking everywhere for you."

Daniel tucked the pistol behind his back. His sharp exhalation matched hers.

"I'm right here," Janine said. "We just finished the meeting. What do you need?"

In her peripheral vision she noticed Daniel turn a shoulder so he could holster the pistol without Kara seeing the action. He tugged his sweater over his hips. The speed with which he'd reacted astonished her...thrilled her.

"Debbi and Kevin helped me haul decorations upstairs. You said we'd work on the party decorations tonight. Remember?" She closed the door and lowered her voice. "How did it go? Do you know who Pinky is?"

"Not yet. Have you heard anybody say anything?"

Kara displayed hands darkened by dirt and dust. "I've been rooting around in the basement ever since I got off shift. I haven't heard anything. What am I listening for?"

"You'll know when you hear it," Daniel said. "I have a feeling that by tomorrow morning everyone will have something to say about Pinky."

Janine couldn't resist. "And you, dear. Don't forget, they'll have plenty to say about you."

THE FIRST FALLOUT from the meeting struck Janine the next morning while she filled a carafe of coffee. George Hornberger, called Chef by everybody, stormed across the kitchen, yelling at her. A short, dark, thick-necked man, he appeared to swell, toadlike and venomous. His Austrian accent thickened until he was nearly incoherent.

Janine arched an eyebrow. "Pardon?"

Gesticulating wildly, dark eyes blazing, Chef stomped his feet and hollered. Janine understood he was upset about Brian. The kitchen was Chef's territory and as far as he was concerned, anyone who worked in the kitchen belonged to him. Used to his tantrums, she waited patiently for him to run out of steam.

"You are absolutely correct," she said. "I should have spoken to you before I questioned Brian."

He scowled suspiciously and shook a thick finger at her face. He slowed his speech as if remembering he spoke English. "Bringing you man troubles in here, not allowed! Baking, roasting—too much to do. Work dark to dark, not life easy like you, big boss lady. All this man thing, too many problems!"

It took her several seconds to work through his tortured syntax before she realized he blamed her love life for upsetting the kitchen staff. Heat flared on her face and she bit hard on her inner cheek. She refused to argue with Chef; refused to humiliate herself with an explanation. She looked around the large kitchen. The people who were hard at work preparing the day's fare kept their backs to the scene between Chef and Janine. "Where is Brian?" She prayed the young man hadn't quit.

Chef jerked a thumb over his shoulder and told her Brian was unloading supplies from a truck. She tuned out the criticisms he directed at her.

"Pinky is a serious threat," she slipped in when he paused to take a breath. "If I can't stop him, we will close the resort in order to protect our guests." Behind her, Daniel lingered near the doorway. She knew he was studying the reactions of the kitchen workers.

Chef's eyes widened so whites showed all the way around the irises. She was surprised he'd heard a single thing she said. She nodded firmly. "That's right. We'll shut the whole place down."

"'Cause you play man against man?"

"Because Pinky is a seriously deranged criminal and I'm afraid he's going to hurt someone. You, sir, will cooperate in my investigation."

Seeing him gearing up for another tantrum, she flung up a hand and leaned in close. He shied like a spooked horse. For his ears only, she said through her teeth, "If you say one more word, I will make you eat every syllable. I am not in the mood!"

He opened his mouth, exposing his teeth. No words emerged.

She grabbed the full carafe and two cups, and stalked out of the kitchen.

Daniel fell into step beside her. He looked amused, and admiring. "He really is crazy. He was even scaring me, and I couldn't understand a word he said."

"He's more trouble than he's worth," she grumbled. "One of these days he's going to take that temperamental artiste crud too far and I'll can him." An empty threat. He was a wizard in the kitchen, creating culinary masterpieces. Because of him the restaurant was always packed with diners. He'd be throwing temper tantrums unchecked into the next century.

She unlocked her office door. "So what do you think? If Brian is Pinky, would he go whining to Chef about me?"

"I don't think so. But then again, he might think it's the way he's supposed to act. That's the thing with sociopaths. They have no emotional base. They're like parrots. Instead of mimicking words, they mimic emotions."

"We don't know for sure that Pinky is a sociopath." She passed a hand wearily over her eyes. A nasty nightmare had plagued her sleep last night. In the dream she hadn't escaped the fire. Her father hadn't escaped, either. She had frantically tried to beat out the flames on his body while he told her how disappointed he was in her performance.

The nightmare haunted to her. "Are we making any progress at all?"

"Pinky isn't obsessing about your father. That's progress."

"Why is he still hiding?"

He showed his palms. "I don't know."

She leveled a hard gaze on him. "You're the expert. You're supposed to know."

"We're not dealing with a machine or a computer program. In Pinky's head, anonymity controls you. Secrecy is the key to his delusion. He believes you're conspiring with him."

"That's absurd." It was also incredibly creepy. She scrubbed her arms against the itchy sensation crawling over her flesh.

Daniel opened an employee file. "Brian has a gap in employment."

She imagined Brian had been pudgy and awkward all his life. Perhaps the teasing and tormenting from other children had created a monster. "He's only nineteen. Gaps are expected."

"He's been steadily employed for the past three years except for one three-month period. Which just happened to occur during the time you lost the Day-Timer."

She took the file and perused the dates. Brian hadn't explained the three-month gap on the application form. "He didn't work at the restaurant where I was having lunch that day."

"He didn't list it on his résumé. That doesn't mean he wasn't there."

"It should be easy enough to check—"

"I did check."

Surprised, she sat down hard. Her chair squeaked.

He helped himself to coffee. He wore a dark blue sweater today. The color looked good with his shiny brown hair and suntanned skin. She wondered what color boxer shorts he wore. Last night and this morning he'd been vigilant about keeping his robe closed. Such wayward thoughts disturbed her. Daniel Tucker's underwear was of no concern to her.

"The restaurant was one of those trend chains, owned by an investment group out of Texas. They opened three restaurants on North Academy Boulevard within a year. All three went out of business within a year. The investment group has broken up and they're all suing one another. I hired a private investigator in Texas to hunt down the employee records for me, but he's not having much luck. With all the litigation going on, cooperation with us is a low priority."

"Why didn't you tell me you hired a private eye?"

"You have your job, I have mine. I told the police about the restaurant and gave them the name of the guy who managed it. We'll see if it turns into a solid lead."

A knock on the door startled Janine. Daniel was on his feet in an instant. He moved to the side of the door and opened it about three inches. It was Juan Hernandez. The good-natured maintenance supervisor wasn't smiling this morning.

"Craig Johnson quit on me."

Janine invited the man inside. Juan told her how Craig had cleaned out his room and left without a word to anybody. Where he'd gone, Juan hadn't a clue. And yes, both Lanny Lewis and Jason Bulshe had complained bitterly about Ms. Duke's unfair and unwarranted accusations. They were threatening to quit, too. The entire maintenance crew was up in arms.

Hurt tightened her chest. Didn't anyone care about her dilemma?

"I'm sorry about Craig. But Pinky threatened my father's life."

Juan's mouth dropped open. "What do you mean he

threatened the colonel? I thought this guy was your ex-boyfriend?'' He glanced at Daniel. ''Jealous, you know?''

She could have groaned. ''Pinky is not and never has been my boyfriend. I don't even know who he is. He's made two specific death threats against the colonel. He's threatened to kill Daniel, too. That's why we've hired deputies to patrol the resort.''

''Guess I heard wrong. Everybody is saying…'' His face reddened. ''Damn.''

Janine quashed the urge to ask what everybody was saying. She did not want to know. ''Pinky works here. I'm fairly certain he lives here, as well.''

He raked his fingers through his black hair and made a soft, confused-sounding noise. ''It can't be any of my boys. I vouch for them all.''

''He fooled me. He can fool you, too.''

''What exactly did Lanny and Jason say to you?'' Daniel asked.

Juan cracked a grin. ''Can't use that kind of language in front of a lady. I can tell you this, sir, you aren't real popular.''

''Did either say anything about the colonel?''

Looking inward, Juan shook his head. ''Ain't ever heard nobody talking bad about the old man. Everyone loves the colonel, Ms. Duke. You know that.''

Everyone except Pinky.

''I'll keep my ear out, ma'am. I hear anything about Pinky, or anyone trash-talking the colonel, I'll let you know.''

After Juan left, Janine rested her chin on a fist. Maybe the nightmare had been a warning. Her sister Megan believed in the power of dreams, swearing people who paid attention to dream warnings could avert disaster. A heavy feeling infused her body, a sense of impending doom. ''Now what?''

"We keep pushing. Even deluded sociopaths have buttons. We'll find Pinky's."

She dropped her hands to the stack of papers on her desk. "Not today. I must go to the Springs. I have a million and one details to take care of for the party."

"Good. It'll give me a chance to talk to J.T."

She'd forgotten that along with rousting stalkers, Daniel had a business to run. She opened her organizer book and checked the addresses where she needed to go. She envisioned a map of Colorado Springs in order to most efficiently plan her day. She could drop off Daniel at his office, run her errands and with any luck get back to the resort by dinnertime.

"Let's set up some surveillance cameras."

"Pardon?"

"J.T.'s an expert in electronic security. He can set up some cameras. One outside your bedroom door. The dormitory. Maybe one over the front desk so we can see who's putting notes in your message box."

She searched his face. Surely he was joking.

"Why are you looking at me like that?"

"This is a resort, not a prison."

"I know it sounds extreme, but it's not. We'll set them up in public areas. Video only, no audio. No invading privacy."

"Setting up a camera in the dormitory is invasive."

"Not inside, outside. That way we can see who goes in and out. It protects your innocent employees."

She saw his point. If Pinky vandalized something in the middle of the night, they'd be able to establish alibis. She didn't even want to think about catching somebody lurking around outside her bedroom. "Won't Pinky see the cameras?"

Daniel laughed. "You have no idea what kind of gadgetry is on the market right now. Nobody but you, me and

J.T. will even know they're there. I guarantee it.''

She didn't like it, but didn't see where she had a choice.

ON THE TWO-HOUR DRIVE to Colorado Springs, Daniel played a tape Pinky had sent her. He pointed out the references to secrets and the theme of undercover love. On this particular tape Pinky had recorded a song where the singer assured his lover he'd be watching every move she made. Janine had heard the tune hundreds of times. For the first time she paid attention to the lyrics. A stalker's lament.

She would never again enjoy a pop song about unrequited love.

In the city, as usual, everything took more time than Janine wanted it to. It took two hours for the liquor supplier to run down the location of the champagne she'd ordered months ago. The supplier assured her the wine would be shipped to the resort that day. A visit to the florist chewed up another two hours.

Janine and Daniel stopped by the party-supply store. The custom-printed napkins, balloons and streamers for the Victorian romance party theme were ready. She purchased extra gold-and-ivory tablecloths, and gold lamé place mats. After that, they visited a hobby store to fill Kara's supply list.

"You're actually having fun," Janine told Daniel as they lugged bulging bags of cloth, candles and Victorian theme decorations to her Jeep.

"I like to shop." He flashed an endearing smile. "I like shopping with you."

Despite some hassles, she'd had fun today. No worries about Pinky spying on her. No looking over her shoulder in apprehension. Nobody glaring at her as if she were the enemy, or worse, as if she were an idiot with an out-of-control love life. Daniel proved an affable companion, interested in her errands—interested in her.

"What?" he asked.

Caught staring, she averted her face.

"Forget something?"

She sorted idly through the ring of keys and smiled to herself. "First day I've had fun in I don't know how long. You actually are a nice guy."

He leaned a shoulder against the Jeep. "Told you so."

He'd done more than tell her, he'd proved it. She wondered why she had such difficulty accepting him. Why her impulse was to think the worst. Time after time he acted gallant, charming, loyal and protective. He was everything she admired: patient, pleasant, even-tempered and quick-witted, but never a pushover, never weak. She suspected the flaws she so persistently sought had more to do with herself than with him. The insight disturbed her. "I think we can be friends."

"Just friends?"

Leave it alone, she warned herself. She couldn't help it. "For now."

Chapter Nine

Janine and Daniel drove to the studio where J.T. waited for them. The martial arts studio didn't look the way she'd expected. She'd imagined something flashy, but it was an unassuming gray building with a small sign next to the double glass doors. Full Circle Karate was emblazoned over a logo that pictured a dragon biting its tail. The noise inside astonished her. High-pitched yells and shrieks bounced off the walls.

She peeked through a doorway. A man and a woman guided children through exercises. With each movement the kids yelled at the tops of their lungs, and bare feet clomped the mats. At another doorway she paused to watch a woman kicking the snot out of a man wearing heavy padding. Her bare foot thudded against the padding while her ferocious shouts rang from the rafters. A dozen or so women watched the action as they knelt at the edges of the mats.

"Self-defense," Daniel said. "It's a great class. You ought to take it." He guided her through a doorway marked For Employees Only.

"I'm not athletic." She couldn't shake the image of the woman kicking the instructor. She'd looked so powerful and self-assured.

"That's the cool thing about karate. It teaches you to use what you have. We have one student who's in a wheelchair.

She's no sissy, trust me.'' He walked through an open door-way and called, "J.T., my man!"

J.T. McKennon rose from a crouch and closed a filing cabinet drawer. He wore black trousers and a red T-shirt marked with the Full Circle logo. He opened his arms for Janine. She hugged him and offered her cheek for a kiss. He searched her face, his eyes questioning. "How are you doing?"

"I've been better. I take it Daniel filled you in about Pinky?"

J.T. grunted. "No luck rooting him out?"

"Not yet." She slid a small smile toward Daniel. "Did he tell you about his truck?"

Daniel grumbled and flopped onto the chair behind the desk. He idly sorted through a bundle of mail while he told J.T. about the vandalism and the death threat.

J.T. whistled softly. "At least it wasn't your Vette."

A Corvette. It figured Daniel would own such a fancy sports car. She imagined it was bright red, probably a convertible.

Janine asked to use the telephone. The men moved to the doorway to give her privacy. When she reached her father and he sounded normal and healthy, such a rush of relief washed through her she sagged on the chair. He assured her that all was well, but he groused about the rumors and gossip circulating through the staff.

"Any problems?" Daniel asked.

"All is well. Nothing in the mail, nothing in my box. Is that a good sign or a bad sign?"

"As long as your dad is okay, we'll take it as a good sign."

Rhythmic squeaking preceded the appearance of a wheelchair. Frankie McKennon pushed her stepson into the office. At the sight of the tiny boy in the wheelchair, Janine forgot her woes.

Little Jamie McKennon had been in a terrible car accident which had killed his mother and put him in a coma for nearly four years. Despite having little use of his legs and left arm, and with the left side of his face paralyzed, he was the happiest child she'd ever known.

Frankie kissed her husband and shrugged off her coat. Janine's gaze locked on her cousin's swollen belly. Her baby was due in two months.

"Look at you!" Janine cried.

"Please don't look at me," Frankie said. "I feel like a tomato on toothpicks."

Daniel slid an arm around Frankie's waist and loudly kissed her cheek. "I think you're gorgeous. When will you dump your old man and run off to the Bahamas with me?"

"If I send J.T. on one more midnight run for ice cream and Fritos, he'll *pay* you to take me." She winced and clutched her belly.

J.T.'s face twisted in concern.

"I'm okay." She laughed and playfully pushed her husband away. "He's kicking me in the bladder, that's all."

Daniel placed a hand on Frankie's belly. He appeared delighted by the activity going on underneath her maternity sweater. "We've got a future kick-boxing champ in here, J.T."

"Tell me about it," Frankie said anxiously. "Take off Jamie's coat. I'll be right back." She rushed out of the room.

Janine crouched before Jamie. "Ga-deen!" he cried joyfully. "Ga-deen. Gammy? Gampy?" He called Elise Gammy and the colonel Gampy.

"Gammy and Gampy aren't here, slugger," she said. "But you get to see them on Saturday. We're going to have a big party. Won't that be fun? Cake and balloons and presents."

He bounced on the chair and wriggled so much she nearly tore a button off his coat. She finally got the coat off his arms and he grunted beseechingly for her to pick him up. She hugged him until he squealed. "He's getting so big, J.T."

"Strong, too." J.T. rolled out the desk chair for her to sit on. He ruffled his son's silky blond hair.

Frankie returned, looking much relieved. Her smile had a hesitant but knowing quality. Janine guessed her cousin knew exactly why she was here with Daniel. She also suspected Frankie hadn't merely happened to show up at this particular time.

She rocked Jamie on her lap and inhaled his clean-little-boy scent. At her age, she figured her odds of finding a decent husband and becoming a mother were slim. Still, holding Jamie and seeing Frankie so gloriously pregnant filled her with bittersweet longings.

"Jamie and I just dropped in to see if J.T. would take us out for hamburgers. If you, uh, I mean—"

"I know J.T. told you about Pinky."

"Well…" Frankie grinned sheepishly at her husband.

"You girls chat while I talk to J.T.," Daniel said. The men left the office.

"You girls?" Janine mocked and rolled her eyes. She bussed Jamie's neck until he giggled. "Your mama won't let you grow up to be a macho knucklehead, will she?"

Frankie carefully settled on a chair and stretched out her legs. "So how bad is it?"

"Pretty bad. Pinky burned down the garage where the colonel stored his old Jeep and he destroyed Daniel's truck."

Frankie winced. "Was anybody hurt?"

Janine played patty-cake with Jamie. She and Frankie had grown fairly close in the past year. Even so, she didn't know how much to say or how Frankie would react. "No one was hurt," she said. "We're getting the situation under control."

"Good thing you have Daniel," Frankie said. "He's a great guy." She glanced at the door. "The greatest. He treats J.T. like a brother. And I've never met anybody so generous in my life. The only way we were able to buy the house was because Daniel paid J.T. a fat bonus. He didn't have to."

Jamie gabbled something, but Janine couldn't understand what he wanted.

Frankie hoisted herself off the chair. "He wants down." A square mat covered with red vinyl hung by straps on the wall. She laid it on the floor. From a cabinet she brought out a lumpy leather ball and a pair of thick, polished wooden sticks. Once on the mat, Jamie used his good arm to pull himself atop the ball, where he rocked back and forth on his belly. Frankie closed the fingers of his weak left hand around a stick.

"He's a terrific baby-sitter, too. He loves Jamie."

Janine laughed, more at her cousin's overt matchmaking than at the way Jamie used a stick to pound the mat. His progress amazed her. The last time she'd seen him he couldn't hold anything in his left hand. "I can't believe how strong Jamie is."

"He'll be walking before we know it. So, no comment about Daniel?"

Janine recognized the signs. The blissful gleam in the eyes, fiddling with a wedding ring, the beatific smile. Invariably, whenever friends or relatives got married, her single status became a sorry condition in need of repair.

She knelt next to the mat and picked up the other stick. Jamie began jousting with her. "I'm not interested in a relationship right now."

"You don't think he's…cute?"

"Cute as a bug. But I'm not in the market."

Jamie slid off the ball. Janine reached instinctively to help him, but he scowled and waved her away. She sat back on her haunches and rested her fists on her thighs. Frankie held her breath until Jamie climbed back on the ball. Both women exhaled in relief.

Frankie caressed her belly, smiling dreamily. "The first time I met Daniel, I thought about you. He actually appreciates smart women. He doesn't play those fragile-male-ego games."

She figured he appreciated long legs and large breasts even more. The uncharitable thought shamed her. "I hired him to help with a problem. Nothing more."

"You haven't even thought about it? Look me in the eye and tell me you don't imagine what he'd—"

"Stop it, Frankie! Shees. I know he's nice, and smart, and yes, extremely attractive. But I'm not interested in a quickie affair. I don't operate that way."

Her cousin bristled as if genuinely offended. "He isn't like that."

"Hate to burst your bubble, but yes he is. He's been hitting on me since we met."

"Uh-uh! He isn't interested in quickie affairs, either."

"Please." Her position felt shaky, but she stood her ground, anyway. "He can have any woman he wants, and I imagine he isn't picky about taking whatever is offered."

"I can't believe you're saying that." Frankie's voice crackled with fierce protectiveness. "He's not some—" she glanced at her son—"*S-L-U-T*. He's a lot more serious than you think. And," her voice lowered, "he's looking to settle down. All he needs is the right woman."

The idea intrigued as much as it unsettled her.

Daniel and J.T. returned. "My ears are burning," Daniel said. "Talking about me?"

Frankie leveled a smug smile on Janine, as if daring her to prove her wrong about Daniel. Janine suspected she couldn't do it, no matter how hard she tried.

He shoved his hands in his pockets and rocked on his heels. "We have good news and bad news. The good news is, J.T. doesn't see a problem with installing surveillance cameras."

"And the bad news?"

J.T. answered. "There aren't any local suppliers for that type of equipment. I'm going to check around and see if anyone has stuff on hand I can borrow. Otherwise it'll take at least a week to get it shipped in."

Janine rested her face on a hand. The more she'd considered the idea of capturing Pinky on videotape, the more excited she'd grown. Disappointment weighted her soul.

Daniel dropped to a crouch beside her and rested a companionable hand on her shoulder. "J.T. knows everybody who's anybody. He'll come up with something before the party." He beckoned to Jamie with his fingertips. The boy poked at him with the stick.

Janine watched the rapport between the boy and man. Daniel seemed to understand everything the little boy said—no easy task since Jamie's facial paralysis garbled his speech. He'd be a good father. Thinking such a thing gave her a funny feeling.

"We're going to dinner," J.T. said. "Care to join us?"

"Love to, but I need to get home. I don't want to fall asleep on the road." She scooped Jamie into her arms and covered his face with kisses. He kissed her enthusiastically in return. "I'll see you Friday, slugger. We'll have tons of fun at Gammy and Gampy's party."

A wave of melancholy rolled through Janine as she left the studio. Daniel offered to drive. She strapped on the seat belt and snuggled inside her coat, cold more from leaving the warmth of her cousin's than from the temperature. She'd tried marriage, failed miserably, and over the years convinced herself that a career was enough. She didn't need a man or romance or children.

When she died, would anyone remember fondly how well she'd managed the resort? How well she managed the books? Her expertise in handling suppliers? Always Aunt Janine, never Mom. Her heart felt empty.

Daniel patted her knee. "Don't sweat it. J.T. will come through for us."

"Pardon?"

"The cameras."

She watched passing traffic and brightly lit stores and restaurants. "I know he will."

"You looked bummed."

Bummed described her mood exactly. She studied his profile. Lights from traffic and the dashboard outlined his straight nose and strong chin. Could he be lonely? It didn't seem possible. Then again, it didn't seem possible she was lonely, either.

The trilling of her cellular phone broke her thoughts. She pulled it out of her purse and opened it. "Hello?"

"Where are you?" her father asked.

The edginess in his voice set off alarms. "We're just leaving the Springs. What's the matter?"

"We've had an incident. Pinky has made his displeasure clear yet again."

DANIEL SURVEYED THE DAMAGE inside the small room on the second floor of the lodge's east wing. Kara had been using this room to create and store the decorations for the anniversary party. Pinky had thrown a major tantrum while Daniel and Janine had been in the city.

Shredded fabric, lace, ribbon and paper littered the floor. Broken fabric flowers lay as if storm tossed. Strings of lights had been cut into pieces and the bulbs were ground into the carpet. Pinky had emptied jars of paint, rubber cement and white glue all over the floor, walls, furniture and finished decorations.

"That disgusting little…" Janine picked her way through debris. "How could he?"

Kara snuffled loudly. Her eyes and nose were red. She swiped at her face with a tissue. She picked up a ripped gold-foil heart, edged in lace. "I worked weeks on this stuff. He trashed everything!" She flung the heart on the floor. "I'll kill him!"

Daniel cringed inwardly. The very first thing he should have done was insist that locks in the east wing be changed and the new master keys issued to family only. Imagining what might have happened had Kara walked into the middle of Pinky's tantrum sickened him.

"What time did you find this?" he asked the young woman.

"Around seven-thirty. Debbi and I finished shift at six-thirty, then we ate, then we came up here to work on the decorations. And—and—" She flung both hands wide. "We found this!"

"Were you in here earlier? Before you went on shift?"

"This morning. Debbi, Kevin and Carol were helping me." She pushed a cut piece of light string with her toe. "We untangled all the lights and replaced all the burned-out bulbs."

"What time did you go on shift?"

"Noon."

"Did you see Jason, Lanny, Devon, Ellen or Brian in the east wing?"

"Brian works in the kitchen," Janine said. "He's always in the east wing." She rubbed the pads of her fingers against her temples. The thin skin under her eyes had a greenish cast.

Daniel's shame deepened. He should have been more aggressive in setting up security measures.

Glum-faced, Kara shook her head. "We were really busy this afternoon. Both those big ski-tour groups checked out. The Barker wedding was today. Their reception started at three o'clock. It's still going on in the ballroom. A million people were in and out of the lobby. It was a zoo."

Daniel stepped through the door and studied the hallway. The east wing of the lodge had two floors, not including the attic. The Dukes and their managerial staff lived on the second floor. Two stairwells led to the first floor. Another led to the attic. Anyone who wanted to sneak around up here unnoticed could easily do so.

He faced the room, recognizing a textbook example of rage in action. He could almost see Pinky at work, his face flushed, teeth bared, eyes glazed, shredding, flinging, kicking and destroying. Most telling were the ripped hearts scattered like broken petals. Pinky hadn't missed destroying a single heart.

Why?

Janine's room was two doors down. The same master key that fit the lock for this room fit the lock to hers. Pinky should have broken into her room and attacked Daniel's belongings.

Janine touched his hand. "What is it?"

"This isn't right."

She drew her head warily aside. "What are you thinking?"

"He should have attacked me."

"Maybe he's scared of you." She brushed a hand over the pistol on his hip. "He might have noticed you're armed."

He chewed his inner cheek. This was wrong, all wrong, but he couldn't pinpoint why it felt so wrong.

Janine poked his arm. "When you're this quiet, you scare me."

"Yeah, Daniel." Kara sounded subdued. "You're scaring me, too."

"Pinky is like a train on tracks. Rigid, focused. That's what makes this kind of stalker self-destructive along with being destructive toward others. A delusion is addictive. Deviation from it is damned near impossible without serious intervention."

"I don't understand."

"I don't, either. And I don't like it. We switched Pinky onto another track. He should be worried about me." He snatched up half a torn paper heart. "But something switched him back."

"He's mad at the colonel again?" Janine shook her head in fervent denial. "No! He's supposed to leave my father alone."

"Kara," he said. "Have you been talking about the anniversary party?"

"Everybody is talking about the party." A tear trickled down her cheek, and she swiped it away.

"Is anybody complaining about the extra work? The overtime?"

"No." Her lower lip trembled. "The kids helping me with the decorations are using their own time. Even Chef is excited about the party. The cake he's making is a masterpiece." Her words trailed into a wail. "Why did Pinky have to go and do this?"

The three trudged downstairs to the family dining room where the managerial staff had gathered. All of them had seen the damage, and the mood was grim.

Cody Hodgkins spoke up. "Devon Hightower isn't your culprit." His huge mustache bristled. "Day long, he never stepped foot inside the lodge."

"How do you know?" Daniel asked.

"Up until about three o'clock he was guiding horseback tours. Six, eight folks, each out for an hour-long ride. Didn't even take time for lunch. After that he was cleaning tack. I told him to cut loose for supper around six."

"You're positive he never left the tack room?"

Cody fiddled with the broad brim of his felt cowboy hat. "Wasn't breathing down his neck, but every time I passed the door, there he was, up to his elbows in saddle soap. Repaired a hackamore for me, too, and splicing rope like that takes doing. He took his supper with me. He isn't Pinky. I stake my own job on it."

Cody might have missed the boy being away for a few minutes, but it had taken Pinky longer than a mere few minutes to vandalize the room upstairs. Daniel caught Janine's attention and nodded.

"I believe you," Janine said. She looked to the head housekeeper. "What about Ellen Schulberg?"

In her trim black suit with a crisp white blouse, the head of housekeeping looked like a department store manager. She worked a finger under her blouse collar and tugged at it. "Ever since you told me you think she might have vandalized your boyfriend's car, I expressly forbade her to step foot in the east wing."

"Shift ended at two-thirty. Where was she after that?"

"I don't know."

"Who's on housekeeping in the east wing today?"

"Pat and Kathy. I already talked to them. They didn't see anything out of the ordinary."

"Chef, what about Brian?"

He told Daniel that as a baker's assistant, Brian began work at three o'clock in the morning. He finished his first shift at nine o'clock in the morning, then resumed working at four in the afternoon. Which gave him four unsupervised hours for mischief making.

Juan Hernandez claimed Jason Bulshe had spent the entire day repairing a balky sump pump in the lodge basement. Lanny had the day off. Juan didn't remember seeing him today.

Daniel whispered in Janine's ear. "We have to search their rooms."

Her expression tightened, and the skin under her eyes looked even more sickly green. "Colonel," she said. "I'm going to search the dormitory."

A murmur of protests filled the dining room.

"The entire dormitory. I won't single people out. I won't embarrass any individual."

"I refused to grant the police permission to search indiscriminately," the colonel stated. "I am not certain this is the best strategy now."

"Your objection is noted, sir." She tossed hair off her shoulders. "I'm doing it, anyway." She glanced at her watch. "Cody, go to the dorm right now. Ask everyone to leave their rooms and wait in the hallway. The rest of you, if you have anyone who lives in the dorm and is working right now, pull them off duty. We'll check their rooms first so they can get back to work."

"I have not granted permission," the colonel said.

"I'm not asking, sir." She leaned both hands on the long table and stared directly into her father's eyes.

"The privacy of—"

"To hell with their privacy!" she shouted. She slammed the tabletop with a fist. "Pinky is endangering the entire resort and the fifty-nine people who are doing their jobs. He is threatening *you!*"

The old man snapped his mouth shut, but he pulsed with angry energy. His eyes were Arctic ice. "I do not approve."

"Noted, sir. I take full responsibility for this." Janine swung her glare on the managers. "I want all of you to let your people know that it is me, not the colonel, who is forcing the issue." She nodded curtly. "Take care of your people. I'll be in the dorm in twenty minutes. I expect every door to be standing open. And nobody is to take anything out of that building."

As the group filed out of the dining room, Janine stopped them. "I want a key inventory, too. On my desk, first thing in the morning. I want to know the exact location of every single key in this resort."

Even Chef left quietly.

Daniel stared at Janine. She was of average height and weight, but at this moment she was a Valkyrie, an Amazon, a crusading general who knew her objective and to hell with public opinion. Admiration swelled his chest.

Elise rested her hands on her husband's broad shoulders.

"Are you absolutely certain you aren't overreacting, Janine?"

"You saw what he did to the decorations, Mom," Kara said. "Pinky overreacted, not us."

"He's mad at you again, Colonel." Janine looked to Daniel for confirmation. "He's mad about the party. Let's go, Daniel."

On the short walk to the dormitory, Daniel asked, "Ever gone Dumpster diving? It's an experience you'll never forget."

"No cute talk. I'm not in the mood."

"If we don't turn up anything in the dorm, we need to look in the Dumpster."

She laughed bitterly. "It's Monday. Our trash is picked up every Monday."

Damn.

"Why is he doing this? Why won't he show himself?"

Daniel figured Janine spoke rhetorically. In any case, he had no real answers for her. She was frustrated, scared and angry—as was he. If Pinky had trashed her bedroom she wouldn't be half this upset.

He slowed his step so he walked behind her. Head high, spine straight, she swung her arms widely as she walked. Her shoes snapped and crunched on the graveled path. A woman of purpose. A woman very much in control of her life. A woman capable of deep, and dangerous, anger. A most unusual victim for a stalker.

Like any predator, stalkers selected their prey carefully. They had a sixth sense about victims whose backgrounds or personalities made them vulnerable to abuse. Daniel's stalker had intuited that while Daniel took no guff from males, he was a total marshmallow with women and children. When she failed to control him with persistence, she'd committed suicide. In a way she'd won, because not a day passed when the image of her limp body swinging off the balcony railing didn't haunt him.

Power and control—stalkers confused those feelings with love. They couldn't force their victims to love them, so they controlled them instead.

Pinky had figured out Janine's weakness. How simple it would be for Pinky to knock on the colonel's door and shoot when the old man answered. Or follow him in a car and run him off a mountain road. Or ambush him in one of the lodge's many rooms and beat him to death.

There, Pinky could say, *I control the lives of those you love—now you have no choice except to love me!*

He and Janine entered the dorm. Built long and low, it had sixteen sleeping rooms, three communal bathrooms and a large common room with kitchen facilities and an entertainment center. Cody was waiting. Every door on both sides of the long hallway stood open. Young people, some appearing confused, some angry, waited in the hallway.

Daniel spotted Jason Bulshe, Ellen Schulberg and Brian Cadwell, but not Lanny Lewis. Ellen wore a short robe and fuzzy slippers. She rubbed her eyes as if she'd been sleeping. Brian wore a white tunic over black trousers. The front of his tunic looked as if he'd been in a spaghetti sauce explosion. Jason wore jeans and T-shirt, and also looked as if he'd been sleeping.

At the first room, Janine raised her voice so everyone could hear. "I have reason to believe a criminal lives in this dorm. If any of you have an objection to this search, say so now. I will respect your wishes, but if you refuse to let me search, you will be asked to vacate the dorm."

No one objected, and Janine entered the first room. Daniel watched. The room was about ten by twelve feet with a single window, a double closet, two narrow beds, two upright dressers, several chairs and two desks. The occupant had decorated the walls with animal posters and animal-print throws on the furniture. Janine searched the closet, drawers, clothes hamper and both desks. She lifted the mattresses on the beds. She checked the trash can.

Nothing.

Room by room she went through the dorm. Each room was as individual as its owner. Some were tidy and spare, some were messy and cluttered. Most had been decorated to reflect its occupant's tastes and interests.

Daniel studied the suspects. Brian Cadwell acted nervous and upset. While Janine searched his room he babbled about a movie he'd seen. He skipped through words like a kitten tearing through a box of Christmas ribbon. Cody finally told him to shut up. Ellen hovered on the verge of tears.

Lanny Lewis wasn't present, so Cody accompanied Janine as a witness. She found nothing incriminating in his room.

When Janine reached Jason's room, the young man leaned against a wall, his arms folded and his eyes hooded.

"You don't say much," Daniel said.

"She's the boss," the kid replied. He stared at the ceiling. "She can do what she wants."

Short hairs lifted on Daniel's nape. At least half the teenage boys who began martial arts instruction from him possessed this smug, hostile, arrogant attitude—an attitude Daniel took great delight in dispelling.

He studied Jason's room. The kid didn't have a roommate, but both beds were made up with military precision. The walls were bare, as were the surfaces of the desks and dressers. The only signs that anyone lived in the room were clothes in the closet, a digital clock and a cheap boom box.

"Ever been in the military, Jason?" Daniel asked.

The kid stared distantly. "No."

"Jail?"

Jason turned his head slowly. His eyes were blank. "No."

Janine stepped out of the room. "Thank you, Jason. I'm sorry for disturbing your sleep."

If Jason had been sleeping, then he'd been snoozing on

the bare floor. Neither bed showed so much as a dimple. Daniel noticed him making a point of not looking at Janine. The alarms in his head blared like a Klaxon warning signal.

"Where are the coveralls you wore today?" Daniel asked.

"In the washing machine."

"Show me."

"Screw you."

"Show me," Janine said.

Jason pushed away from the wall and stalked down the corridor to a bathroom. He straight-armed his way through the swinging door.

A washer and dryer sat against the far wall. Jason jerked open the lid of the washing machine then stepped back and folded his arms. Janine pulled two pair of jeans and two coveralls from the machine. The dark green coveralls were much-mended and stained. Daniel spread them out and searched for signs of the acrylic paint Kara had been using for the decorations. He found colored stains on both coveralls, but there was no way to tell by looking if the stains came from craft paint.

From the corner of his eye Daniel caught a trace of a grin on Jason's face. *Screw you twice,* his expression said.

Janine resumed searching the dorm. She found nothing that pointed to Pinky.

Mike Downes waited for them outside. Clouds blotted out the stars. A stiff breeze sounded like highway noise as it rushed through the trees. Janine informed the deputy they hadn't found a damned thing. They returned to the lodge.

Sounds of revelry rolled from the ballroom. People in formal dress milled about in the lounge. The sight reminded Daniel that they had only days until the big anniversary party. Destroying the decorations could be a mere precursor to what the stalker might do at the party.

Once in Janine's office, Daniel spoke to the deputy. "Jason Bulshe is off, way off."

Janine plopped onto the sofa and dropped her face on her hands. She clenched her hair, and white knuckles showed through masses of chestnut curls. "I can't fire him because you have a hunch. Why is he *off?*"

"I've got a better suspect for you," Mike said. "Your cook, Cadwell. He's got a juvie record. Breaking and entering when he was fifteen."

Adrenaline rushed through Daniel like electricity.

"I talked to the FBI, too. They say a lot of stalker types get popped for crimes like B&E, peeping and burglary." A grim smile creased his cheeks. "I'll take hard facts over your hunches, Daniel. Brian Cadwell is your man."

Chapter Ten

Not finding anything during the dorm search bugged Daniel. Jason's attitude incriminated him. Brian's lies on his employment application about not having a police record incriminated him. Lanny's no-show possibly incriminated him. Even mousie little Ellen remained a suspect.

Then it hit him. He knocked a fist upside his head. "I'm an idiot! Pinky's stash."

Janine and Mike stopped talking. Both blinked owlishly at him.

"His I-love-Janine stash. We know he has your Day-Timer. Chances are he's collected other souvenirs, too. He's too smart to keep them in the dorm."

"Souvenirs?" Janine wrinkled her nose. "What kind of souvenirs?"

Daniel recollected everything he'd ever read or heard about erotomanic stalkers. Much like serial killers who collected souvenirs from victims in order to relive their crimes, erotomanic stalkers often did the same in order to remain close to the object of their twisted affections. "Stuff he's collected from you. Things you've written. Knickknacks, pieces of clothing."

Color drained from her face. "A hairbrush?"

"That would be quite a treasure. According to his letters, he loves your hair."

Color returned in a rush, pinkening her cheeks. Her eyes glowed with feverish light. "I lost a hairbrush. Right out of my bathroom! I went nuts looking for it." A shudder rippled through her entire body. "Come to think of it, I've lost several items in the past few months. Little things, dumb things. The hairbrush, a bottle of perfume, lipstick, a pocket journal."

His mouth filled with a nasty sourness. "First thing in the morning, we're searching the lodge. We'll search the entire resort inch by inch if we have to. Can you help, Sergeant? If we find the stash, you can lift fingerprints."

"I'll clear it with the sheriff."

With nothing left they could do that night, Daniel and Janine retired to her room. She spent a long time in the bathroom. When she came out, she'd changed into her robe. Her eyes were red and swollen, and her complexion was blotchy. Daniel's heart ached for her.

Common decency said to vacate her room and leave her be; Pinky dictated otherwise.

"Are you okay?"

"Dandy."

"I'm sorry."

"For what?"

"For not getting a handle on Pinky."

"I haven't been able to figure out who he is in a year. I don't know how you expected to do it in a week." She pinched the bridge of her nose. Her shoulders hitched. "I hate him so much. He's forcing me to do things... You don't know how humiliating it was to search the dorm. I hate people who abuse positions of power. Now I'm one of them."

"You aren't like that. Don't—"

"I put my hands in underwear drawers! I rifled through personal papers." She clutched the back of a chair and looked ready to fling it across the room. Instead, she hung her head, so damp tendrils of hair fell over her face.

"We'll find him."

"Before or after he's destroyed my life?"

"Before. Get some sleep. You look exhausted."

She pointed with her chin at the television set. "What are you watching?"

An old movie played. He didn't recognize any of the actors. "I don't know." He aimed the remote at the television set to turn it off.

"Leave it on. If you don't mind. I can't sleep."

He patted the couch cushion. "Have a seat." Warily she did so. "Put your feet up."

She used the remote to flip through television channels. When she reached the old movie again, she tossed the remote as if to say, I give up. She lifted her feet onto his lap. The robe fell open to reveal her legs covered by gray sweatpants. Her toenails gleamed with bright red polish.

He began working on her right foot. He used the flats of his fingers to stroke the length of the tendons, manipulating and warming the fascia. "Nice feet. No bunions, no corns. You don't wear stupid shoes."

Her eyelids lowered. A thin smile softened her mouth.

"I see wrecked feet all the time. I'm surprised some women can even walk."

"You have a foot fetish?"

He went to work on her toes, spreading them gently and working his fingers between the joints. She sank farther down on the cushions. "I notice feet. It's my business. You, my dear, have terrific feet. Strong arches, good conformity. Cute toes." He used both hands to work her ankle and stretch the muscles. He could tell the massage had the desired effect when her foot went as limp as a sleeping puppy.

He took his time, enjoying the feel of her silky skin and the way strain abated from her face. Her eyes closed, which was a good thing, because if she got a glimpse of his crotch, he was in trouble. He massaged both feet.

"Want me to do your back?"

"No," she murmured in a drowsy voice he felt all the way to the center of his bones.

"It'll feel good."

Her eyelids fluttered. "You're trying to seduce me."

"Yeah, so what's your point?"

"I'm too old to play games." She slipped her feet off his lap and stretched her arms high over her head. The satin molded around her breasts. Daniel's eyes glazed. His groin throbbed. Animal lust roared in his ears. He wanted to pounce on her, ravish her.

The tip of her tongue slid over her upper lip. "Truth is, you are tempting."

Progress! "You can seduce me if you want."

She rose, took a step, then uttered a low *mmmm* of sheer pleasure. She used her right foot to stroke her left leg. If a herd of dancing elephants burst into the room right now—pink elephants!—he couldn't have torn his gaze away from the sensuous action of her feet.

"Pardon the cliché, but I'm not that kind of girl. Quickies don't interest me."

He passed a finger diagonally over his chest then held up three fingers in a Boy Scout salute. "I'll take all night if you want."

Her laughter whispered over his skin and through his soul. "Thanks for the massage. It really did help."

"I'm going to figure you out, Janine," he warned her. "When I do, you're mine."

"There is nothing to figure out. Besides, I have Elliot. He's all the man I need. Now good night. We have a lot to do tomorrow."

Daniel doubted if comfy old Elliot could make her purr the way she'd been purring during the foot massage. He resigned himself to keep a curb on his desire until Pinky was taken care of. After that, getting rid of Elliot should be a breeze.

"IT'S LIKE A LABYRINTH down here," Daniel said.

Janine opened a door to reveal the wine cellar. She'd been thinking the same thing about the basement under the lodge. "The original lodge, without the wings, was built in the 1920s for a hunting club. During the Depression, the owners tried to keep it profitable by turning it into a speakeasy. They built hidden rooms to hide liquor. But the roads were bad and the G-men were good. The investors lost everything."

Though the wine cellar was well lit with banks of overhead lights, she used a flashlight to peer into corners. Daniel discovered the dumbwaiter connecting the cellar with the restaurant upstairs. Noise trickled down the shaft. Janine envied the carefree diners in the restaurant above.

"How does this work?" he asked.

"The old-fashioned way. A rope pulley."

Gears squeaked when he manipulated the rope that raised and lowered the elevator platform. A cloud of dust made him sneeze. "A man could fit inside."

"And plenty of people have tried it. Especially boys." She flicked the flashlight beam at his face. "You're supposed to be searching, not contemplating a ride in the dumbwaiter."

He grinned, unrepentant. "I was thinking about Pinky."

"Sure you were." His smile distracted her, reminding her of the foot massage he'd given her last night. Common sense said to ignore his flirtations. Common sense meant little when he was the only person with the power to make her feel good these days.

They found nothing in the wine cellar, just as they'd found nothing in the laundry room, boiler room or in the many storage areas. A sense of vulnerability swamped her. Two sets of stairs led from the basement to the east wing. Two more led to the main lodge. Another set of stairs led to the outdoors. The dumbwaiter in the wine cellar could be used by a determined stalker, as could the laundry chutes and the small, automated supply elevators servicing the kitchen and west wing. The lodge had as many holes as a wedge of Swiss cheese.

Janine paused at the door to the laundry room. Muggy heat radiated from the constantly running washing machines and commercial-size dryers. Plumes of detergent-scented mist curled through the doorway. She eyed the wide openings of the chutes. A bundle of sheets fell from one and landed inside a canvas-sided cart.

Daniel touched the small of her back. "What are you thinking?"

"If Pinky is dumb enough to use the laundry chutes." She pointed out a woman loading bundles of fresh linens into a small elevator that carried clean linens up to all three floors of the west wing. "Or the laundry elevator. He could slip into the west wing through one of the side doors, go down through here and then slip over to the east wing without anyone seeing him."

"Or enter through the door from outside." He looked around. "A person could live undetected down here for years. Hmm, I wonder where Lanny Lewis really was yesterday?"

Eager to get out of the basement, she hurried for the stairs. "Juan said Lanny was visiting friends in the Springs."

"Ask Mike to check out Lanny's alibi. If nothing else, we can eliminate him as a suspect."

"I think we can eliminate Ellen, too. She was on-shift when Pinky set the garage on fire. The more I think about it, the more difficult it is to imagine Ellen being able to slip away from her duties long enough to follow us around."

When she reached the main floor she heaved a sigh of relief to be out of the gloomy basement. She wiped her grimy hands against her sweatshirt and brushed away spiderwebs.

After a busy weekend, the lounge seemed deserted.

Housekeeping personnel took advantage of the midweek lull to power clean the floors and furniture in the lounge and lobby. Jason Bulshe balanced atop a ladder. He changed lightbulbs in a chandelier.

Janine's mouth turned unpleasantly dry. Last night he'd seemed like a completely different person from the cute young man who always acted so eager to please.

Daniel grunted. Eyes narrowed and jaw tight, he looked dangerous. His muscles flexed against her arm, radiating coiled power. She suspected he'd like to get Jason alone in a locked room so he could beat a confession out of him.

She hated suspecting Jason. Juan was upset already about Craig Johnson quitting. Having two more of his staff under suspicion didn't help matters. He hadn't said a word when he'd given her a key inventory this morning.

Janine didn't know what to do about Jason. She couldn't fire him without cause. He'd never done or said anything in the past to make her uncomfortable.

The young man stepped down a few rungs. He stared at her, unsmiling, blank-faced. She wanted to scream at him, to demand he tell her if he was the creepy little sneak trashing her life.

Daniel suddenly slipped a hand under her hair and grasped the back of her head. His long fingers splayed, holding her fast. Before she had time to protest, he kissed her.

His lips against hers shocked her to her toes. He held her head firmly and slipped his other arm around her waist. His kiss was tender, a sweet press of his closed mouth against hers. His warm, masculine, earthy scent overwhelmed her, flooding her body with erotic heat. Her eyelids drifted downward of their own accord. She sighed deep in her throat and her mouth relaxed, her lips parting.

He slipped his tongue in tentative exploration along the slick inner rim of her lower lip. He tasted like spring water. He smelled of shaving cream and a hint of mint, their subtleties blotting out the smells of dust, cleansers and lemon furniture oil. Her pulse thudded in her ears, deafening her to the sounds of vacuum cleaners and people talking. She touched her tongue to his and every nerve in her body snapped to life, tingling with sexual greed.

She pressed upward. Every memory of previous kisses disappeared. Any kiss in her life had been but a mere prelude to this kiss. A kiss reaching far beyond the gentle laving of his tongue and sharing of heated breath. A kiss that stopped time. A kiss that reached deep within and plucked her soul. Each beat of her heart echoed *I want... I want...*

He pulled away, suckling on her lower lip, his heavy exhalation hot against her cheek. She stared into his eyes. Soulful, tender, sexy eyes—had she ever seen eyes so beautiful?

A snicker pierced her daze and she snapped her head toward the source. A housekeeper dusted a potted plant. Head down, staring fixedly at her task, the girl obviously fought laughter.

Reality returned with a jolt. Janine remembered where she was and more important, who she was. Where the lobby had seemed deserted before, now it seemed crammed full of people, all of whom had witnessed the kiss.

She pulled from Daniel's embrace. It took every ounce of willpower she possessed to not break into a run. Head high, cheeks burning, she crossed the lobby, past the grinning young women working the registration desk and into the east wing.

She never lost her head around a man—never, never, *never!* She called the shots, she set the boundaries, she remained in control. Being swept away by passion was for weaklings and romantic fools. Sexual desire was like any other bodily appetite—moderation was the key.

She fumbled through keys, searching for her office key.

"Janine?"

"You didn't have to do that," she whispered harshly. She jammed the key in the lock and turned it hard. She shoved the door open and stomped inside.

"Engage and enrage, that's the plan," he said, closing the door behind them. "If Jason didn't take me seriously before, he will now."

Hurt knotted her insides. The kiss had been a ploy, nothing more. All part of Daniel's grand plan.

She whirled on him. "Improvising?"

"Yep," he replied, smugly.

She grabbed the front of his sweater. "Improvise this!" She kissed him.

His immediate response thrilled her. He wrapped both arms around her, crushing her against his body. Her fingers tangled in his sweater. He kissed her with bruising force. A full mouth kiss, wet and hot and arousing. Her teeth scraped his. Blood rushed in her ears. She wanted this, she wanted him. All of him. He backed her against the desk, never breaking the kiss. She couldn't breathe, she didn't need air. All she needed was him. The erotic thrusting of his tongue, the press of his hands against her back and under her hair, the grind of his pelvis against hers. He was aroused; knowing she aroused him inflamed her.

His mouth gentled. She slowed her tongue to match his rhythm and savored the sweet taste of his mouth. She worked her hands upward, over the soft knit of his sweater and found the rough masculinity of his cheeks. She touched his earlobes with her fingertips and a low pleasurable noise rumbled in his throat.

He kissed and kissed her, one moment soft and questing, the next hard and deep. Her breasts grew heavy, the ache matching the one in her groin.

The desk was sharp against her backside. She squirmed until she perched on the edge. He made that exciting noise again. When she hooked a leg around his, pressing their bodies tighter, he groaned. His hardness threatened to drive her mad. Denim scratched her suddenly sensitive thighs and she wanted to rip off her jeans—rip off his jeans.

He broke the kiss. She thrust her fingers into his hair. Thick but silky, it flowed over her hands like water. His eyes had darkened to chocolate sparked by embers.

"Do you mean this?" he asked, caressing her back. His fingers lingered over her bra strap.

The uncertainty she heard melted her from the inside out. She cupped his cheek. "I don't know what I mean," she answered honestly.

Her life suddenly felt as barren as the walls in this office or the tidy desktop. She had it all: a career, a great home, a close family. Without love, though, she had nothing.

"I can't keep holding you like this. I'll go nuts."

She traced the strong line of his cheekbone. She wanted him to go nuts. Common sense returned and she patted his cheek. "You better back off."

He nodded graciously and did so. His hands trembled.

Her hands trembled, too. She clutched the edge of the desk. "This isn't the time or the place. You realize that, don't you?"

He fingered his lower lip and smiled, his entire face softening. "Give me a time and place. I'll be there."

She should make him promise to never do anything like that again. No more touching. No more teasing. Put their relationship back on a strictly business level. Her thoughts drifted instead to the Honeymoon Hideaway, especially Cabin A with its carved bed and oversize marble bathtub built for two. She wanted to lick champagne off every inch of his gorgeous body. She wanted to tear off his fancy boxer shorts with her teeth.

She swiped hair off her face. She didn't look sexy, but she felt sexy. He was sexy—so sexy the sight of him physically pained her.

Loud voices in the hallway beyond the door drew her attention. A shriek, unmistakably coming from Chef, made her jump off the desk. Daniel flung out an arm, preventing her from opening the door. He opened the door enough to see out.

Chef bellowed something about Nazis.

Daniel led the way to the kitchen where Helmsley held Brian Cadwell by the arm. The young man's face looked formed of bread dough and his mouth hung slack. A pair of sheriff's deputies had their weapons drawn. Brandishing a wickedly sharp meat cleaver, Chef screamed threats. Kitchen workers cowered behind worktables.

The colonel arrived. "What the devil is going on here?"

Janine wanted to know the same thing. As tempting as it was to allow the deputies to shoot Chef, she stalked across the kitchen and stuck a finger in his face. "Put that down immediately!" Perhaps from shock, or perhaps because he suffered a rare bout of common sense, Chef slammed the cleaver onto a chopping block. *Clunk.* Chef grumbled under his breath, and his face turned bright red, but he crossed his arms and stood quivering with rage.

"Now, Mr. Helmsley, what are you doing?"

The investigator looked between her, the chef and the cleaver. He nodded curtly at the deputies. They holstered their weapons. "I've asked Mr. Cadwell to come with me to the sheriff's department. I'd like to ask him a few questions."

"Your basis for questioning is what exactly?" the colonel asked. "Why have you bypassed the chain of command?"

"Do you want to tell your boss, Brian, or do you want me to tell him?"

Tears rolled down Brian's fat cheeks.

"Seems our young friend here has some hobbies he failed to mention when we talked before. He likes to set fires in trash cans. He's got a thing about ladies' underwear, too."

Janine's mouth dropped open. Daniel cocked his head, studying Brian as if he were some exotic insect.

The colonel took one stiff step then another. His eyes glittered with fearsome light. With each step drawing him closer to Brian, the young man shrank. The colonel halted his advance and stood at parade rest, his feet apart, and his hands locked behind his back. "Are you the miscreant who's been harassing my daughter?"

"No," Brian sobbed. "I swear. This is all a mistake. I didn't do anything!"

"So let's go clear up those mistakes," Helmsley said.

"You can't question him here?" the colonel asked. "You may use my office."

"Brian has already agreed to go with us. He'll come quietly. Won't you, Brian?"

Flanked by the deputies, Helmsley led Brian out of the kitchen. The investigator refused to answer questions. Janine followed the group to the rear entrance of the east wing, then stood in the doorway and watched until they drove away. She considered Brian weasely and socially inept, but found it difficult to envision him locking her in the garage and setting the building on fire.

Not daring to believe her problems with Pinky were over, she accompanied her father to his office. Like a shadow, Daniel followed. The office was large and airy, with a window offering a view of the forest.

Daniel moved close to the glass-fronted weapons safe that displayed the colonel's collection of shotguns and rifles. Some were antique war weapons, but most were the weapons the colonel used in competition shooting. A shelf next to the safe displayed dozens of trophies, plaques, medals and ribbons the colonel had won for marksmanship.

"Is Brian our culprit?" the colonel asked.

"Many stalkers begin their careers with petty crimes," Daniel replied. "Homicide profilers consider setting fires part of the triad."

"Triad?"

"Common traits in the childhoods of serial killers. Bed-wetting, fire setting and cruelty to animals and smaller children. Erotomanic stalkers share similar traits. I'll ask Helmsley about the ladies' underwear. It might have to do with the B&E the sergeant told us about."

"B&E?"

"Brian was arrested for breaking and entering when he was fifteen. Looks like the cops found some other incidents."

"Why wasn't I informed of this, Janine?"

"I didn't have enough information."

"Why not? It's your job to know who works for us."

Janine bristled. Bad enough her father decided to blame her for the fracas in the kitchen. To chew her butt in front of Daniel infuriated her. "I don't give out top-secret clearances."

"Didn't you check references?"

"Of course I checked references! I always check references. What do you want me to do? Hire a private eye to verify applications?"

"Perhaps your policies need review."

Her policies? His policies! "In the past eight years I've hired hundreds of people! Other than some minor incidents, which I might remind you are no worse than any of the stunts some of your soldiers used to pull, you've had no complaints."

Daniel cleared his throat, loudly.

"Stay out of this!" she snapped.

She searched her father's implacable face. He always held her to a higher standard than he demanded of anyone else. He never cut her any slack. Ever since she'd confessed her troubles with Pinky she'd felt his blame in countless little ways.

"You blame me for Pinky, don't you? You think I encouraged him. That I hired him on purpose."

"All I am saying is, perhaps it is time to review your hiring policies and make adjustments—"

"You are blaming me!" She slapped her hands atop his desk. "Go ahead, admit it. You think this is my fault. I know you're thinking it, so go ahead and say it."

His nostrils flared. Hot color rose on his throat. Anger billowed around him like a thundercloud. *Good,* she thought with dark satisfaction.

"You must admit," he said quietly. "You do have a history of mistreating men. Look at what you did to Eric."

Her mouth snapped shut. If he'd jammed a twelve-inch butcher knife into her chest she couldn't hurt any worse.

All of her accomplishments meant nothing. All her successes may as well have never happened. She'd divorced precious, perfect, pathetic Eric, and that, as far as he was concerned, made her forever a failure.

Hatred rose with such heat and fury it left her shaking. She loved her father desperately. She lived for his approval. She yearned for his respect. She compared all other men to him and judged them by his standards of honor, integrity, strength and loyalty. At this moment, facing his disdain, knowing she'd never be good enough for him, she hated him.

She stormed out of the office and slammed the door.

Chapter Eleven

Daniel rarely lost his temper. He had better things to do than stomp around while anger burned holes in his gut. In this instance, however, he wanted to take the colonel outside for the Daniel Tucker version of slap and tickle.

Struggling for control, he reminded himself that some genuinely nice people, through ignorance, said extremely stupid things. *Why did you lead him on? He was only being nice. You shouldn't have hurt his feelings. He's sending nice presents and sweet letters, you should be flattered. Why did you make him so angry? He must be sick to act that way, you didn't have to be mean.* Even cops, judges and probation officers who witnessed firsthand the damage stalkers wreaked on innocent lives could be appallingly insensitive.

"She is not to blame, sir."

"This is not your concern. You are dismissed."

The colonel must have put the fear of God in every soldier who ever stood before him. But Daniel had faced down enraged men armed with guns or knives. He'd been questioned by attorneys who used such slimy tactics in court that he'd felt sick for days after testifying. He'd even faced down self-righteous fathers.

"Only Pinky knows why he selected Janine as a target. He knows why he's compelled to control her. He knows how he lied and fooled her into hiring him. *Only* he. To think otherwise victimizes Janine as much as Pinky does.''

The colonel's gnarled hands clenched into meaty fists atop the desk. He sucked air like a racehorse.

"I know how stalkers operate," Daniel continued. "It's a game to them. They feel a right to harass. They manipulate and lie. They strip away a victim's privacy and sense of safety. Because they want something, they give themselves a license to destroy an innocent life.'' He leaned both hands on the desk.

"As if having a nut terrorizing them isn't enough, victims have to put up with crap from friends and family. They suffer at the hands of a justice system more concerned with the rights of criminals than with the suffering of victims.''

"Point taken," the colonel said through gritted teeth.

"Nobody asks to be stalked. Nobody wants it. Nobody who hasn't been stalked can understand the kind of hell your daughter is going through right now. She needs your support, sir.''

"You're a brash young man."

"I've been called that and worse."

The colonel drew in a lungful of air and forcibly relaxed his hands. His eyes softened, slightly, and so did his mouth. "I get the distinct impression you care about my daughter.''

At the moment he didn't feel so good about that caring. He wasn't used to being rebuffed and found it astonishing when she told him no. His persistent pursuit of her seemed suddenly, uncomfortably close to stalking behavior.

"Yes, sir, I do care about her very much." She had a right to say no. He had an obligation to accept no.

"I do not approve of the way she's handling this matter.''

"Considering the circumstances, she's doing a good job.''

Elise Duke burst into the room. Daniel spun about, re-

flexively grabbing his pistol and placing himself between
the door and the colonel. At recognizing Elise, he relaxed,
but his heart pounded. Didn't any of these people know
how to knock?

"What in the world is going on? Chef is saying Nazis
dragged Brian away, and Janine is gone."

"Where did she go?" Daniel pictured Janine alone in
the surrounding forests, vulnerable to Pinky's attack. Short
hairs lifted on his neck. "What direction?"

"I have no idea where she went. I tried to catch her, but
she drove away. Will somebody please tell me what is going on?"

"THANKS FOR MEETING ME on such short notice," Janine
said. "I really needed to talk to a friend."

Brow twisted, lips pursed, Elliot looked her up and
down. "You look awful, darling. I've never seen you like
this."

She wore a grubby sweatshirt and jeans. Her hair was a
mess. She wore no makeup. His disapproval annoyed her,
but she passed it off as his normal fussbudgeting. "That's
why I asked you to meet me here. I'm not dressed for
anyplace nice."

His face skewed in an expression of open distaste as he
looked around the diner. A hostess led them to a booth.
Elliot brushed off the bright orange plastic bench seat. He
unbuttoned his jacket and held his tie so it wouldn't touch
the table when he sat down. "Coffee," he told the hostess.
"We don't need menus."

"I'd like a menu," Janine said. "I'm starving."

"They use frozen food here. And I imagine the kitchen
is none too clean."

Janine smiled apologetically at the hostess. She accepted
a menu. She studied the brightly illustrated selections and
sensed she'd made a mistake in asking him to meet her
here. Elliot despised fast food and chain restaurants. He

also despised being interrupted at work. They were not a spontaneous couple. He generally made dates a week or more in advance. She rarely called him at work. He disliked having his routines disrupted.

She slipped a hand into the side pocket of her purse where her cellular phone rested silently. She should call home, or at the very least turn on the phone so her family could call her. She'd hoped the long drive into the city would give her time to calm down and think rationally. She'd hoped to defuse some of her stress. With every mile she'd traveled, misery and hurt deepened over the colonel's unfairness. She didn't care if she never returned home.

The coffee arrived and Elliot declared it wretched. He didn't like the little plastic containers of creamer. He mused aloud about whether children with sticky, germy fingers had played with the sugar packets. Janine ordered a cheeseburger, then, more to annoy Elliot than from desire, asked for a side of onion rings.

"You don't like onion rings."

What did he know? She loved greasy, gooey, to-hell-with-watching-her-weight food. She rarely indulged, but that didn't mean she didn't like it. She wished Daniel were here. He'd eat onion rings with her and relish the taste. He wouldn't be prissily flicking minuscule crumbs off the tabletop, either.

Elliot was usually a charming date, always impeccably dressed with impeccable manners to match. In appearance he reminded her of the actor William Hurt. Nice looking, but not particularly handsome. He was pleasant, a good conversationalist, and never pressured her. Compared to Daniel, he was an insufferable prig.

She'd never seen him so irritable before. Daniel never got irritable. "Thank you for being here."

"You sounded so distraught, I canceled a very important meeting for you. What is the matter?" His expression said, *This had better be worth it.*

Her chin began to tremble and her eyes burned with impending tears. She unrolled the paper napkin from the knife, fork and spoon and pressed it against her eyes. She breathed deeply until certain she wouldn't cry. Elliot stared fixedly out the window. Daniel would have offered comfort. She dabbed the napkin at her lips and wondered if they looked as well-kissed as they felt. Elliot's kisses felt like the dry busses of a favorite uncle.

"My whole life is the matter," she said. "Oh, Elliot, everything has gone wrong. Everything!" Encouraged by his silence, she told him about Pinky and Daniel. She spoke haltingly, slowly, trying as much to make sense of what was happening to herself as to make Elliot understand. The cheeseburger and onion rings arrived. She dumped ketchup on her plate.

"Wait a minute," he interrupted. "Who is this Daniel Tucker again?"

"He owns some martial arts studios here in town. A friend of my cousin's. He's also an expert on stopping stalkers."

"And you hired him to provoke Pinky?" Elliot polished a spoon with a napkin. "I find it difficult to believe that you don't know who this Pinky fellow is."

"He won't let me know who he is."

"You've been accepting his letters and gifts for over a year and you don't know who he is?"

His skepticism appalled her. She paused with a mouthful of cheeseburger. She chewed hastily and washed it down with water. "I haven't accepted anything. He tried to murder me!"

"You're being rather melodramatic."

She wondered how melodramatic he'd feel if he'd been trapped inside a dark, smoky, flame-filled garage. She touched the remains of the scratch on her forehead. If it had been Elliot, rather than Daniel, in that garage, she'd be dead.

"You lead men on, darling. Look at what you do to me."

"Pardon?" Appetite gone, she pushed the plate aside.

"You run hot and cold, and send mixed signals. How am I supposed to act when you're smiling one second then acting as if I've trod on your toes the next? Now be truthful. You've flirted with this man and now you've wearied of his attentions." He smiled as if they shared a secret joke. "I doubt Pinky appreciates being twisted around your little finger any more than I do."

As hurtful as it was, she understood her father's position. Since she'd never been able to tell her father exactly what had happened between her and Eric, he'd been left to think the worst. But she didn't understand Elliot at all.

"I have never led you on."

"From day one you've set the terms for our relationship. It's always whatever you want, and how you want it. You never take my feelings into consideration. You're more than happy to let me buy you dinner, but you give nothing in return."

"That is not true!"

"And now I find out you've been carrying on some kind of fling. What am I supposed to think?"

She grabbed her purse and pawed through it in search of her keys. "I can see this is a mistake."

"Are you living some sort of double life? You never visit my home. You won't allow me to visit your home. What is it you're hiding from me?"

She snatched the bill off the table, grabbed her coat and purse and scooted out of the booth. "Goodbye, Elliot."

"I canceled a meeting for you."

"Don't worry, I'll never do it again."

He rose, towering over her. She resented him using his height in an attempt to intimidate her. "What is that supposed to mean?" he asked.

"It means," she replied quietly, "I thought you were my friend, but I now realize you are not. So, goodbye." Head high, she crossed the restaurant and presented the bill to the girl behind the cash register. Ignoring Elliot, she paid the bill and walked outside. A headache pounded in her temples. She missed Daniel with a yearning so powerful she ached down to her toes. He never spoke hatefully to her. He never accused. He sympathized without pitying her.

Elliot followed her to the Jeep. "We need to talk about this."

"I've known you for years, but now... I don't know you at all."

"What do you expect from me? I find out you're carrying on with some deranged boy who sets fires. Then you hire some martial arts fanatic to live at the resort, but you never even called me."

She blinked slowly. Hadn't Elliot listened? Perhaps he'd been thinking about the meeting she'd forced him to miss and had heard only enough to feel jealous. She climbed behind the wheel. "Goodbye."

He caught the edge of the door. "I love you, Janine. There, I've declared myself. All I need from you is a promise that you will stop seeing other men." He challenged her from behind his wire-rimmed eyeglasses.

Uncertain whether to laugh or cry, she jerked the door out of his grasp and hit the door locks. She drove out of the parking lot.

Love, she thought bitterly. Elliot hadn't the faintest idea what love was. He was as deluded as Pinky.

"HERE." Kara handed Daniel a small cardboard box. "Put the colored bulbs in here. Leave the clear ones on the strings."

Daniel popped colored minilightbulbs off the strings of Christmas lights. Every few seconds he glanced at the open door and listened for the crisp clicking of Janine's heels on the floor. Janine hadn't called, so either she didn't carry a telephone or it wasn't turned on. Throughout the long day he'd surreptitiously checked on the locations of Jason, Lanny and Ellen to assure himself Pinky hadn't followed Janine.

No word yet on Brian. Criminals, he mused. Cops took homicides and attempted homicides very seriously. Suspects were always astonished by how much information a determined investigator could dig up.

"She'll be okay," Kara said.

"Huh?"

"Janine. That's why you keep looking at the door, right?" Kara had done a good job of cleaning up after Pinky's temper tantrum, and now made progress in restoring some of the decorations.

"I've never seen her so upset."

Kara idly opened and closed a pair of scissors. Glitter sparkled on her face and hands. "She doesn't do stupid things. If that's what you're worried about." She lowered her voice. "What did the colonel say to her? I know he said something. He's the only person who can tick her off like that."

He concentrated on the lightbulbs. Kara had brought up nearly a hundred strings of minilights. All of them needed their colored bulbs replaced with clear bulbs. He didn't want to gossip about the colonel and Janine. Still... "Who is Eric?"

Kara nearly dropped the scissors. "Eric Collins?"

"Your father mentioned Eric, and Janine went off."

"Oh." She held up a pasted-together heart. "Eric is her ex-husband. The colonel only mentions him when he's really mad. No wonder she left."

Hurt pinged his innards. She'd never told him she'd been married. "She was married? When?"

"Long time ago. She never, ever talks about Eric. So whatever you do, don't bring him up. She's really touchy about it."

He had figured out that part already. "What happened?"

Kara set the heart aside and busied herself with a sheet of gold poster board. "Only she knows. They started out perfect. Eric was a captain, a West Pointer." She rolled her eyes. "Gorgeous. I was only a kid, but man! And the colonel thought Eric walked on water. He actually encouraged them to get together. If you know my dad at all, you know that doesn't happen very often. He hates everybody we girls date."

"Was he one of your dad's soldiers?"

"An officer," she corrected with a smile. "The colonel was a battalion commander, and Eric commanded one of his companies." She sighed dreamily. "Their wedding was like a fairy tale, so romantic. All the men in dress blues. Guys with sabers. Megan and I were bridesmaids.

"Then Eric got transferred to Germany. I thought they were the perfect couple. But then Eric had an accident."

"What kind?"

"He was a Cavalry officer, on border patrol. His driver wasn't very experienced. He rolled the Jeep down a mountain." She touched the side of her face. "Eric's face got smashed and he lost a leg. He almost died."

Daniel suppressed a reflexive shudder. He liked his body, his body liked him. Imagining mutilation and the loss of limbs gave him the willies.

"They brought him back to the States." She frowned. "I don't know what happened exactly. We were living in Kentucky. Mom flew up to D.C. all the time to help Janine out. Eric was getting better. But one day Janine showed up and said she'd left him. They got divorced."

Daniel sifted the information through his brain. No matter how he looked at it, he kept coming to the same conclusion: Janine had deserted her invalid husband. Her mutilated, wounded - in - the - line - of - duty, no - longer - handsome - and - perfect husband.

"I asked her what happened. Once. Never again. She won't talk about him." She hung her head, looking abashed. "I shouldn't have told you. Don't tell her I told you, okay?"

He wished she hadn't told him, too. He didn't want to make the mistakes his parents made, and he didn't want to hang around people who acted like his parents. His mother allowed no one other than herself to be the center of attention. Refusing to admit her age, she insisted Daniel call her Marie, never Mom. His father collected beautiful, flaky wives whose amorality and penchant for affairs matched his own. Deep within that old storage locker of childhood hurts he could still hear the shrieking, weeping, accusatory battles of adults who refused to grow up.

Dumping an invalid husband was something his mother would do. In fact, she had dumped husband number three when he got cancer. She couldn't handle the stress, she'd claimed.

He finished a string of lights, coiled it neatly, then picked up the next. Janine dazzled him. Dazzled him enough, perhaps, for him to attribute qualities to her he only wished were there.

He sensed a presence a second before Elise appeared in the doorway. She looked tired and deeply concerned. Forty years of marriage, Daniel thought. She was what he'd been imagining Janine would be like in forty years. Lovely and serene, proud of her children and still deeply in love with her husband.

"Daniel? Janine is on the telephone. She wishes to speak to you."

He set the lights aside and rose. He swiped his grimy hands on his jeans. "Is she all right?"

"I think so." She handed him a cordless telephone. "This whole Pinky business is so very hard on her, isn't it?"

"You have no idea, ma'am." He put the phone to his ear. "Where are you?"

She chuckled softly. "Gee, Dad, did I miss curfew?"

She sighed heavily into the phone. "I'm in the parking lot. I'm—I'm scared to get out of the car."

"Be there in a sec." He hung up and handed the phone to Elise. "She's waiting outside. I'll get her."

He found Janine seated in the Jeep. He understood why she didn't want to walk alone. The staff parking lot was next to the dormitory. He heard the door lock click, and she gestured for him to get in.

A cold front had rolled over the mountains, and after the sun set the temperature had dropped below zero. He scrubbed his arms. "Brrr!"

"The weather forecast says we might get some snow." She rested her arms on the steering wheel. Parking lot lights illuminated her profile. Her long lashes cast shadows beneath her eyes. "That would be nice. This place is so pretty when it snows."

She sounded tired, distant and very sad. He squeezed his biceps, refusing to give in to the urge to touch her. "Where have you been?"

"Colorado Springs. I met Elliot. Then—" she jerked a thumb over her shoulder "—I went shopping. Party supplies."

His abdominal muscles clenched. Kiss him senseless in her office, drive him wild, then run straight into the arms of her boyfriend. It sounded exactly like something his mother would do. She had called her relationship with Elliot casual. Maybe she meant she was casual about sleeping around.

"I should have called," she said.

"Everyone was worried. Especially your mom."

"I know." She rested her forehead on her arms. "I just had to get away."

"To see Elliot." He winced, wishing he hadn't said that.

"That was an impulse." She laughed ruefully. "I should know better. I'm not so good at improvisation."

He perked up, his foolish heart hopeful. "Elliot wasn't happy to see you?"

Her shoulders hitched. "That's an understatement. I interrupted him at work. Then he said Pinky is my fault and I must be leading him on. He all but accused me of having an affair."

Daniel brutally shoved aside relief. What Janine did with her life was of no concern to him. As attractive as she was, as much as he desired her, he wasn't stupid enough to believe people changed. She had hired him for a job, he would do that job, and nothing more. He sensed she needed to talk, but he didn't have the stomach to listen to complaints about her love life.

"It's cold out here. Let's get your stuff inside." He opened the door and hopped out, automatically looking around for any potential danger.

"Daniel?" She leaned over to peer at him through the open passenger door. A thin line appeared between her eyebrows.

"Come on, Ms. Duke. I can't do my job with frostbite." She grabbed her purse and left the Jeep.

Elise Duke met them at the door. She hugged her daughter, relieved Daniel of a few plastic bags and accompanied them upstairs. Janine passed off her mother's questions with monosyllabic answers. She never mentioned Elliot.

Kara appeared delighted by Janine's purchases. She urged Daniel to help her unpack and sort boxes of lightbulbs, craft paper, bundles of fabric flowers, yards of lace and other colorful miscellany.

"You need to speak to your father," Elise said. "He's worried about you."

"I doubt that very much."

"Janine, please—"

"He never cuts me any slack! He never lets me forget a mistake, and he treats every screw-up like an act of treason. He blames me for Pinky."

"You know how he is when he's frightened. It's difficult for him to admit he's worried about you."

Janine snorted disparagingly. "He's afraid I'll make him look bad, that's what he's afraid of."

"You're being unfair."

"So is he!" She met Daniel's eyes; he recognized torment and looked away. "I'm not apologizing to him, Mom. Not this time. I am sick and tired of begging for his forgiveness." She thumped her fist between her breasts. "God help me if I can't live up to his standards. Why can't he just accept me the way I am?"

"Oh, dear." Elise grasped her daughter's hands. "He loves you more than life itself."

"He's got a funny way of showing it." Her voice cracked and wavered. "I'm sorry I worried you today. It was stupid. But I'm not apologizing to the colonel. For once in his life, he can apologize to me." She turned her back on her mother and stared at the floor.

"Very well," Elise said with a sigh. "At least you're home safe." She hugged her daughter again, smiled wanly at Daniel and Kara, then left the room.

"Are you okay, Ninny?" Kara asked. She appeared braced for a storm.

"Fine. Did anything happen that I need to take care of?"

"Everything is under control." She patted Daniel's arm. "He's been helping me with the decorations."

"A man of many talents." She sank onto a chair and rolled her neck. "Who's probably regretting he's smack in the middle of our little family soap opera. I'm sorry you have to keep witnessing our spats."

He passed off her concern with a careless wave. "You ought to see my family in action. You Dukes are rank amateurs in the dysfunctional Olympics."

Kara perked up. "You have a crazy family? How so? You seem really normal."

Before he could indulge her love of gossip, Mike

Downes arrived. "Hi." His smile focused on Kara. "Your mom said you were up here."

"You're in uniform, so it must be official," Kara said tartly. "Do you have news about Brian?"

"I brought him back to the resort. He's waiting downstairs. I figured you'd want to talk to him, Janine."

Daniel and Janine rose. She appeared excited, but he knew if the cops had released Brian then the kid hadn't confessed to arson. "What's the story?"

"My opinion? The kid's guilty as hell. Unfortunately, the state boys can't charge him. They asked him to take a polygraph, but he refused and demanded a lawyer. When the mouthpiece showed up he made them cut Brian loose."

"What about his criminal record?" Janine asked.

"Property crimes. All of it was handled in juvie court. But we aren't talking run-of-the-mill kid capers. He set a neighbor's storage shed on fire. He was only twelve at the time. There were other suspicious fires in the neighborhood, but the cops couldn't connect them." He smiled tightly, humorlessly. "Brian's mommy was real good at protecting her baby from the bad old policemen."

"What about the B&E?" Daniel asked.

"Same neighbor whose shed he torched, a woman living alone. He broke into her house and stole her underwear. When the cops popped him they found quite a stash under his bed."

"Eeeyew!" Kara shuddered.

"Brian spent a year locked up. He got some therapy. Personally, I think juvie hall made him a smarter criminal. He acts like a sniveling little crybaby, but he's one hard kid. Helmsley couldn't crack him." His face crinkled with a smile. "Helmsley is royally PO'd."

"What about a handwriting exemplar to match him up with the Pinky letters?" Daniel asked.

Mike grumbled, looking disgusted. "Nada. The lawyer told him to get a warrant. Figure the odds on that."

Janine chuffed indignantly. "But why?"

"Because no hard evidence connects Pinky to the arson. Judges don't like fishing expeditions. Unless we find evidence, we won't get the warrant. Without the warrant, no evidence." He showed his palms in hapless apology. "It's the system."

"Do you think he's Pinky, Mike?"

Mike jutted his chin at Daniel. "Ask the expert. All I can say is I don't like the kid and I wouldn't want him working for me. He's squirrel bait from the get-go."

Daniel mulled over the information. "He fits the profile. Harassing a neighbor for so long means he's prone to obsessive behavior. He lied on his application, so you have to fire him, Janine. But without proof that he's Pinky we can't obtain a restraint order under the stalking statutes. The best we can do is pop him for trespassing if he returns to the resort."

"He won't quit stalking, will he?" Mike asked.

Daniel hated having to say what needed saying. "No. There's a chance I can intimidate him. But if the cops and the threat of prison don't scare him, then I don't know how he'll react to me. We need to institute some extreme security measures."

"Like what?"

"Buttoning up the lodge for one thing. Install one-way emergency doors in the wings. Lock the main doors after hours. Lock the entrances to the basement. Hire a security-trained doorman."

Janine staggered as if he'd punched her. "I'm supposed to turn the lodge into an armed fortress?"

Mike cleared his throat. "I agree with Daniel. If Brian returns we can get him for trespass, but that's only if we catch him. You can't get a restraint order without cause. We can't prove Brian threatened you."

"So I have to act like a prisoner in my own home? Completely disrupt the operation of the resort? Live the rest of my life looking over my shoulder?'' She pointed a trembling finger at Daniel. ''Find another plan!''

''We still have a few options. The first is, we haven't found Pinky's stash yet. I know it exists. It has to exist. There's sure to be some clue to Pinky's real identity.''

''And if there isn't?''

He studied Mike. He'd come to the conclusion that the sergeant was a good cop. He was smart and he cared deeply about the Duke family. ''I'll handle Brian.''

Mike stood taller. A frown furrowed his brow. ''If you mean what I think you mean, then you better be very careful. That punk knows the law.''

Janine shifted her suspicious gaze between the men. ''What do you mean? What are you going to do?''

''Put a tail on him. Twenty-four hours a day, seven days a week. I know some guys who'll give Pinky second thoughts about returning to Elk River. If we catch him mailing pink envelopes or if he starts calling, we can use the law against him.''

''And when Brian charges you under the stalking statutes?'' Mike asked.

''You let me worry about that.''

''So we have to wait for him to make another move?'' Janine looked as disgusted as Daniel felt.

Even knowing that falling into the what-if trap was useless, Daniel felt guilty. He wanted to stop Pinky. He wanted Janine to live her life as she wished, without fearing a madman lurking in the shadows. He no longer cared about being a hero in her eyes, but he cared deeply about stopping one more stalker from ruining one more life.

''Intervention time,'' he said grimly. ''Mike, mind being somewhere else while I chat to Brian?''

The sergeant checked his wristwatch. ''I'm off shift. Maybe Kara could use some help in here?''

''Give me your office key, Janine. Wait thirty minutes before you come downstairs. Then follow my lead. I want

to convince him the problem is me, not you.'' Seeing the
protest forming, he raised his right hand. ''And no, I will
not touch him.''

She worked a key off a ring and handed it over. Her
fingers grazed his. Electric tingling rippled through his skin.
He wanted so much to embrace her and assure her he'd
keep her safe. He wanted to gaze all night long into her
violet eyes.

He brutally reminded himself he'd fallen in lust before.
He'd survived, as he would survive now, sore but un-
damaged. What he couldn't survive would be repeating his
parents' idiotic mistakes.

With the key in hand he headed downstairs. He took his
time, formulating what he was about to say and how he
was going to say it. He needed to convince the kid that the
Daniel Tucker brand of stalker-busting held the power to
make Brian's miserable life unbearable.

The corridor in front of Janine's office was deserted.
Brian Cadwell was gone.

Chapter Twelve

Daniel grasped the door frame and leaned into the room. Janine, Mike and Kara looked surprised to see him. "Brian has disappeared," he announced.

Janine dropped a string of lights and jumped to her feet. "What do you mean?"

"I checked the kitchen. I went through the entire east wing. Asked everybody. Checked the lobby. No one has seen him."

"He's probably in his room." She grabbed her coat off a chair. She shoved her armed into the sleeves. "You don't think he ran away, do you, Mike?"

"Could be," the deputy replied. "We'll catch him in the dorm."

The three of them hurried down the back stairs. They met the colonel at the rear entrance. He wore a coat, and his cheeks were ruddy from the cold. He looked grimly satisfied. He stopped at the sight of them and snapped into parade rest position. "I see you've decided to resume your post, Janine."

His coldness broke her heart. She shook off the pain. "We're looking for Brian Cadwell. Have you seen him?"

"I have."

She heaved a sigh of relief. She'd been imagining Brian disappearing into the bowels of the lodge, going underground to wreak his havoc, committing terrorist acts with impunity. "Is he in the dorm?"

"You needn't concern yourself with him any longer. I have mustered him out and personally supervised his departure from the grounds."

Janine gave her head a shake, unable to believe what she'd heard. Bad enough her father blamed her for Pinky's behavior, but to discount the danger? "You didn't."

"I spoke to Mr. Helmsley on the telephone. He informed me about Brian's criminal record. I will not tolerate lying, nor treason in our midst. I have discharged the boy and forbidden him from ever returning."

"Where did he go?"

"That is not my concern." He nodded crisply and dropped his arms. "Nor is it yours. I will handle all necessary paperwork first thing in the morning."

"You shouldn't have done that," Janine whispered. "We think he's Pinky."

"After hearing Mr. Helmsley's report, so do I. You need concern yourself no longer." He glared down his nose at Daniel. "I've had long experience in handling troops, sir. Where young men and trouble are concerned, I've seen it all. While I understand where you may think your brand of skullduggery serves its purpose, vast experience proves the best solutions are generally the most obvious. Quick, clean, efficient. Problem solved."

"But—"

"End of discussion, Janine. I expect you to finalize your agreement with Daniel so we may all get back to normal." He marched away.

As one, Daniel, Janine and Mike watched his erect back and arm-swinging stride.

Janine turned to Daniel with such a helpless, frightened look in her beautiful eyes he nearly melted. Confusion racked him. How could she so cavalierly dump a husband, yet care so deeply about her family?

"We're right back where we started. Brian will blame my father for firing him."

"We can still turn him. Mike, you said he's a mama's boy? He'll probably run to her so he can lick his wounds. We can get her address off—"

"His mother is deceased," Mike said. "According to Brian's shtick, he's a poor little orphan boy with no one to protect him. I'll double-check with the office."

Daniel didn't like this one little bit. Throw in stressors like losing a job, getting hassled by the police and having no place to go, and a stalker may as well carry a sign saying, I Am Going to Kill Somebody Now. "I'll go through his employee file and see what I can pull off it." He lowered his gaze to the floor, envisioning the labyrinthine basement below. He prayed Brian, with vengeance and betrayal burning up his brain, didn't worm his way back into the lodge.

"HIS FORMER EMPLOYERS liked him. Chef liked him." Safe in her room, Janine sat across the table from Daniel. A late-night talk show played on the television. Wind howled past the windows, giving her chills despite the warmth radiating from the furnace registers. "Fine, he lied on his application, he lied to the police, but he hasn't been in trouble for years. Maybe he learned his lesson. Maybe the therapy helped. Juvenile records are sealed for a good reason. Most kids who do stupid things grow out of it."

"You can't wish him away," Daniel said without looking up from Brian's employee file. "I know you don't want to lock down the resort, but you can't take chances."

Panic rose in her throat. She envisioned happy, friendly, hospitable Elk River transformed into an armed camp. What came next? Mounting metal detectors at the doors? Going through rooms with bomb-sniffing dogs?

"I'll find Brian," he said. "I'll put a tail on him. If he pulls anything stupid, I'll catch him."

She clung to the promise in his voice. She pushed away from the table and paced. Her fingertips trailed over a dresser, and she wondered if Brian had stolen underwear from her. She jerked her hand off the dresser and scrubbed the back of it until her bones ached.

"Get some sleep." He yawned and covered his mouth with his hand. "There's no more we can do tonight."

"My head hurts," she complained and looked to him hopefully. She wanted him to massage her scalp…to hold her. Kiss her and comfort her and make her feel safe. The encounter with Elliot had been a wake-up call. She wasted her life by playing it safe in the romance department. Armoring herself against pain kept joy at bay, as well.

Maybe Daniel Tucker wasn't the man for her. She'd never know for certain unless she gave them a chance. She edged toward him. He watched her, his gaze steady but unreadable. She mustered a wan smile, the best she could manage. "My neck is stiff, too."

His eyes glazed. His hands curled into fists. Then he smiled brightly and jumped to his feet. He took a wide step to the side. "Sleep will help. You look exhausted. We can think more clearly in the morning." He sat on the couch where he'd already made up his bed.

His deliberate avoidance astonished her. He sounded different, somehow cold. She rubbed her upper arms slowly. He didn't remove the robe until he was under the covers. He never looked her way.

She walked slowly to the bed. When he failed to speak, sadness washed through her. He turned out the light next to the couch. She crawled under the covers and turned off the light on the bed table. The utter darkness gave her a little shock of fear. She growled at herself for acting like a baby. She wasn't afraid of the dark. She turned her gaze to the door, though, where a thin slash of light showed under the door. "Good night."

"Night, Ms. Duke."

His neutral tone offered no clues as to whether the formality was meant to tease or not.

She sat up and turned on the light. "Are you mad at me?"

"No, ma'am."

Ma'am? He snuggled under the covers and closed his eyes. The 9 mm glinted on the floor beside him. "Are you sure you aren't mad at me? You seem…different."

He opened one eye. "Everything is cool. Now get some sleep."

She snapped off the light and flumped back against the pillows. He was angry! Everyone else was angry at her, so why not Daniel, too? She tried to sleep, she longed for sleep, but sleep eluded her. She listened to the wind battering the lodge. She held little hope that a decent snowfall would transform the resort into a winter wonderland for the party. February tended to be the driest month of the year.

She tossed and turned for what felt like hours. She listened to Daniel's deep, even breathing. She fantasized about his beautiful body and the touch of his hands against her skin.

A stealthy noise alerted her and she snapped upright. She strained to identify the source. A shadow rippled through the light shining under the door. She sprang off the bed, noting in passing that the digital readout on the alarm clock read 2:08. At the door, she pressed her ear to the wood and listened. She heard only her hammering heart.

She debated opening the door to peek into the hallway. If someone was actually out there, she'd die—if not figuratively, then quite possibly literally. Her mouth dried and her tongue stuck to her palate.

Her bare foot brushed something on the floor. Her calf muscles recoiled. She groped and found a square of stiff paper. She ran her fingers over its outlines. It felt like an envelope.

A light flared. Daniel sat up, the gun in his hand.

Janine's fingers lost all strength. A bright pink envelope fluttered to the floor.

Daniel leaped off the couch and ordered Janine into the bathroom. She scooted for safety. When he heard the click of the door lock, he raised the Luger to shoulder level, drew a deep breath and eased open the bedroom door. Adrenaline ripped through his veins and heightened his senses. Dim lighting shined at both ends of the hallway.

Mike, he thought, heart sinking. The deputy was posted outside the colonel's bedroom. Horrible images of a bloody lawman rose in his brain. He drew another deep breath, prepared for the worst, and stuck his head out the door.

Down the hall, Mike Downes slumped still and silent on a chair. The chair back rested against the wall. Arms crossed, chin to chest, with a magazine draped over his thigh, the deputy slept. Daniel stared until convinced he saw Mike's chest rising and falling. He sidled out of the room, shifting his gaze back and forth. Gooseflesh broke on his bare back. Every hair on his body stood at attention.

"Mike!"

His harsh whisper startled the deputy awake. The chair legs thumped on the floor. The magazine slipped off his lap. Mike looked around wildly.

Daniel lowered the pistol to his side. "You missed the party, man."

"Huh?" He blinked blearily.

Wondering when was the last time the deputy had a good night's sleep, Daniel clucked his tongue. His mouth tasted funky. "Pinky was here. He slipped a letter under Janine's door."

"Here?" Mike asked stupidly. Cursing a blue streak, he scooped his hat off the floor and unsnapped his holster. "I can't believe I fell asleep. You're sure it's Pinky? Which way did he go?"

Daniel shrugged. The little sneak could be anywhere by now. He returned to Janine's room. He slipped on the terry cloth robe before he knocked on the bathroom door and gave her an all-clear.

"Did you see him?" she asked angrily. "Is it Brian? How did he get past you, Mike?"

The young man hunched his shoulders and pulled his hat brim through his fingers. "I fell asleep."

"Oh, for—" She snatched the envelope off the floor and ripped it open. She extracted a sheet of pale pink paper, covered front and back with crabbed handwriting. "I can't read his garbage," she said, the words trailing into a groan.

Daniel took the letter. Pinky's brazenness angered him, but didn't surprise him. The stalker had proved his determination over and again. The letter's tone surprised him. Pinky commiserated with Janine about the shadows under her eyes and the way she neglected her appearance. He urged her to wear the red silk Donna Karan suit, assured it would make her feel better. He also suggested she trim her hair. Split ends were showing. He said a vacation might not be a bad idea to take her away from the stress of her overbearing father and his countless demands. For three paragraphs he spun an adolescent fantasy about the two of them hiking the Appalachian trail, sleeping under the stars and communing with nature.

The final paragraph chilled his blood. He read it aloud.

"I passed every test. I'm ready for the main event now. I bow before your wisdom even though it's been hard, love. I confess, I've faltered and had my doubts. But I know how proud you are of me. I see in your eyes how much you care. Your smiles give me courage. Every day is a challenge to live up to your expectations. I can do it. I have the right stuff. It's time to make our love public."

Janine paused in her aimless pacing. The wind had died, so the room was quiet. Her breathing sounded harsh and ragged. "What tests?" she asked. "What does that mean?"

"He knows I'm a ringer," Daniel answered. "I don't know how he knows, but he does. Damn it."

Mike took the letter. His eyes flicked over the words, and his lips moved silently. His face darkened until he looked as dangerous as a mean drunk spoiling for a bar fight. "This doesn't make any sense. Sounds like Ms. Duke knows exactly what he's doing."

"That's part of his delusion." Daniel jammed his hands in his pockets. Muscles flexed in his arms and shoulders. He went rigid. "Whoa! Let me see that again."

Mike and Janine crowded Daniel to read over his shoulder. He stuck his finger on mid-page and read aloud, "'I am grateful for your modesty.' Modesty?" He turned a wondering gaze on Janine and cocked his head.

"He's congratulating you on using me to test his devotion. Then he's glad you're modest?" He swept his gaze over her sweatshirt and fleece pants. He turned his face toward the ceiling.

Curious, Janine looked up, too. Like all the rooms on the second floor, it had exposed log beams running across the heavily textured ceiling.

Daniel pointed up. "What's above your room?"

Short hairs lifted on her nape. No way did she want to think what his question led her to think. "The attic."

Gaze on the ceiling, Daniel walked slowly back and forth. At her bed, he leaned far over the mattress until he rested on both hands, his neck craning. He hopped onto the bed and stretched, reaching for the ceiling. His fingertips barely brushed the bottom of a beam. "Look at this."

Janine turned on the overhead, then peered closely at where he pointed. Finally she saw it, a fuzzy pink tuft.

"Insulation," Daniel said. "There's a hole in the ceiling."

Janine's belly seemed to drop to her toes; her gorge rose. The tiny hole was directly over the side of the bed on which she slept. Pinky had been spying on her. Sneaking stealthily about in the attic, peering through the hole, watching her. The view that rose in her mind was of herself, her face slathered in cold cream, her hair bristling with fat pink rollers, while she read a racy novel and watched an old movie on television. Maybe all those times she'd imagined noises in the night hadn't been her imagination after all.

She had a right to privacy. She deserved her privacy. For Pinky to so casually strip it from her was an offense for which he'd receive neither pity nor compassion. Murderous rage displaced her fear.

The three of them carried flashlights up to the attic. Daniel and Mike had their weapons drawn. None of them made a sound—though Janine was positive if Pinky lurked nearby, then surely he heard her pounding heart. Daniel urged her to stay behind him. He kept reaching back with his left hand as if checking she followed.

She found the control panel and turned on the lights. In the nanosecond before the bulbs flared, she prayed Pinky was up here. He'd be wishing for the mercy of a bullet by the time she finished with him.

White cloths covered upholstered sofas and chairs. Metal shelving held boxes of old papers and books, table lamps, flowerpots and other miscellany. A row of hooded lamps hanging from the central room beam formed more shadows than illumination. Dust motes swirled around the light fixtures. Mustiness was undercut by the flavors of ancient potpourri and mothballs.

Daniel and Mike shone flashlight beams into corners. She strained to hear suspicious rustles or clunks.

"The floor," she whispered and pointed her flashlight at footprints in the dust. The men crouched to examine the prints.

"Looks like he's wearing socks," Mike said. "Clever." He shone the flashlight at an angle that highlighted the faint prints. "Not many people come up here, do they?"

"We use this for long-term storage. Anyone up here for a good reason would wear shoes." She got her bearings in regard to where her room was. "Over here." She squeezed through upholstered chairs stacked two high and covered with cloths. The dust on the floor had been disturbed recently. She hunkered into a crouch to search for the peephole.

On hands and knees, the three searched between the stacked chairs. Their bobbing heads formed a macabre shadow puppet show on the walls. She kept checking to make sure only three shadows flickered on the walls, not four.

"Loose board," Mike announced. He held up a piece of planking. The insulation beneath the board lifted like a flap and a ray of light beamed upward through a tiny hole.

Janine peered through the hole. The view it offered astounded her. She could see her entire bed, the bedside table and nearly to the door. "He's played us for jackasses all along. Spying on us, listening."

"Looks like it." Daniel peered under a furniture cloth. "His stash is here somewhere."

Between two chairs, their cushions removed, stacked so it formed a sheltered niche, Mike discovered Pinky's shrine to Janine. The centerpiece, placed like a bible, was her Day-Timer book. A used candle was stuck to the middle of the book. Soot stained the chair upholstery above it and wax pooled on the organizer's leather binding. Over it, pinned to the chair was Janine's college graduation photograph.

She peered curiously at the photograph, uncertain where Pinky might have acquired it. The only photographs she kept in her room were photos of friends and snapshots she'd taken on vacations. He could have stolen it from her parents' room, or even Kara's.

Surrounding the photograph were newspaper clippings about Elk River. Each mention of her name was highlighted in pink. She recognized her missing hairbrush, a lipstick tube, and a small spiral notebook she'd used as a journal. Pens, slips of paper, a key and a used cloth napkin weren't personal, but they disturbed her on a deep, instinctual level.

"Don't touch anything," Mike warned.

"Here's more," Daniel said. He held up a corner of cloth. On another chair seat was a flat-woven basket. It contained pink stationery, a roll of stamps, pens and greeting cards. A clipboard was propped against the inner chair arm.

Janine pictured Pinky, seated in the dark, burning a candle in homage while he penned declarations of sick love.

"Roust Juan out of bed." Mike lowered the cloth over the make-shift shrine. "Have him padlock the attic door. I'll call the sheriff. He'll get the state boys over here to collect the evidence."

Daniel looked around the attic. "We can trap him."

"No can do. We don't know how often Pinky comes up here. You could spend weeks sitting in the dark while he's making trouble elsewhere. Uh-uh, this is all the trap we need. We'll get fingerprints. Match up the footprints."

"If the fingerprints don't belong to Brian? Then what?"

"You said Brian is Pinky."

"Maybe. Or he could be a goofball who got caught in a lie. If they run the prints and come up with zilch, then what? Get fingerprints from every employee? What about those who refuse? You couldn't get a judge to sign a warrant for Brian's handwriting exemplar. Where will you find one who forces everyone to give fingerprints?"

"I can't withhold evidence."

"Pinky warned us about the main event. That means the party. I'm not willing to trust Janine's life or the colonel's life to the bureaucratic process."

"Gentlemen!" Janine waited a beat until certain she had their attention. "We can have it both ways. Mike, ask the sheriff to make sure the people who collect this stuff are very discreet. Daniel, call J.T. and have him set up a surveillance camera. It doesn't have to be one of those special little models. There are dozens of places we can hide a camcorder."

The men exchanged a glance.

"If Pinky comes back up here, we'll catch him on tape. If he doesn't, the police will figure out who he is by the fingerprints. Can we do that?"

"Sounds like a plan to me," Daniel said.

Mike grumbled, but agreed.

"Hold off calling the sheriff until morning. I don't want to disturb my parents...or alert Pinky if he's still lurking around."

"I have to call in. If Brian is prowling the premises, we can pick him up."

"Of course, but I don't want anybody in the attic right now. We'll wake up everybody on the second floor."

Mike announced he was going to search the lodge. Daniel insisted he guard the colonel's suite. Seeing yet another argument about to commence, Janine issued orders. Mike would resume the post; she and Daniel would search the lodge. They wanted to argue with her, but she held her ground. This was her resort, her responsibility—and there was no way in hell she would allow Daniel to roam around alone.

AT THIS HOUR OF THE MORNING the lobby and lounge were silent and dimly lit, with only enough lights turned on to assure safety.

"Kind of spooky at night," Daniel said, sotto voce.

"It didn't used to be." A shudder rippled down her spine and a rush of fear raised the hairs on her arms. "How long do you think he's been spying on my room?"

"Try not to think about it."

"You try not thinking about it." She waited for him to take her hand or to drape an arm over her shoulders. When he did neither, hurt pinged her heart. She fiddled with a flashlight, turning it on and off, assuring herself the batteries were strong.

"You ready for the basement?"

"No," she replied honestly. "But let's do it." She hefted the flashlight. If she found Brian Cadwell in the basement, she intended to brain him first, ask questions later.

She and Daniel descended into the basement. They searched every room, niche, corner and hidey-hole. Several times she trod on his heels. Her heart pounded until her chest ached, and she wondered if she'd have a heart attack before morning. Other than working herself into a raging case of the screaming meemies, nothing was accomplished.

Daniel turned the flashlight on her face. "Are you cold?"

She noticed her teeth chattered. She clenched her jaws. She had goose bumps on top of goose bumps, but the basement wasn't cold. Heat from the boiler room, laundry room and myriad pipes insinuated itself into even the most remote rooms. "I'm scared." Her voice was husky and small.

"I'm high on adrenaline myself. Let's get out of here."

She watched him walk away, his footsteps quick and soundless, his posture alert. She'd all but held up a flashing sign saying, Hold Me. Could he truly be that unforgiving over the way she'd run off? She'd apologized. What more could he ask?

He stopped abruptly. His hair gleamed in the tricky light of the bouncing flashlight beams. "Do you hear something?"

Only the inane questions in her heart. She hurried to catch up to him. At the staircase, both of them took the stairs two and three at a time.

They checked on Mike. He stood in the hallway outside her parents' suite rather than sit on the chair. He assured them that the sheriff had dispatched two patrol cars to check out the resort and nearby roads for Brian's car.

An inspection of the upper floors of the lodge proved as fruitless as the basement search. Housekeepers and the kitchen crew were coming on duty. Everyone denied seeing Brian Cadwell. She noticed Daniel keeping his distance

from her. No more "cupcake," no more playing the lover.
She felt abandoned.

Morose, irritable and frustrated, she ended up in her office. She dropped onto the sofa and threw her feet up on
the arm. Her eyes felt as if she'd walked through a sand-
storm. Her head throbbed. She wanted some coffee, but
couldn't bear facing Chef right now.

"Now what?" she asked.

Daniel sat behind her desk and pulled the telephone in
front of him. "I'll call J.T."

"It's too early."

"He'll be up."

Her parents would be in the dining room by now, eating
breakfast, unaware of the sickening discovery she'd made
in the attic. She hoped Mike hadn't told the colonel about
the latest note, the hole in the ceiling or Pinky's shrine.
After the way her father had handled Brian, no telling what
he would do about Pinky's night-crawling. Shut down the
resort, possibly—cancel the anniversary party, definitely.

If he did, damn it, that meant Pinky had won. That meant
he'd jerked her strings, made her dance—it meant he
owned her.

She closed her aching eyes and listened to Daniel speak
to her cousin-in-law. His voice soothed her, his smooth-
but-animated tenor was like a psychic massage, working
some of the kinks from her soul.

Come over here and hold me, she telegraphed silently. *I
really, really need you to hold me....*

poling finished reading. Daniel, seething because Jean Metcalfe's specifically discouraged the firm poker with a redhead, and changing the color on the resort's theme was wing. The colonel finished his easy ingrates' poses for decisions ways.

Her father refused to discuss the changes with Janine. Apparently, attached only to the list of chores he needed, downgraded. Janine settled in reply to her questions and comments. She continued the work of colonel employees without breaking his mood. He thought so. Janine kept chilling her ear. "Quit it," and shrugged the feelers. She placed

Chapter Thirteen

Crappy day. A day that belonged in Janine's should-have-stayed-in-bed Hall of Fame.

Helmsley had taken charge of Pinky's stash and peephole. Crime technicians collected the items as evidence. Seeing the techs in action had exhilarated Janine. Everyone wore rubber gloves. They photographed footprints, the shrine, makeshift writing desk and peephole. They bagged each item and tagged it. They dusted the attic for fingerprints. At last, a real break in the case.

And then Helmsley told Janine he doubted if the evidence would point to arson, attempted murder or the vandalism of Daniel's truck. Which meant even if he proved Brian and Pinky were one and the same, the best-case scenario meant Brian might go to jail for a year for making death threats—if a judge decided that the threatening letters fulfilled the requirements of the antistalking statutes.

Finding the stash and the latest letter had an energizing effect on the colonel. To Janine's surprise, and suspicion, her father openly recruited Daniel as the resident security expert. The resort would hire security guards for the anniversary party. Wearing tuxes so as to mingle unobtrusively, they'd patrol the lodge. During the party, Mike Downes, J.T. and Daniel would provide security inside the ballroom. The colonel also agreed to lock down the resort. The new policy included instituting Daniel's security measures. Juan Hernandez spent the day outfitting the attic door with a padlock and changing the locks on the rooms in the east wing. The colonel ordered one-way, emergency doors for the lodge wings.

Her father refused to discuss the changes with Janine. Never openly affectionate in the best of times, he now acted downright cold. Juan grunted in reply to her questions and comments. Chef pretended she didn't exist. Employees went out of their way to avoid her. Daniel kept calling her ma'am. Guilt and anger mingled in her chest. She passed the day rubbing her breastbone and wondering if she had heart problems.

Frustrated and depressed, she escaped to her room and turned the new dead bolt. The sight of shiny brass deepened her depression. She should quit and leave Elk River. It took no special talent to do her job. Her parents could easily find another manager. She'd disappear, change her name, cut off her hair and get fat. Live in a cheap apartment and work in a coffee shop. No one would miss her.

She filled the bathtub with hot water and herb-scented bubble bath. Knocking on the bedroom door grew increasingly urgent, but she sat in the tub until the water cooled. When she left the tub, wrinkled and still morose, the knocking continued. She wrapped her robe around her damp body and went to the door.

"Go away!"

"It's Daniel. Are you all right?"

She opened the door. Brow drawn, his mouth thin-lipped in a scowl, he glowered at her. She ignored the fluttering of her stupid heart, passing it off as yet another symptom of an impending cardiac infarction. He'd been so excruciatingly polite today she had no reason to yell at him. She wanted to yell at him—longed to hold him and kiss him.

"I've been standing out here for an hour."

"So I'll pay you overtime." She knew why everyone

else was mad at her, but hadn't a clue as to what bothered Daniel. She wasn't sure she wanted to know.

"I can't protect you if you keep running off." He shut the door. The dead bolt clacked. "I've never dealt with a stalker exactly like Pinky before. But I know he's extremely dangerous. He will kill you. Or your father. Or some other poor schmuck who interferes with his fantasy. Do you understand that?"

His lecture rasped her irritated nerves. She picked up a paperback novel and debated throwing it at him. She dropped the book on the desk. Wet tendrils of hair itched her neck. She gathered the stray strands and tucked them into the knot on top of her head.

"I've never lost a client. I don't intend to lose you." He placed a hand on her shoulder. "Do you hear me?"

"Leave me alone."

"I know this is rough on you."

His gentle voice hurt worse than a physical blow. "You don't know anything," she murmured. She shrugged from beneath his hand and faced him. Wanting him so much hurt most of all. His embrace, his silly jokes, that sense of connection she feared she'd never feel again.

Though she fought it, her chin trembled and her eyes watered. She wished he'd leave—she yearned for him to stay.

He cupped her face in both hands, his long fingers protective and gentle. A sound rose from his chest, a plaintive rumble her entire body responded to. He kissed her, closed-mouthed, sweet. She kissed him back and used her tongue in an invitation he immediately accepted. Long and slow, they engaged in a mutual laving, a tender sharing. In his kiss she found a promise that though her life might shatter, he would be there to help her pick up the pieces.

Long after he stopped kissing her, he held her face. She opened her eyes and sighed. She slid her gaze at the bed and lowered her lashes.

Daniel jammed his hands in his pockets. He cleared his throat, then shot her a grin. "Sorry about that."

She reeled as if his hands had been holding her upright. "That?" she repeated stupidly.

"I've got a bad habit of getting too deeply involved with my clients." He rapped his skull with his knuckles. "Can't seem to learn professional detachment."

His words were rushed, choppy; his voice was raw. She got the distinct impression he lied. "There's something going on between us, Daniel, and it has nothing to do with Pinky. We need to discuss it."

He shook his head and pulled a face. "Nah, not at all. This is my fault. I got too deep into the boyfriend role."

The remnants of good feelings from the kiss wisped away, leaving her angry, embarrassed and cold. "You're lying."

Color rose on his sculpted cheekbones. He actually blushed!

Now that she'd stopped lying to herself, she acknowledged he was the sexiest, most desirable man she'd ever met. He was a man of deep courage and boundless good humor. An intelligent man, sensitive enough to examine the depths of his own soul. A good man. An exciting man. A man she very much wanted to get to know better. A man with whom she could fall in love. "Why are you lying to me?"

"All right, all right, straight up. I have been lusting after you. The first time I saw you, I wanted to take you to bed." Hands in pockets, shoulders hunched, he stared at his boots. "I wanted you, so I thought you wanted me, too. That makes me as bad as Pinky."

Some fine actor, she thought in disgust. He was a lousy liar. "Pardon?"

"You're a fine woman, but you have your life, I have mine. Never the twain shall meet and all that. You've got good old comfy Elliot. I respect your choice and apologize for any disrespect I showed you before.''

Words, words, words—he held her at bay with a barrage of words. Verbal karate. "I broke up with Elliot," she said coolly.

His eyebrows lifted. "Because of me?"

His guilty tone wounded her. Why should he feel guilty? Because his kisses made her feel alive and cherished? Because she'd found promise in his eyes and joy in his company? "Don't flatter yourself."

"A beautiful woman like you. You'll find another guy."

Her back muscles stiffened, but no muscle or sinew—not even leaden armor—could protect her from the barb.

In his mind her looks summed up her entire being, and he forgot her character, feelings and thoughts. Love, commitment and loyalty meant nothing to her. Men were toys, one as good as the other. She couldn't be trusted.

She couldn't be loved—except from afar by a sociopathic nut.

DANIEL WARILY WATCHED Janine bustle about the room. With her makeup expertly applied and every hair in place, she slipped on a dark red woollen blazer over an ivory silk blouse and tailored black trousers. Low-heeled pumps made little noise on the thick carpet. She checked her appearance in a wall-mounted mirror. Her face a neutral mask, she pulled hair from beneath her collar and adjusted the lapels. All night long he had suffered second thoughts—and third and fourth and fifth thoughts along with a hefty dose of regret.

He'd hurt her. He hated himself for it. No matter how much he intellectually justified the rightness of his withdrawal, his heart said otherwise. Breaking up with Elliot proved she was casual about relationships. She'd dumped an invalid husband. What other proof did he need that she wasn't the woman for him? An affair with her would go nowhere. Hoping for her love made him as foolish as his parents.

She fastened a watch on her wrist. She wore no other jewelry. Her clothing was classic and expensive, but not flashy. The suit didn't say, "Look at me, I'm sexy and beautiful," it said, "Take me seriously." It occurred to him that even if she wore dumpy tweeds, horn-rimmed glasses and skinned her hair into a priggish knot, she'd still be beautiful. She couldn't help it.

He remembered her holding Jamie McKennon. Daniel had heard cruel comments and witnessed repulsed stares from insensitive boobs who couldn't see beyond Jamie's paralysis and garbled speech to recognize his tremendous personality and boundless capacity for love. Janine loved Jamie and accepted him, damage and all.

Unable to stand it, he asked, "Why did you break up with Elliot?"

"None of your business."

"You need your friends right now. I thought he was your friend."

"I thought so, too."

Her hurt came through loud and clear. Urgency rose in him to know the truth. "What happened to your marriage?"

She stilled. Her cool expression turned gelid—her face a carving in pale marble. "Looks like my little sister has been running her mouth again." She dabbed a pinky at the corner of her lip.

"She said you never talk about Eric."

"I don't. So drop it."

He tried to catch her eye in the mirror's reflection. She studiously avoided him. "What was wrong with him?"

She heaved a deep sigh and turned around. Arms crossed, her eyes blank, she regarded him. "Nothing. In fact, the two of you have a lot in common. I think you would have liked him."

He sensed an insult in there somewhere. "Why the divorce?"

She lifted a shoulder. "You'd have to ask him."

Not the answer he expected, nor could he interpret it. Her chin lifted a notch. Behind the Ice Queen he saw the vulnerable woman who so enchanted him. He curled his hands into fists, battling the urge to touch her.

She huffed a bitter laugh and averted her gaze. Her lower lip trembled for a moment before her mouth curved in a tight smile. "All right, you want the story? We were married for two years, then Eric got hurt. He lost a leg and the vision in one eye. He nearly died. I could help him with his physical injuries, but he lost something inside. I couldn't help him with that."

"So you gave up on him?"

"He gave up on me." Her voice lowered so he had to strain to hear. "As soon as he recovered well enough to leave the hospital, he filed for divorce."

Daniel squirmed inside.

"He accused me of not being able to cope with a cripple. The fact was, he couldn't live with himself. He thought I was going to desert him or cheat on him, so he dumped me."

"Didn't you fight the divorce?"

"Fight how?" She sniffed loudly and cleared her throat. "He wouldn't talk to me, he wouldn't see me. He refused counseling. When I forced confrontations, he either threatened physical violence or refused to speak at all." She flicked hair off her shoulders and her voice raised. "But he's a great guy. Just ask my father."

"Losing a leg. He must have been depressed."

"If so, he recovered nicely. Three months after he threw me out, he married his physical therapist."

Daniel scraped his thumbnails over his jeans. Unable to face her, he listened to her soft footsteps as she gathered items off the table. She waited for him to open the door.

When he gave her the all clear, she walked down the hallway. He fell into step beside her.

A million questions lodged in his throat. A million and one apologies.

"Do you think Pinky will cause problems at the party?" she asked.

"We're prepared if he does." He practiced apologies in his head. All sounded lame. He'd misread and underestimated Janine from the beginning. How could he apologize for that?

"Assuming the party goes off without a hitch," she said crisply, "then I'd like some recommendations for a permanent security staff. In the meantime, you'll move into another room. With the new locks and access to the attic cut off, I'm safe alone."

At her office he opened the door and peeked inside. She flicked on the computer's power source. She opened a date book and flipped through the pages. "The security guards you've hired. Can they remain on the job until I hire a permanent staff?"

"I think so."

"Good. You'll leave on Sunday then." Her fingers flicked over a calculator's keys. "If you don't mind, let's renegotiate our original business deal. The value of a Honeymoon Hideaway package is approximately two thousand dollars. Your time and expertise is worth more than that. I'd prefer dealing with you on a cash basis. How much is your time worth?"

"Don't do this, Janine."

"Business is what I do. It's what I'm good at."

Her wounded violet eyes ripped at his heart. "I'm sorry, okay?"

"For what?"

"For...everything!"

"Pinky isn't your fault," she said. Her coldness jabbed him with icy knives. "Despite the setbacks, your expertise is valuable. I feel confident what you've done will eventually lead to an arrest. In any case, my safety and my father's safety are assured. You've done your job.''

He sank onto the sofa and dangled his hands between his knees. Her prickly pride annoyed the hell out of him. His shame made him feel like a bum.

"Well? What's your time worth?"

"I want the honeymoon."

"Out of the question. After the party, I don't expect to ever see you at Elk River again."

"I'm not your enemy."

The ice cracked. Raw pain softened her eyes, and her chin trembled. She spun the chair and typed on the computer keyboard. "You aren't my friend, either."

"We have a deal. We shook on it."

"So sue me."

"All right, tough girl, maybe I will."

She ignored him. He huffed and noisily shifted on the sofa, crossing his arms and legs. She continued to ignore him. Daniel hated being ignored. He especially hated not knowing what to do. When they left the office for breakfast, she paid him no more attention than she did to her own shadow.

Her parents and sister were already seated at the long dining table. A small television was tuned to the weather channel.

Elise smiled at her eldest daughter. "We have a storm coming in, dear. They're predicting snow."

"I'll make sure Cody gets the sleigh polished up and ready to go," Janine said. She spoke past her father, her gaze never lighting on his face. "I'll call Mr. Torskell, too, and see if his pond is frozen enough for a skating party. I can arrange it for Sunday."

"That would be delightful." Elise laughed. "Especially for General Greene and his family. They've been stationed in Arizona for so long, I imagine they've forgotten what winter is like." She patted her husband's hand. "Do you remember what fun we had with George and Lucinda over in Germany? George was a wonderful skater."

"How long has it been since you've ice-skated, Mom?" Kara asked.

"Seems like a hundred years. Not since you children were small." She sighed dreamily. "I am so looking forward to this weekend. It's been so long since we've seen everybody. This is truly the best present you could have given us, Janine."

Janine lowered her face and toyed with a spoon in a bowl of oatmeal.

"Forty years.... Seems like only yesterday." Elise walked her fingers up the colonel's arm. He continued to watch the television, but he smiled. "Do you know, I almost didn't marry your father."

Kara hooted a laugh. "You never told us that!"

The colonel harrumphed.

"I was only twenty, still in college. My parents objected, saying he was too old for me, we didn't know each other well enough, and I'd hate being a military wife. And," her voice lowered dramatically, "they wanted me to marry another boy. Steve Wincoop. Your father punched him in the nose because Steve treated me rudely."

Even Janine joined in the laughter. The colonel's ears turned red.

"How long did you know each other, ma'am?" Daniel asked.

"Three weeks. Of course, the minute I saw him I knew he was the one. I never had a single doubt." She lifted his hand and kissed it with a smack. "I would have married him that very day, but it took some time to convince him my parents were wrong. Such an honorable man."

"Your determination was formidable even then, dear." He chuckled into his coffee cup.

Elise winked at her daughters. "He never stood a chance against me."

"Still don't," the old man muttered.

Enjoying the banter, Daniel watched the weather reports while he ate. January and February in Colorado, even in the mountains, were generally dry. This winter had been unusual, though, and skiers were ecstatic over deep snow-pack and fresh powder almost every week. Yellow, green, blue and red radar displays showed a slow-moving storm building in the south and moving north. He prayed for enough snow to discourage Pinky from slinking around the resort.

He prayed he came up with a way to apologize to Janine so they could start over. Like her mother had known she'd found her soul mate the first time she met the colonel, Daniel felt the same way about Janine. She was the one, but after his idiocy, convincing her might prove impossible.

Back in her office, the silent treatment continued. He began feeling very sorry for himself. He had standards. She couldn't blame him for trying to live up to them.

"Your parents set quite an example," he said.

She pushed hair out of her face and kept working on invoices. "Uh-hmm."

"They're the opposite of my parents." When she didn't reply, he pushed onward. "They don't know commitment from moon rocks. I like your parents. They're good people."

"Yes, they are."

"Look at me."

"I'm busy, Mr. Tucker. If you need something to do, go help Kara in the ballroom. She's putting up decorations."

"I'm your bodyguard."

"Aren't bodyguards strong and *silent?*"

He snatched a sheet of paper off her desk and began folding it into a paper airplane. He tossed it with a sharp downward wrist flick. It zoomed through a loop-de-loop, and he snagged it out of the air.

She leveled a glower on him. "Do you mind?"

He tossed the plane at her, and it sailed lazily over her head, ruffling her hair in passing. "Not at all."

"Are you looking for a fight?"

"If that's what you want, I'm game." Excitement coursed through his veins. He wanted to fight it out, clear the air and start over. He intuited she wanted the same. They had something special going, something worth developing. She knew it as well as he did.

The telephone rang. She sniffed haughtily and answered. A dazzling smile replaced her prim frown. "Megan!" she cried. "How are you?...You're in Denver?" Still smiling, she listened to her sister. "No, I won't tell them you're coming in early. Mom will love it. Is Tristan with you? And William?" She gave a start and frowned. "What big surprise? Will you quit teasing me? Oh, fine, be that way. I'll see you in a few hours, sweetie. Bye."

She hung up and sighed happily. "My sister and her husband are arriving early." As if forgetting she hated Daniel, she practically bubbled. "I haven't seen them in a year. They have a working ranch and it's difficult for them to get away. Not that Megan ever wants to leave. She loves Wyoming. She says she has the best anniversary present ever, but she won't tell me what it is. She's such a tease."

She pushed away from the desk and hurried to the door. Daniel rose to follow, floating on her aura of happiness.

In the lobby, at the registration desk, she spoke in a low, conspiratorial tone. "Megan is coming in early, Debbi. Is Cabin C available yet?"

Debbi searched her computer files. "Sorry, Ms. Duke. The guests in C don't check out until tomorrow. Cabin B is open, though. Shall I put Megan there?" She giggled. "It'll be so much fun seeing her again. It's been forever!"

"If she gets nostalgic for her honeymoon cabin, we can

switch her later. Don't tell anyone she's coming. She wants to surprise my mother.''

''My lips are sealed.'' Debbi typed rapidly. She cautiously eyed Janine. ''I saw the cops were back yesterday, Ms. Duke. Are you okay?''

''I'm fine. Thank you for asking.''

She reached over the counter and patted Janine's hand. ''That Pinky guy made a big mistake messing with us at Elk River. We're all behind you, ma'am. All for one, and one for all.''

''Why…thank you, Debbi.'' She rubbed the back of her hand as if uncertain what to make of the employee's touch.

Debbi turned her smile on Daniel. ''I'm glad you're taking care of her, Mr. Tucker. A boss like her is one in a million.''

Color rose on Janine's cheeks. Daniel took the opportunity to slip an arm around her narrow waist. When she didn't push him away, he rejoiced. ''You have my word,'' he said. ''Nobody is getting past me.''

''Ahem,'' Janine said. ''How is everything looking for Friday and Saturday, Debbi? Any problems?''

''Not one, ma'am. All the rooms will be ready. The shuttle buses are reserved. Everything is perfect.'' Debbi giggled. ''Two hundred guests! It's going to be the greatest party ever. I can hardly wait.''

''Same here.'' Janine eased away from Daniel's arm.

Daniel spotted Mike Downes crossing the lobby. He wore civilian jeans, a flannel shirt and a sheepskin coat. A broad-brimmed cowboy hat covered his hair. His cheeks were bright red from the cold. He hadn't worked extra duty last night and looked as if he'd gotten some sleep. He raised a hand in greeting and quickened his step.

''You look like you have good news,'' Janine said hopefully.

''Mostly good news.'' He smiled at Debbi, and the girl lowered her eyelashes. ''Can we talk in your office?''

Once in her office, with the door shut, Mike announced, "The Colorado Springs police picked up Brian Cadwell."

Janine clasped her hands. "Where?"

"At his grandparents' home. They dropped in to question the grandparents, and Brian showed up. He doesn't have a good explanation for where he's been since he supposedly left Elk River. Helmsley is on his way to question him."

"Where does he say he was?" Daniel asked.

"I don't know the details. He might have wanted his grandparents to give him an alibi, but the cops got there first."

"How does Helmsley justify questioning him?"

"Suspicion of breaking and entering." Mike shrugged. "Personally, I think he's jumping the gun. There's no word yet on what the techies found. That kid won't crack without hard evidence slapped in his face."

"How long can they hold him on suspicion?"

"Twenty-four hours, maybe."

"So he'll be out in time for the party." Groaning, Janine dropped onto her chair. She passed a hand over her eyes.

Daniel pondered a game plan. If he knew for certain Brian was Pinky, he'd wait at the jail for Brian's release. He and Brian could have an in-depth discussion, man to man. He couldn't risk leaving the resort until he knew Pinky's identity for certain. "What's the holdup on the fingerprints?"

"Ask Helmsley. The sheriff dropped the entire case in the state's lap. Budget, you know how it goes." Mike then asked where Kara was. Janine directed him to the ballroom.

After the deputy sergeant was gone, Daniel mused, "He's got a thing for your sister, eh?"

"Poor thing. She's been ignoring him for years. I don't know why. He's terrific."

"Must run in your family."

"Don't start on me, Daniel."

No more "Mister." He took it as a good sign.

Chapter Fourteen

"Janine! Kara!" The joyous cry echoed in the ballroom.

Nearly dropping a clipboard, Janine spun about. Employees paused in their work of hanging lights and streamers and setting up tables to transform the ballroom into a Victorian Valentine. Janine tossed the clipboard on a table and rushed toward Megan. Kara whooped and jumped off a step stool. The three sisters met in the middle of the room and tangled in an exuberant hug.

Pushing back so as to better see, Janine looked her sister up and down. Megan's face was suntanned and glowing. Her cropped hair looked as chic as it was practical. At spotting the pointy toes beneath her jeans, Janine laughed. "Cowboy boots?"

"They're comfortable." She hitched a jeans leg to show off the dark red leather with fancy stitching. A woollen coat concealed her body, but Janine suspected she sported a Western shirt and probably a big silver belt buckle, too. "You ought to try them, Ninny. You'll never wear anything else."

Megan's husband sauntered toward the group. Tristan carried his felt cowboy hat in his hand. Janine hugged him and kissed his cheek. "I'm so disappointed William couldn't come this weekend," she said. "The colonel really loves that kid. We all do."

"Between school and basketball, he couldn't get away. He wants me to ask you about coming down here to work this summer. He's earning money for college. Did Megan tell you? Arizona State accepted him into the engineering college."

"That's wonderful! We'd love to have him." She hugged his lean waist and smiled fondly as her younger sisters tried to out-talk each other.

She noticed Daniel watching the reunion. A poignantly sweet expression marked his face. She hardened her heart against him. Let him lust after some other woman. She didn't need him or his poor opinion of her. She'd rather live alone the rest of her life than yearn for a man who'd break her heart.

Elise, hauling her husband by the hand, hurried into the ballroom. An uncharacteristic squeal ripped from her mouth, and she ran to her middle daughter. The group hugging began all over again.

Tristan and the colonel clasped hands, renewing and re-inforcing their friendship. Sweet pleasure infused Janine's soul.

"I can't stand it anymore," Megan cried, unbuttoning her coat. "Hey, Mom, Colonel, look what Tristan did!" She tore the coat open. Megan had always been thin and athletic, with the perfect runner's build. Her rounded tummy was as obvious as a snow pile on asphalt. "Happy anniversary, Grandpa and Grandma!"

Elise clapped both hands to her mouth. Tears glimmered in her eyes. "You're pregnant?" she whispered. "A baby?"

Tristan swung his head, grinning bashfully. "Near four months along, Mom. Her keeping it a secret hasn't made for easy living. She about busted a gut every time she talked to you on the telephone. Happy anniversary."

Overjoyed for her sister and brother-in-law, Janine kissed each in turn, then stepped back to give her parents room.

Emotion rose in her throat. She envied her sister's marriage, which in its own way was as strong and solid as her parents'. She envied Megan's pregnancy and joy. Soon her brother and his wife and their twin babies would be here. Then her cousins, aunts and uncles would arrive, most of them happily married and busy with children. Loneliness settled over her shoulders like a shawl.

Daniel stood next to her. "So this is Megan and Tristan." He whistled appreciatively. "He's a big guy."

"Former bull riding champion." Her husky voice appalled her. She couldn't look at Daniel. For a brief time she'd imagined finding happiness with him. When would she learn?

She introduced Daniel to Megan and Tristan. Since she hadn't told them about Pinky, she faltered in how to explain his presence. Finally she settled on "friend." She wished he were her friend. She wished he could be more.

Linked arm in arm, with everyone chatting at once, the family left the ballroom. Janine hung back, saying she had work to do. She retrieved the clipboard, then stared numbly at the to-do list. The letters jumbled, making little sense.

"Are you all right?" Daniel asked.

"Couldn't be better."

"So you're going to be an aunt. Congratulations."

Ever an aunt, never a mother. "Thanks," she replied weakly, and turned her attention back to decorating the ballroom.

She managed to avoid her family until dinnertime. She sat quietly at the table. Megan and Kara had been, and still were, the best of friends. Giggling like teenagers, they traded stories while Elise beamed at her daughters from across the table. Janine sensed Megan's interest in Daniel; she sensed, too, Kara was dying to tell her sister everything about him. She figured before the night was over Kara would have told Megan and Tristan all about Pinky.

Her headache returned full force and she excused herself.

At her door Daniel placed a hand atop hers. She reveled in his touch and loathed herself for the reaction.

"Are you really throwing me out?" he asked.

She canted her head, indicating the room next door. "You have the key. Make yourself at home."

"Janine, I—"

"Good night," she interrupted and slipped into her room. She shut the door, but the sight of his beautiful penny-colored eyes lingered in her mind until she finally, fitfully fell asleep.

The next morning she awakened to the sound of heavy machinery. Excitement building, she drew back the window draperies. Fat snowflakes, the size of quarters, drifted in a filmy curtain across the land. Employees plowed the parking lot. She flipped on the radio. The weather forecast called for four to six inches. Childlike giddiness made her clap her hands and twirl on her toes. She envisioned sleigh rides and snowball fights and children making snow angels and the ballroom full of candles reflecting off the wintry wonderland outside.

She dressed in a hurry and found Daniel waiting outside her door. Reading the newspaper, he sat on a chair. Mauve circles accentuated the bags under his eyes, and the lines in his cheeks had deepened. If she loved him and he loved her, she would haul him outside to play in the snow and they'd laugh. Her good mood vanished.

"Have you been sitting out here all night?"

He folded the newspaper. "No."

She bit back the urge to call him a liar, and steeled her heart against sentimental gratitude for his protectiveness. "Is the room okay?"

"Bed's more comfortable than your couch."

Perversely, his irritable note pleased her. "I have a lot to do. Most of our relatives will arrive today."

She noticed his hair was slightly damp and his cheeks were freshly shaved. His fawn-colored sweater brought out the bronze tones in his skin and hair and eyes. She knew she'd never again be able to smell his brand of soap without thinking about him. Her insides went soft as images of sex—images of Daniel loving her—taunted her.

She was about to do something stupid. She abruptly turned and walked down the hall.

At noon her brother and his family arrived. By the time Ross pushed the double stroller holding his twins in from outdoors, the children's woolly hats were covered in snow.

"Whew!" Ross exclaimed. "It's getting nasty out there."

Janine greeted her brother and sister-in-law before she crouched to begin unbundling the babies. Not quite two years old, the twins babbled excitedly. Kara, Megan and Elise entered the lobby. Their noisy kissing and hugging gave Janine a measure of privacy with her niece and nephew. Rosie, the dark-haired girl, and Hank, the tow-headed boy, enchanted her. As soon as she lifted Rosie out of the stroller, the toddler wrapped her arms around Janine's neck and covered her face with slurpy kisses. Her brother howled in indignation.

His mother freed him from the stroller.

"You look a tad frazzled, Dawn," Janine commented.

"You wouldn't think two such short people could get into such big trouble. I swear, they conspire about ways to drive me crazy." Dawn set Hank on the floor, and he immediately ran to his grandmother. Elise scooped him into her arms.

A while later, J.T. and Frankie arrived. Frankie carried her stepson while J.T. carried the folded wheelchair. Frankie's sister, Penny, trailed them, laden with luggage. Seeming to float cloudlike, radiating joy, Elise enlisted aid in arranging the lounge furniture to make a play area for the children. Hank and Rosie treated Jamie like a big doll. His laughter rang from the rafters.

Frankie flopped gracelessly on a chair. "I didn't think the van was going to make it. The roads are terrible."

Janine anxiously eyed a window. The snowflakes, no longer fat and lazy, sheeted from the sky and clung icily to the windowpanes. They had their promised six inches of ground cover, but still the snow came down.

All through the afternoon the Dukes' relatives arrived. Aunts, uncles, cousins and in-laws, many of whom Janine hadn't seen in years, filled the lodge and kept the resort employees hopping. Children played in the lounge while their mothers kept an eye on them and caught up on family news. Teenagers roamed the hallways and grumped about the weather making it impossible to ride horses or hike the forest trails.

The snow kept falling. Juan and his crew operated snowplows; they barely stayed ahead of the storm. Man-made drifts at the edges of the parking lot piled higher than the vehicles. Realizing she hadn't seen her father in a while, she worried he was outside helping the crew.

She found the colonel in his office. He glowered at the television set where the weather channel gave continuous reports. She rapped her knuckles on the open door. "Colonel? Walter is here. He's asking for you."

"Weather anomaly," he said.

His mood bothered her. Usually he was in the middle of any gathering. For all his stiff airs, he genuinely loved people, family especially. "Pardon?"

"An unexpected front shifted and is moving in from the north. The storm is stalled over central Colorado and along the Front Range. We could receive as much as three feet of accumulation."

She groaned. A little snow, just enough to hitch up the sleigh or build a snowman, that's all she wanted. She peered through the horizontally blowing snow to see the thermometer mounted outside the window. The red line hovered at three degrees above zero.

"Chain laws are in effect over the passes."

"If this was March, I'd worry. You know February storms never last long. It'll be fifty degrees tomorrow." She eased to his desk and picked up a paperweight, a colonel's silver eagle insignia encased in acrylic. "What's really bothering you?"

He slowly swiveled his chair. Even in his late seventies he was a handsome man with a firm jaw and steely eyes as bright as crystals. "I've done you a disservice, Janine."

She bounced the paperweight from hand to hand.

"I'm an old man, but I hate to think I'm set in my ways."

She curled her lips over her teeth to prevent a smile. He'd been born set in his ways.

"My mission in life has always been to protect my family. Your mother, you girls, even Ross despite his insurrection. It's difficult for me to let go."

She looked at him then, finding him solemn. Remnants of anger drained away. "I know."

"Hiring Daniel hurt my feelings."

Surprised he'd make such an admission, she set down the paperweight. She eased a hip atop his desk. "Hurt—? No, that's not—"

"I realize what your intentions were. If I weren't such a prideful old man, I'd applaud your efforts. But I am prideful, and when you didn't tell me about Pinky, didn't give me a chance to protect you, I..." Looking disgusted, he shook his head. "I failed you."

"I never meant to hurt you." She reached for his hand. He entwined his fingers with hers. His skin felt like crisp paper. "Pinky made me feel like a failure. He threatened you. I'd rather die than let anything happen to you."

His mouth curved in a gentle smile. "Your mother claims you and I are cut from the same cloth."

"I consider that quite a compliment."

"As do I." He squeezed her fingers. "I'm ashamed of

placing my pride before your well-being. I am proud of you. Your performance is outstanding.''

She risked revealing her deepest heart wound. Not speaking about her failed marriage had become a habit, but the concealed truth was like an imbedded splinter, festering and souring. She wanted him proud of her in all things. ''What about Eric?''

He looked away, and the smile thinned into a grim line. ''I'm certain you had good reasons to leave him.''

Her eyes burned as if filled with hot sand. Her throat ached. Pride was her flaw as well as his. Out of pride, she'd allowed him to think the worst of her. Perhaps, she considered, her refusal to confide in him had hurt him worse than the divorce. ''He dumped me.''

''Speak up. What did you say?''

She licked her lips and cleared her throat. ''I said, he *dumped* me. I never wanted a divorce. I loved him. I knew we could work out our problems, but he wouldn't try.'' She withdrew her hand, her head bowed beneath the weight of old shame. ''He threw me out. I was always too embarrassed to tell you.''

He handed her a tissue. She dabbed at the corners of her eyes.

''I thought Eric and I were forever, but after the accident he changed. He stopped believing in me, stopped trusting me. He wouldn't give me a chance to work things out.'' Looking back with a more mature perspective, she realized her ex-husband had feared being less than a man. He'd rejected her not because he hated her, but because he hated himself. ''I felt like a failure. A reject. Sometimes I still do.''

The colonel called her ex-husband a foul name, his demeanor so defiant she didn't dare chide him about his language. ''Your mother claims I am, at times, unapproachable. I suppose I have no one to blame but myself.''

She lifted a shoulder. "I guess I'd rather have you mad at me than feeling sorry for me."

He loudly cleared his throat and looked away for a moment. In his silence Janine found a measure of peace. When he stood, she impulsively hugged him. He stiffened then hesitantly patted her back.

"I love you, Daddy." She pressed her cheek against his scratchy sweater, which smelled of laundry soap.

"I, uh, ahem, I love you, too. You say Walter inquired about me?"

Janine squeezed his ribs and stepped back. "And he's richer and meaner than ever. How did a nice guy like you ever end up with a brother like that?"

He lowered his most disapproving glower on her. She laughed and poked his arm with a stiff finger. "You know it's true. He's out there smoking cigars. Stinky, nasty cigars in front of the kids! You need to counsel him on proper behavior."

She hooked her arm with his, and they strolled out of the office. She teased him about his younger brother, knowing his grumbling and gruffness hid laughter.

IN THE LOBBY, Daniel looked around for Janine. He assured himself Brian was Pinky, and he was safely in custody in Colorado Springs, far from any opportunity to make trouble. Still, nagging unease plagued him. He wouldn't stop being uneasy until the fingerprints proved conclusively that Brian was the culprit.

Kara had other plans for him. Despite her ditzy mannerisms, she was sensitive to the tension between Daniel and Janine. She seemed to have made it her mission to set things right. She kept him circulating in the lobby and lounge, introducing him to her relatives. "This is Janine's boyfriend," she announced. "He owns two martial arts studios." Not bothering to clarify the situation, he made small talk. With the exception of a stout, grouchy old man Kara called Uncle Walter, everyone was friendly.

Daniel grasped Kara's hand. "Excuse me, kiddo. I need to find—"

"There's Bob and Bobbi! The coincidence is an incredible hoot. Roberta and Robert Robertson. Can you believe those names?" She dragged him across the floor and introduced him to her cousins. Within minutes he knew Bobbi Robertson was an artist; Bob Robertson was an engineer; their daughter wanted to be a model, since she stood nearly six feet tall.

Daniel spotted Janine. She and her father entered the lobby, arm in arm. The colonel bent to whisper something in Janine's ear and she laughed. The intimacy of the gesture warmed Daniel from the inside out, building hope. If she could make up with her father, maybe she'd make up with him.

An icy draft rushed through the lounge. Wind howled and snow swirled through the open front door. A figure appeared in the doorway. Snow and ice crusted his legs to his knees. Clumps of snow dripped from his hat. The lenses in his glasses were fogged, making him look bug-eyed. He lurched a wobbly step, grabbed the door and pushed it shut. He slapped his bare hands against his sides.

"Who in the world is that?" Kara mused.

"Not a relative?" Instantly suspicious, Daniel looked the stranger up and down. He stood around six feet four inches tall, and swayed as if the wind still battered him. Melting snow and ice pooled at his feet.

Kara trotted across the floor to greet the man. He clumsily tugged his glasses off his face and blinked myopically at her.

Daniel strode toward Janine. She stared past him and her mouth went slack. He followed her stare.

"What is he doing here?" she whispered.

"Who?"

She scowled and raked both hands through her hair. "Elliot."

Daniel eyeballed the stranger with heightened interest. This was good old, comfy Elliot? Kara helped the man out of his coat and aided him in brushing snow off his trousers. A tweed sports jacket hung from slender shoulders. His hair was sandy and lank, cut short. He looked like Ichabod Crane.

"I am going to kill him," Janine muttered, and stalked across the lobby.

"Darling!" Elliot cried. He slid his glasses back on his face. They immediately fogged. "The weather is horrible. I've been on the road for nearly five hours. Then my car slid into a ditch. I had to walk a good half mile in the blizzard. I thought I was going to freeze to death." He pulled a handkerchief from inside his jacket and wiped off his glasses.

Daniel sneered. What kind of man carried a hankie these days? Despite his height, there wasn't much to the man. He was skinny, and his hands looked soft. Not much muscle tone.

Kara peered suspiciously at her sister. "You two know each other?"

Arms crossed, chin lowered dangerously, Janine nodded in affirmation. "Elliot Damsen, my sister Kara."

"Very nice to meet you, Kara—at long last." He reached for Janine, but she stepped out of reach. "I braved a blizzard for you, darling."

"Which speaks poorly of your intelligence. What are you doing here?"

"I'm here to see you. Our little tiff was ridiculous."

"Maybe to you." She glanced over her shoulder at the crowd. No one seemed to be paying much attention. "Go home."

"My car is in a ditch." He rubbed his reddened hands briskly. "Besides, I believe the highway is closed."

She loosed a long sigh. "Do you have a change of clothing?"

"I wasn't expecting to get caught in a blizzard."

"Kara, find him something dry to wear. And get him a cup of tea."

"Loose black darjeeling, brewed four minutes," Elliot said. "With honey. Raw honey. I can't abide anything processed."

Daniel curled a lip. He couldn't fathom what Janine saw in this guy. But the fact that Elliot had braved a major storm to be by her side said he felt their relationship was anything but casual. Daniel slipped an arm around her slender waist. Feeling her disapproval, he smiled and stood his ground. The gesture wasn't lost on Elliot. His mouth fell open.

He thrust out a hand. "Nice to meet you, Elliot. I'm Daniel Tucker. Too bad you came all this way for nothing."

Elliot tucked his right hand into his coat pocket. "The karate fellow."

Before Daniel could formulate a snappy retort, Janine pulled away. "You're dripping," she said. "Get warmed up. Then I'll speak to you in my office." She stalked away.

"Yeah, a drip," Daniel muttered. He followed Janine.

Once in the privacy of her office, she turned on him. "How dare you act like a jealous boyfriend!"

"I am jealous."

She gave a start. Her mouth formed a fetching *O*. She began twisting a hank of hair around her finger. "You have no right."

"So what?" He advanced on her. She backed around the desk. "We have an issue or two to work out, but we'll do it."

"I haven't the slightest interest in pursuing a relationship with you." She struck the chair and sat down hard.

"You're lying like a dog." He clutched the chair arms, trapping her.

She shoved at his wrists and tried to peel back his fingers. "Get away from me!"

"Look me in the eyes and say that."

"I will not tolerate this, this—bullying!"

"Says one bully to another. You're not scaring me off this time, honey."

She clamped her arms over her chest. Fire crackled and snapped in her eyes. Straddling her legs as he did put him in a vulnerable position. He suspected she knew it. If she kneed his groin, he'd consider it a small price to pay for the pain he'd caused her.

"I made a mistake," he said.

"You've made a lot of mistakes."

"So I'm human, sue me. But if you don't accept my apology, you'll make the biggest mistake of your life."

She bent a wrist and touched a finger prissily to her chin. She batted her eyelashes. If not for the seething anger radiating from every pore, the gesture might have been coquettish. "You're right, I'd miss out on a night of wild sex with you. My goodness, how shall I ever recover from the regret?"

"One night, huh? Is that all you want?"

"That's all you want."

He recalled saying something to that effect. Eating those words tasted nasty. "I lied."

"It didn't sound like a lie." Her shoulders relaxed and she dropped her gaze. He wanted to flutter kisses over her tender eyelids. Hold her close and never let her go. "You let me down, Daniel. I needed you and you acted like a jerk."

He withdrew from the chair. Resting his backside against the desk he regarded her glumly. He'd known he made her angry and felt bad about it. Her wounded feelings made him feel lower than a worm.

"I began to believe you knew me. Understood me. I

thought when you looked at me I was more than just a pretty face. I thought you were different.''

Her accusations hit home. He cringed inside.

''I work hard at not repeating my mistakes,'' she said, her voice low and sure. ''I don't deny the attraction I feel for you, but acting on it would be a mistake.''

''It's not just physical attraction,'' he protested. ''It's deeper than that. You know it.''

''I don't know it.''

Her stubbornness frustrated him. He'd been in reasonably long-term relationships. He'd dated more women than he could remember. He'd been through breakups and making ups. Never once had he begged. He wanted to beg now, throw himself at her mercy, toss out his pride. Grovel. Squirm. Eat dirt.

''You know what your real problem is? It's not that people don't understand you. You're afraid someone will get to know who you really are.''

''That's absurd!''

''Is it?'' He flung out a hand. ''You hide behind this office. Behind those power suits. That cool businesswoman air. You hide from your own family. Do you realize what you did when Debbi was nice to you yesterday? You actually blushed. You don't know how to act when people treat you like a human being.''

''That's...absurd.''

He stabbed a finger at her. ''I know you're human. I know you bleed just like the rest of us mortals. That's the real problem, isn't it? I got under your skin and you just can't stand it.''

''Shut up.'' She pinched the bridge of her nose.

''And that you're-so-beautiful thing? The part where I only care about you because I'm smitten by your beauty? In case you haven't noticed, you might be Miss America, but your little sister is Miss Universe.''

She gasped.

Her open surprise heartened him. "Kara is one incredibly beautiful young lady. Those long legs, that hair, those eyes. She's the stuff dreams are made of." He wolf whistled. "Your other sister isn't bad, either. I haven't seen an—um, rear end like that in a long time. Hate to say it, honey, but you don't have a lock on the gorgeous department."

The fire faded, and good humor softened her eyes. She covered her mouth with a hand. "You're a wretched man," she whispered through her fingers. "Do you honestly—?"

Juan Hernandez poked his head into the office and tapped on the door. "Ma'am?"

She swiveled the chair. Her knee brushed Daniel's. Electric shocks of pure desire arced along his nerves. They hadn't resolved anything, yet; he resented the intrusion.

"Yes, Juan, what is it?"

He leaned wearily against the doorjamb. Moisture turned his dark blue parka black. Pearls of water quivered on his mustache and eyebrows. He looked exhausted. "The snow's winning, ma'am. It's coming down faster than we can scoop it up. Got ten-foot drifts out there."

"Oh, dear. How much snow is there?"

"A good four feet and it's still coming down. It's worse than that storm we had back in October. The temperature is six below and dropping. The wind is gusting at forty miles an hour. Trees breaking right and left."

"Have you told the colonel?"

"I was on my way, but saw your door open. I can't keep my boys out there any longer. They're beat and they're cold."

Janine flipped on a radio. A weather reporter dubbed the storm the Friday the Thirteenth Blizzard. Up to six feet of snow covered some mountain areas. Colorado Springs reported two feet of snow at the airport. The state patrol had declared chain laws in effect over Monument Hill on Interstate 25. Highways 24, 50, 160 and just about every other highway through the southern Colorado mountains were closed. The storm had stalled over southern Colorado and the snow would continue throughout the night. Another twelve to thirty inches of snow were predicted.

"All I wanted was a sleighride," Janine murmured. Half smiling, she chuckled. "All right, Juan, shut down the machinery and get the crew inside. I need you to keep a path cleared to the generator house in case we lose power. Other than that, leave the snow alone."

Juan left to relieve his crew. Janine looked up at Daniel. "I'll deal with you later. Right now I have work to do."

In the lobby she rang the desk bell and called for attention. Voices stilled. "Well, folks, I'm so glad you were all able to make it. It doesn't look as if anyone else will. We're snowed in, and the storm isn't finished with us yet."

Low murmuring rippled through the lobby and lounge. An excited undercurrent amused Janine. Some of her out-of-state relatives looked at her as if she'd ordered the storm just so they could get a taste of a real Rocky Mountain winter.

"I'll be moving those of you in the Honeymoon Hideaway into rooms in the lodge. Don't worry, we have plenty of food. So eat, drink and be merry. Any of you who enjoy cross-country skiing should have a great time tomorrow."

Elise approached her daughter. "Is the storm affecting the airports in Colorado Springs and Denver?"

"I haven't heard. But Highway 24 is closed. The storm should be over by morning. The party will go on."

Seeing her father head toward the east wing, Janine intercepted him. "Where are you going, sir?"

"To inspect the generator house. In case—"

"I'll handle the generator and the supplies and seeing to everyone's comfort. Get back there and mingle. Mom, order him to have some fun."

She headed for her office, her mind buzzing with the million and one details needing her attention. Elliot called her name, and she winced. Seeing trouble brewing on Dan iel's face, she nudged him in warning. He claimed to know her, so he had better remember she hated public scenes.

Elliot stalked across the floor like a wading stork, each step careful and deliberate. As he neared, she saw he wore socks, but no shoes. The elasticized legs of dark blue sweatpants barely covered his calves. An Elk River sweatshirt billowed over his slim frame. The sleeves were too short. Fearing she might laugh, Janine pressed a hand to her mouth.

"I can't find shoes for him, Ninny." Kara turned wide, too-innocent eyes on Daniel. She smiled sweetly. "He wears a fourteen and a half extra narrow."

Janine knew darned well that, shoes aside, Kara could have found a sweat suit that fit Elliot properly. She slid a glance at Daniel, daring him to laugh. Once certain she wouldn't laugh, she said, "I'm afraid you'll have to make do, Elliot. We're snowed in. Your shoes and clothes will be dry by morning. The road should be open by then, as well."

The maintenance crew trooped into the lobby. Wet, coated with snow, their faces concealed behind fur-trimmed parka hoods, they toted luggage. Juan waved at Janine. "They was already wearing snowsuits. Told housekeeping we'd clear the Honeymoon Hideaway in exchange for a round of beer."

"Thank you, Juan. You can put a second round on my tab." Already thinking about where to relocate guests, she turned toward the registration desk.

Elliot grabbed her arm. His fingers dug painfully between her muscles. "Do not dismiss me."

Janine saw Daniel's hand flash, but didn't actually see him touch Elliot. Still, the man yowled like a stepped-on cat and grabbed his elbow. He hopped from foot to foot. His face turned bright red. Daniel stepped between her and Elliot. He coolly eyed the taller man. A muscle twitched in his jaw.

"Put a hand on her again, buddy, and I'll use it for a hood ornament." His smile failed to match the angry glitter in his eyes.

Aware of a hush settling in the lounge, Janine didn't need to look to know everyone watched the drama unfold. She shoved her hands in her blazer pockets. "I didn't ask you to come here. We have nothing to discuss."

"You are very wrong. I've invested three years in you. For you to so casually toss me aside in order to have flings with arsonists and karate freaks is ridiculous." His voice rose. Even employees working in the restaurant could probably hear him. "I will not abide such shabby treatment."

When Janine believed this couldn't get any more humiliating, her brother, brother-in-law, cousin-in-law and father approached the desk like the cavalry riding to the rescue.

"Problem here?" Ross asked.

"Who's the goof, Daniel?" J.T. asked.

The colonel snapped to parade rest, and Elliot seemed to shrink in the face of the old man's glare. "What is the meaning of this?"

Tristan Cayle appeared to be sizing up Elliot, as if wondering how small a bundle he could make of the man.

"More of your lovers?" Elliot exclaimed. "Good God, woman! How many men can you fit in your bed?"

Janine caught Daniel's swinging arm and clung to him for dear life. He practically lifted her off her feet. Tempting as it was to allow Daniel to deck Elliot, the patent attorney believed deeply in using lawsuits to avenge insults. Daniel would lose his lottery winnings as quickly as he'd acquired them.

"I realize your feelings are hurt," she said, "but that doesn't excuse your behavior."

"I'm supposed to excuse yours? I have a right—"

"Season tickets to the symphony don't give you any rights!" she yelled. She turned her fury on her family. "Leave me alone. I'll handle this." She shoved at Daniel.

"You, too. Go get a drink. Eat something. Go away." She whirled on Elliot. He startled and backed a step. She jabbed at his chest with a stiff finger. "I don't know what you're thinking. I don't care what you're thinking. You had no right to come here uninvited. No right to make stupid accusations!"

Elliot kept backing away, she followed, stabbing at his chest. "No right to embarrass me. No right to invade my home. No right to say who I may or may not see."

"Darling, I—I—I've never seen you like this."

"This is the real me. You don't like it, too bad."

"I—I—"

"Put a cork in it, Elliot."

She peeked at her relatives and employees. Some were smiling, but most looked shocked. Her cheeks burned. She'd gone and lost her mind, and now every person who meant anything to her had witnessed it. Had she actually thought Pinky was her major problem? Her own big mouth was ten times worse.

She raked fingers through her hair and straightened her blazer with a tug. To the registration desk clerk, she said coolly, "I'm certain you can arrange new rooms for the guests who were in the Honeymoon Hideaway." With all the dignity she could muster, she walked into the east wing.

Daniel caught up to her while she unlocked her bedroom door. He assured her everyone was asking about her, and wanted to know when she was coming back downstairs.

"I can't go down there. I humiliated myself."

Arms crossed, he leaned a shoulder against the wall. He smiled. "You did great."

"Stop it."

"I'm not kidding. All those people down there love you. They think Elliot is an idiot and you're damned terrific."

"I've botched everything. Pinky, Elliot, the party." *You,* she added silently.

"Pinky isn't your fault. Elliot should realize no means

no. And in spite of the weather, everyone seems to be having a good time. You've got an incredible family. I haven't met anyone I don't like.''

"You're a regular cheerleader, aren't you?''

"Rah, rah. Can I come in? I need to make a phone call.''

She pushed open the door. "To whom?''

"Mike. Or Helmsley if I can find him.''

Short hairs lifted on her nape. "Why?''

"Find out Brian's status.''

"Why?''

"Double-checking, that's all.''

"Brian is Pinky,'' she insisted. "All the evidence says he's Pinky.''

His too-cheerful assurances left her with a sick sensation in the pit of her stomach. The uneasiness lingered, though she assured herself her family wasn't trapped in the lodge with a potentially homicidal madman.

Daniel couldn't reach either Mike Downes or the state investigator. He left messages for both men. Janine made herself return downstairs. Elliot had the decency to be elsewhere, so within a short time she stopped forcing her smile and began to enjoy the family reunion. To her bemusement, her relatives acted as if having men fighting for her favors made her some sort of heroine. Everyone assumed Daniel was her choice, and they liked him. By the time she retired for bed, she felt better than she had in weeks.

When she awakened on Valentine's Day, the uneasiness returned full force. She stared into the darkness. Anxiety fluttered in her belly. Her heart pounded. Finally she realized it was the darkness itself scaring her. No digital clock with bright red numbers glowed at bedside. No band of light shone under the door. Not a glimmer of outdoor lighting reached the edges of the draperies.

Moving in the darkness, she lit a candle. She telephoned Daniel's room. He answered on the second ring. "Power's down. I have to investigate." He assured her he'd be at her door in three minutes.

Together, following the pale light of a gardenia-scented candle, they knocked on Juan's door. A loud crash and equally loud cursing answered. She didn't need to inform him the power had failed.

Janine didn't worry. Juan would have the generators operating before her guests awakened and realized the power had gone out. She didn't worry when she found chaos in the kitchen where Chef struggled valiantly to prepare breakfast by candle and oil lamplight. His normally foul temper now turned vile, the man didn't bother with English, but screamed at his employees in German. Janine had employees fetch battery-operated lanterns from the basement. Mollified, Chef merely snarled when Janine and Daniel helped themselves to coffee brewed the old-fashioned way on the gas range.

Bolstered by coffee, she directed employees in lighting the big fireplace in the lounge and setting lanterns in the hallways for the safety and convenience of guests.

After forty-five minutes, Juan still hadn't returned, and Janine began to worry. The sun rose, offering enough light to see the massive drifts blanketing the lodge. Guests stumbled in the darkness, and she put employees to work providing proper lighting and feeding everybody. The snow piled so high against the restaurant windows it completely obliterated the view. She feared snow blocked the generator house door.

When Juan returned two hours later and informed her that someone had broken into the generator house and destroyed all three generator engines, then Janine worried for real.

Chapter Fifteen

"It must be Lanny Lewis." Janine addressed the men gathered in her office. Her father, brother, brother-in-law, J.T. and Daniel filled the room, radiating heat and anger. Worry, too—all of them worried. "Where haven't we looked?"

Sometime, between the hours of 2:00 a.m. and 5:00 a.m., Lanny Lewis and another maintenance worker had disappeared. The two had been on shift, specifically to watch for power outages and to fire up the generators. During their shift, someone had vandalized the power generators, and the two men had vanished without a trace. They weren't in the lodge, the stables or the dormitory.

Janine's deepest fear was that Lanny—Pinky—had murdered his co-worker, and now played hide-and-seek in the lodge. She curled her fists on the desk, trying and failing to prevent them from shaking.

"What does this guy want?" Ross asked.

Janine swallowed the lump in her throat. They were sitting ducks, all of them. The police couldn't reach the resort. None of them could leave. "Me," she said. "He wants to prove how much he loves me. Daniel, what is he going to do?"

Chewing his lower lip, Daniel gazed distantly. "He's promised to make his love public. I have a feeling it'll involve a grand gesture." He looked up at the colonel.

"Sir, you and J.T. are best buddies now. Joined at the hip. Ross, Tristan, can you handle a pistol without shooting off a foot?" When they nodded in affirmation, he continued. "I want all of us armed. You, too, Janine. Lanny isn't playing games. He's dangerous. After seeing what he did to the generators, I'd say he's setting the stage."

The colonel asked, "With what shall we arm ourselves, Daniel?"

He fingered the Luger. "I saw pistols in your office, sir."

"Antique weaponry, young man, for which I do not at this moment have ammunition. Proper ordnance includes rifles and shotguns. Surely you cannot advocate we prowl the lodge toting rifles?"

"That might tend to panic some people," Ross mused. "Not to mention shouting out loud to Lanny that we're after him. What about you, J.T.?"

J.T. opened his jacket, displaying a pistol snug beneath his arm.

"Do you think Lanny is armed?" Ross asked.

"Other than the ax he used on my truck and the generators," Daniel said, "there's no indication of a deadly weapon. He never mentioned firearms in his letters. We didn't find weapons in his stash."

Janine snapped a pencil in half. "So it's no?" *Say it's no,* she urged with her eyes.

"I don't know. Your dad is right. We can't run around with rifles. The calmer we keep people, the better chance we have of getting this situation under control."

"What about our guests?" Janine asked. Horrible visions of the lodge going up in flames nagged her imagination. Horrible guilt about endangering those she loved most haunted her soul. "The staff? The children? What if Lanny sets the lodge on fire?"

"He'll do something more personal. Something that leaves no doubt that Pinky is in charge."

"It is a possibility," the colonel said.

"Yes, sir."

"All right," Janine said. "We have to clear out the west wing, make sure nobody is alone and vulnerable, or trapped on an upper floor."

"Start the party early," Ross suggested. "That'll keep people busy. No one will have an excuse to panic. Everybody will be where we can keep an eye on them. Plus, we should bring the girls in on this. Frankie, too, J.T. Even pregnant, she'll be good in an emergency."

"Bring them in on what?" Tristan asked. He clenched and relaxed his huge hands. "I'm not putting Meg at risk. No way."

Ross beamed at his brother-in-law. "Not in tackling Lanny. Let them coordinate with the staff. Come up with an emergency evacuation plan. If the nut does torch the joint, we get everyone out, safe and sound."

"Good idea." A chill raised goose bumps on her arms. Small emergency generators in the basement kept the furnaces operating, but to conserve energy, they'd had to turn down the heat. With the west wing so cold, everyone should willingly gather in the main lodge.

They sketched out a hasty battle plan. The colonel and J.T. were to clear guests out of the west wing. They'd also alert the staff about Lanny and give them instructions about raising the alarm. The other four set out to search the basement again.

DOWN IN THE BASEMENT was exactly where Janine did not want to be. Without lights or the heat, the place felt like catacombs. Holding a battery-powered lantern high, Janine clutched the back of Daniel's sweater. Gun drawn, placing each foot carefully, he crept slowly through the corridor leading from the east wing stairwell. Knowing Ross and Tristan searched from the other end, Janine strained to hear them. All she heard was her thundering heart. Lantern light bobbed, reflecting off rough stone walls and highlighting spiderwebs.

Gesturing her to stand aside, Daniel opened a door. The hinges creaked. He lowered into a crouch, weapon ready. She eased the lantern into the doorway.

"Lanny?" he whispered. "You in there, boy?"

Janine wished she had a rifle.

Room by room they made their way through the basement. In the wine cellar, Daniel went straight to the dumbwaiter. He worked at the pulley, trying to release the rope. When he couldn't dismantle it, he jammed a champagne bottle into the mechanism.

"That should keep him from using it."

"Until he figures out the bottle is there."

"I doubt he's in any shape for logical thinking." He canted his head. "How are you holding up?"

"You know those stupid girls in horror movies? The ones who go down in the basement? That's how I feel right now."

"Do you like horror movies?"

She looked around, feeling the walls closing in. "Not anymore."

"How about a comedy? Some good movies are playing in the Springs."

Were it anyone else having this stupid, whispered conversation, Janine wouldn't believe her ears. Since it was Daniel… "Are you asking for a date?"

"Yeah, next Friday. Movie, dinner." He waggled his eyebrows. "Then whatever else strikes our fancy."

"Your truck is still in the shop."

"I have a '57 Corvette convertible. Classic, cherry condition. You'll look gorgeous in it. I am willing to put it on the road just for you."

Hearing a stealthy noise, she crowded him, nearly stepping on his toes. "Can I give you my answer later?"

He slipped between her and the door, the Luger at ready. "Sure."

"Janine?" Ross called softly. "Daniel?"

"Here." He blew a long breath and lowered the pistol. Ross and Tristan entered the wine cellar. "I take it you guys didn't find anything."

Janine felt in her pocket, making sure she had her key ring. "Let's check the west wing. Guest rooms, storage rooms. He has to be somewhere."

But Lanny was not in the west wing. They searched every room on both guest floors. The only person they found was Elliot. He sat on a chair in a twilight gloom, facing a window that offered a view of the leaden sky. He wore his own clothing, now dry and pressed. His shoes gleamed with a hard shine that matched the hard unhappiness on his face. He hadn't shaved. The whiskers added to his ferocious air.

"Go downstairs," Janine told him. "No use sitting up here in the dark."

"No, thank you. I'd like to be alone."

She debated telling him about Lanny. She had no idea what he'd do with the information. Strange thing. She'd dated him for years and didn't know him at all. Yet, Daniel, whom she'd known less than two weeks felt like her best and dearest friend. "It's cold up here."

"I have a coat."

Daniel nudged her arm and shook his head. "No time," he whispered. "Pinky won't bother him."

"Suit yourself," she said.

As they headed downstairs, Daniel asked, "What did you see in that guy?"

"I can't remember." She shot him a warning glare. "I don't wish to discuss it. Okay?"

"Fine by me. Let's discuss Saturday, then. I think next week the gem and mineral show will be in town. I'd like to go. I have a thing for rocks. Never know when I'll find a lucky stone.''

"Pardon?''

"Stay in town for the weekend. If anyone deserves a few days off, it's you. We'll have a blast.''

"I haven't said yes to the movie yet.''

"How else will you get to know me as well as I know you?''

Compared to the silent basement and west wing, the noise in the main lodge nearly deafened Janine. Employees toting trays of drinks and carts laden with food hurried from the restaurant to the ballroom and back again. People in full finery milled about the lounge. Guitar music twanged from the ballroom. Tristan and Ross joined Janine and Daniel. Tristan shut off the lantern he carried and set it on a nearby table. So many lanterns, oil lamps and candles burned, the place was lit up like a ballfield.

Ross gazed at the crowd. "Looks fine to me. Maybe kidnapping your maintenance man was Lanny's grand gesture.''

"We can hope,'' Daniel muttered.

"There's Kara.'' Janine hurried across the lounge. People hoisted champagne flutes in greeting and complimented her on throwing the best party ever. She chuckled to herself. Only her relatives could think she'd arranged for a blizzard and a power outage just to provide an adventure.

At the registration desk, Janine leaned on the counter. Kara stood behind the desk, talking on the phone. She wore a clingy, sparkly red sheath. Huge red-sequined earrings glittered through her hair. She hung up and grinned. "The phone is ringing off the hook!''

So Daniel thought Kara was Miss Universe. Much to her dismay, Janine had to agree. Kara was younger, thinner, taller, and her smile could melt stone. She squashed the feeling of being the wicked queen to Kara's Snow White. "Guests calling to tell us they can't get through?''

"Exactly. I mean, I'm glad they're calling, but Mom is too busy to talk, and I want to party." She leaned on the counter and lowered her voice. "Did you find Lanny?"

"I wish."

"Everybody is keeping an eye out for him. The guys say if he shows his face, they'll take him out." She looked over Janine's jeans and grubby sweater. "Are you going to change clothes?"

"Later. Where is Mom?"

Kara pointed. "With the babies, where else? Over there by the fireplace."

Janine saw her mother talking to a gathering of women. Elise held the handles of Jamie's wheelchair. Ross's son squeezed onto the chair with Jamie; the boys played an odd version of patty-cake. Megan held Rosie in her arms. Soon, Janine thought, Megan would add another grandbaby for Elise to love.

Juan Hernandez burst into the lobby. Snow crusted his coveralls chest high. His lower legs looked like ice blocks. He waved excitedly at her. Daniel and Janine rushed to join him.

"Found 'em," Juan said breathlessly. He panted as if he'd been running. He pounded his chest with a fist. "Snow's six feet in some places. But we found 'em."

"Who?"

"Lanny and Vernon. Honeymoon Hideaway. Cabin A. Trussed up like turkeys and half-froze, but they're okay."

Uncertain she'd heard correctly, Janine peered closely at his face. His cheeks and nose were bright red. Water dripped from his mustache. "Lanny tied up Vernon?"

"No, ma'am. Jason did it. Jason Bulshe. Had a sword or machete and marched them through the snow to the cabin. Damn boy's gone crazy. But the guys are okay. Madder than hell. Can't feel their feet, but they're okay."

Janine looked at Daniel. He looked at her. As one they

spun about and ran across the lounge. "Mom! Where's the colonel?"

Elise pointed vaguely toward the east wing. "He's fine, dear. I know this is horribly upsetting, but—"

"Where did he go? Is J.T. with him? We're looking for the wrong person. Lanny isn't Pinky, Jason Bulshe is! He—"

Elise staggered and placed a hand on the fireplace rim to steady herself. Megan shifted Rosie to her other hip and reached for her mother. The other women closed ranks, looking confused and worried.

"My God," Elise whispered. "Jason told your father Cody and Juan were waiting at the back door. They left a few minutes ago."

Daniel grabbed Janine's hand and practically pulled her off her feet in his haste. "Find Tristan and Ross," she yelled over her shoulder. Machete, sword—she refused to consider the implications.

Inside the wing, near her office, Daniel pulled out the Luger. He released the safety and worked the slide. "Be warned, if he's waving a sword, I'll shoot him."

She wanted him to blow Pinky's head off. "Just don't let anything happen to my father."

They found J.T. at the rear entrance. The big man was sprawled facedown on the floor. Blood glistened on his black hair. A short length of pipe lay next to him. With a cry, Janine dropped to her knees. She fluttered her fingers helplessly over his bleeding head.

"J.T., oh, man. J.T." Daniel crouched next to his friend and jammed his fingers under J.T.'s jaw. He heaved a long shaky breath. "He's alive."

Pounding footsteps made him jump upright. Tristan and Ross approached at a dead run and skidded to a stop. J.T. groaned and struggled to rise. Daniel and Janine helped him into a sitting position. She anxiously searched his eyes. The pupils looked the same size.

"Sucker-punched me," J.T. mumbled and touched the back of his head. "Skinny little bastard sucker-punched me." His voice strengthened, and he sounded more angry than wounded.

"He's hurt," Janine said. "Jason has my father! Did you see them?"

"We didn't pass them in the hall. This door is snow blocked," Tristan said.

Daniel's eyes widened. "Your dad's office." He fished beneath J.T.'s jacket and pulled out his pistol. He thrust it at Ross. "Take care of my buddy, man. Tristan, get on the horn and call the cops. Tell them we have a hostage situation. I don't care how they get here, helicopters, sled dogs, I don't care. Just get here."

"I think I heard Mom say something about a sword." Ross knelt next to J.T.

Daniel shook his head. "I have a bad feeling he's going for the big guns. Literally." He took off at a dead run.

Ignoring her brother's shouts for her to stay, Janine ran after Daniel. She caught up with him in the colonel's office. The door stood wide open. So did the gun safe. A familiar ring of keys hung from the lock. Ammo drawers had been pulled open, and loose bullets and shotgun shells littered the floor. A deer rifle and a shotgun were missing.

People began to scream.

Daniel jerked a shotgun from the safe and thrust it at Janine. "Can you use this?"

In reply she scooped shells off the floor and efficiently loaded the weapon. She jammed extra shells in her pockets. She shut out the sounds of screaming and yelling. She'd never harmed another person in her entire life, but Pinky had her father, and that meant he wasn't human. He was a monster. Daniel grabbed the remaining shotgun and a handful of shells.

They raced after the trail of screams. In the kitchen they found workers hiding under tables and squeezed between appliances. A busboy said Jason had marched the colonel at gunpoint through the kitchen toward the restaurant. Jason toted two weapons, had a sword in his belt and a coil of rope slung over his shoulder. The grand gesture had begun.

More cautious now, Daniel and Janine hurried down the corridor connecting the kitchen to the restaurant. Men and women hid behind and beneath the prep tables. The soft sound of weeping wafted through the air.

"Get out of the lodge," Daniel told everyone they passed. "Get to the stables. Get out!"

Through the now-deserted restaurant they crept. A deathly silence had fallen over the lodge. At the restaurant entrance, Daniel crouched behind a half wall and peered through trailing philodendron vines.

"The ballroom doors are closed," Janine whispered. A bad, bad feeling burned in her gut and worked its way up her aching chest.

A child began to wail. A woman's voice rose in a frantic effort to hush the crying. Janine spotted movement behind the fireplace. She and Daniel stayed low, their weapons at the ready, never taking their eyes off the ballroom doors as they sneaked through the lounge. Men and women lay flat on the floor, hiding behind furniture. Elise and Megan had Jamie, Rosie and Hank on the floor behind the fireplace. Hank screamed at the top of his lungs.

"Where is he, Mom?" Janine asked.

"He forced your father into the ballroom."

"Get out." She stood upright and trained the shotgun bore on the ballroom doors. "Juan? Juan, where are you?"

The maintenance supervisor peeked around a potted plant.

"Get these people to the stable." She urged Daniel to give the shotgun and extra shells to Juan. "If you see Jason headed your way, blow his head off."

Daniel reached the ballroom doors. He pressed an ear against the door.

"Megan, Tristan is calling the cops. Tell him the gun safe is open in the colonel's office. Arm as many people as he can. Where's Frankie?"

"In the ballroom." Megan spoke woodenly. She clutched her belly in a protective gesture. "Kara is in there, too."

Swaying from the horror, Janine clenched every muscle in her abdomen against the urge to vomit. "J.T. is hurt. Ross is with him. Get him to the stables, too. Hurry, Mom, get these people out of here." She ran lightly to Daniel's side and dropped to a crouch behind him, her back to the wall and the shotgun cradled in her arms. "What do you hear?"

"Nothing. Is there another way in?"

"Several." She watched people clear out of the lounge and lobby. "He's not shooting, that's good, right? I mean, psychos in office buildings always go in shooting, right?"

"Right."

She didn't believe him.

"What's the best way in, other than these doors?"

Trying to enter from the outdoors was impossible. Snow piled against the doors and windows. "Men's room." She pulled out her keys. "A storeroom behind the men's room. This way."

They got into the storeroom, which was pitch-black. She felt for the door on the other side that led to the men's room. Her clammy, shaky hands barely held the keys. A lantern illuminated the bathroom. The place was empty.

"Elk River has nice bathrooms," Daniel whispered as they tiptoed to the door leading to the ballroom.

"We do our best." She eased the door open a few inches. An alcove separated the bathrooms from the ballroom. The alcove was empty, too. Beyond the alcove, candlelight flickered, casting shadows on the walls. She listened, but nobody was talking. The silence was so heavy she wondered if any of the thirty or so people trapped by the madman even breathed.

Daniel extinguished the lantern, plunging the bathroom into darkness. "Belly crawl," he whispered in her ear.

She slithered on the slick tile floor, inching toward the arched portal. An icy draft brushed her face. Candlelight dimmed then flickered furiously. Following the source, she saw a sight she'd never wanted to see. A sight burned into her brain, guaranteeing nightmares for the rest of her life.

A door stood open and a mini-avalanche had tumbled snow onto the ballroom floor. The colonel stood, balanced upon a piece of firewood, his hands behind him, his back to the glass-paned door. He wore a noose around his neck. The rope stretched over the top of the heavy door frame and was attached to the door handle. A gold napkin bound his mouth.

Daniel pushed a hand on Janine's back. "Stay down," he whispered.

Daddy, she thought helplessly. Was it the candlelight, or was he quivering? If he lost his balance and slipped, he'd strangle. If he leaned against the door, he'd lose his balance. If he died, she couldn't live.

Daniel urged her to peek around the wall.

Jason Bulshe, twenty years old, a mechanical wizard who'd never given her a speck of trouble, stood on the bandstand. Feet spread, back straight, he glared at the ballroom. In silence, people stared back. Her family and some employees sat at tables, the candles reflecting their fear. Jason held her father's .30-.30 rifle. A shotgun lay at his feet. Her father's ceremonial saber was stuck in his belt. His coverall pockets bulged with ammunition.

Janine scooted back into the alcove. "We cannot wait for the police."

"I know."

"Will he kill me? Is that his intention?"

He gazed into her eyes. His throat worked with a hard swallow. "Yes."

She'd never been athletic like her sister Megan, or charming like Ross, or quick-witted like Kara. Other than fashion sense, she had no particular talents. But damn it, she'd always been her father's daughter, and she refused to sit back and watch him die.

"Got a pocket knife?" she asked. Her father looked her way. His eyes widened. She waggled her fingers at him.

"Uh-huh, why?"

"You still want that honeymoon?"

"Janine…"

"You get my father down from there, and I'll bathe you in champagne myself." Leaving the shotgun, she pushed off the floor.

He tried to pull her back down, but she shook him off. "Reason won't work, logic won't work. What will reach him? How do I make him listen to me?"

"Uh, play his delusion. Acknowledge his love." He glanced at her father. "Be yourself. Show him the real you."

She straightened her sweatshirt. Despite the cold floor and colder draft, perspiration trickled down her back. She raked back her hair. She stared at her father. He stared back, expressionless, but he trembled. The chunk of wood was only about six inches in diameter; disaster was only a slip of the foot away.

She stepped out of the alcove. "Pinky?"

Jason spun about, kicking the shotgun. He swung the rifle to his shoulder. She stood frozen, certain he was about to fire. She heard gasps. Smelled her own rank sweat, mingling with the waxy scent of candles. The burn in her belly flared. He lowered the rifle.

At first her legs refused to cooperate. She told her rebellious muscles firmly: *Move!* so Daniel can rescue the colonel. Arms wide, her palms exposed, she approached the bandstand. Be herself, Daniel advised. Herself wanted to grab a microphone stand and beat Jason to death with it.

"What do you want?" she asked.

He ducked his head shyly and grinned, but he kept a finger inside the trigger guard. "I passed all your tests."

She kept walking past the bandstand, relieved he turned his head to watch her. Either he'd forgotten about Daniel or he didn't care. Armed to the teeth, with more than thirty hostages, he probably didn't care.

"You are flunking this test," she said. "I abhor violence. I thought you were better than this. Smarter."

He shook his head. Shadows danced on the wall behind him. She made herself not look toward her father.

"The tyrant is going down," Jason said. "Just like I promised. I always keep my promises to you. Once he's gone, we can be together. You don't have to be afraid of him anymore."

"You think this is what I want?"

He growled and whipped the rifle to his shoulder. Her insides clenched into such a tight little knot, she thought she'd implode from the pressure.

"I don't care what you want!" he yelled. "Damn you, I've done everything for you! I've devoted my entire life to you. I gave you everything. Did all your little crap jobs, ran your little errands. And you threw it back in my face. What makes you think you're so special, huh? I can have any girl I want."

Not crazy? He sounded crazy as a berry-drunk robin to her.

"What am I supposed to do? I've been respectful, patient. I spent all my money buying you gifts. Then when you pass me in the hallways, you pretend I don't even exist. I'm sick of you treating me like garbage. I'm sick of that damned colonel keeping us apart."

Be herself...Daniel couldn't have meant that. Her true self was a classic type-A overachiever with a bad temper and thin skin. "You're only half right," she said. "The colonel isn't keeping us apart. It's me. I treated you poorly. I acted like a snob."

He lowered the rifle. His eyes frightened her. They were like the glass eyes of a doll. "You're not a snob. You're perfect."

She laughed bitterly. People shuffled restlessly. She didn't dare take her attention off Jason. She prayed no one panicked. "Nobody's perfect, Jason—Pinky, least of all me. You want to know the truth? Especially not me. I'm scared people will think I'm not perfect. I'm scared if they know me, they won't like me."

"You're perfect." The words trailed into a moan.

"I'm not. Don't you understand? What I am is scared."

"You don't have to be scared of me. I love you." He lowered the rifle another inch. His lips worked as if he chewed something.

"That's very…sweet. I'm not really scared of you. It's me. I'm scared if I'm nice to people, they'll think I'm weak. I'm scared of people making fun of me. I'm scared of making mistakes. If you knew what I'm really like, you wouldn't like me at all."

"I do know you! We're soul mates. I love everything about you."

"You know *about* me." She was running out of words. None of her past experience prepared her for a conversation with a madman. She maintained eye contact, willed him to keep his attention on her. "Like, you know I wear the color red. But you don't know why. Nobody knows why."

The rifle bore dipped a few more inches. "Because it's pretty. You look beautiful in red."

She licked her lips. "Truth is, I read somewhere that red is a power color. People take red seriously. Green is actually my favorite color. Green and purple. I like pink, too, but I never wear it. I don't want people thinking I'm silly."

"Honest?" He shuffled his feet and flexed his shoulders

as if they ached. He cut his eyes at the silent crowd. "Why are you telling me this?"

Why, indeed? "For love? People in love know each other. Not just the surface stuff. They know each other down deep. They don't have to be perfect."

"You are perfect!" he insisted and tossed hair off his forehead. Sweat beaded on his face, pooling on his upper lip.

Don't crack up on me, she prayed. Just keep talking.

A clunk made Jason spin around. The log spun a lazy circle on the floor and cut rope dangled limply over the door frame. Daniel shoved the colonel toward the alcove. An animal howl ripped from Jason's throat and he shouldered the rifle.

"No!" Janine screamed as she scrambled onto the bandstand.

A door opening from the opposite direction made Jason whirl. A bullet ripped into the ceiling. The explosion rocked Janine. Pandemonium broke loose in the ballroom, and screaming people scrambled for safety.

Elliot stood in the main doorway, his mouth hanging open and his eyes wide behind his glasses. "This is not a good time, I take it?" he asked stupidly in a squeaky voice.

As if through clear gelatin that slowed every action, she watched Jason bring the rifle to his shoulder and sight down the barrel. She knew, without a doubt, once he murdered Elliot, he'd continue killing. His finger tightened on the trigger. He squinted one eye. He inhaled deeply.

Daniel leaped, right foot extended and struck Jason squarely in the back. Fire flashed from the rifle muzzle. The bullet whizzed so close past Janine's shoulder, she felt the air on her neck. Daniel and Jason crashed into the drum set. The rifle flew out of Jason's hands and spun across the floor. The bass drum banged and cymbals clanged. The snare drum rolled off the bandstand, clattering. The boy fought furiously, twisting and kicking and punching wildly at Daniel.

Janine scrambled after the rifle. Jason rolled free and sprang to his feet. He grabbed a microphone stand and swung the heavy base viciously at Daniel's head.

Daniel ducked and jabbed Jason's belly with stiff fingers. Janine fumbled at the rifle. A spasm gripped her fingers. She kept grabbing and missing. She finally got it off the ground with the business end pointed at Jason. Lips thinned in a snarl, the boy charged Daniel.

Daniel kicked him in the face. One perfect, smooth, too-fast-to-follow kick, slamming the full force of his powerful body into Jason's nose. His foot connected with a crunch. Realizing she held the rifle upside down, Janine twisted it in her hands.

Jason dropped to his knees and swayed. His arms hung loosely at his sides. Blood spurted from his nose and mouth. His eyes crossed. He crumpled silently to the floor and lay still.

Elliot nervously cleared his throat. "I wondered where everyone had gone. I think...I shall leave as well." He turned tail and ran.

Staring at Jason, Janine crouched and laid the rifle on the floor. She wondered if the boy was dead, but then he gurgled. On stiff unfeeling legs, she went to Daniel. His chest heaved, and he ran his hands anxiously over her shoulders and arms as if assuring himself she was all right. All the shouts, questions and crying behind her faded into nothingness. She focused on his beautiful copper-penny eyes.

"Wow," Daniel said. "A woman as crazy as I am. I'm in love. Marry me."

She cupped his dear, dear face in both hands. In front of everybody, despite her father striding toward her, she kissed him fully on the mouth.

JANINE FROWNED AT A RECEIPT, wondering why in the world Chef needed a mandolin. She circled the item in red to remind her to ask him why he needed musical instruments in the kitchen. Familiar whistling floated to her ears and business concerns faded.

Daniel. He'd done more than save her life, in the past six months he'd saved her sanity. After Pinky, she'd suffered such horrendous insomnia and anxiety, she'd finally met with a therapist. She'd been depressed and angry and afraid of her own shadow. Through it all, Daniel stood by her, enduring her moods and patiently helping her recover. She was getting better. She could go days at a time now without brooding over Pinky and the tragedy he'd nearly visited upon her family.

He strolled into the office and plopped an odd-looking plastic thing on her desk. He looked so handsome in his cream-colored linen suit he nearly hurt her eyes. She never tired of looking at him.

"What's this?" she asked.

"It's a toy." He turned it over and viscous blue liquid bubbled and curled lazily as it dripped languidly through a funnel spout. He leaned on her desk and she met him halfway in a kiss.

"Thank you. It's cute...I think." She picked up the strange receipt. "You like to cook, right? Why would a cook need a mandolin?"

"It's a slicer-dicer gadget. Why? You want one?"

"Never mind." Trust him to always have an answer. "But you're early. I still have work to do."

"I have a problem." He flopped onto the sofa and stretched out his legs. "It's serious. Life and death."

She typed a Save command on the computer keyboard. "Oh? What's that?"

"There's this girl. I'm obsessed with her."

She smiled to herself. "That sounds very sad, dear."

"It is. I see her every weekend, talk to her on the phone

every day. Wine and dine her. Impress her with my manliness every chance I get. It's still not enough. I'm lost without her.''

She bit back a laugh. The more time she spent with him, the more she liked him. The more she loved him. He loved her, too. He told her so at least twice a day.

''Has it ever occurred to you that you're greedy?''

He frowned comically. ''Nope. I'm rich, good-looking, a good dancer.'' He ran a thumb under his lapel. ''Snazzy dresser. But not greedy.''

''Don't forget conceited.'' She swiveled the chair and rested an elbow on the desk and her chin on her fist. ''So why is this a problem? Sounds very nice to me.''

''The real problem is, she promised me a honeymoon. She won't cough it up.''

''I told you already, you can have that vacation anytime you want it.''

''No vacation. I want a honeymoon. That's the deal.''

His antics had ceased to amaze her, or so she thought. But an undercurrent of seriousness gave her pause. ''Well, in order to have a honeymoon, you need to get married.''

''Okay.''

Her heart thump-thudded. She loved him so much it frightened her sometimes. The sound of his voice on the telephone left her floating all day. Their dates on the weekends filled her with happiness. He'd changed her whole life, and not just concerning Pinky, either. Around him she relaxed. She experienced joy. As an added bonus, her family adored him.

''Is that supposed to be some kind of proposal?'' she asked tartly.

''What do you want, honey? Flowers, champagne, overpriced ring, bended knee?''

She thought about it. ''Yes, I suppose I do.''

He jumped off the sofa and hurried out of the room.

She stared openmouthed at his sudden departure. When

would she ever learn that she couldn't have her way in all things? She rose to run after him, but he returned.

He carried a bouquet of roses so large it obscured his face. Wheels squeaked on the cart he pulled into the office. It held champagne on ice and two crystal flutes. Attached to the cart were helium-filled, heart-shaped, foil balloons trailing pink, purple and green ribbons. Grinning, he placed the flowers on the desk and the intoxicating scent enveloped her, stunned her.

"Sit," he ordered. She sat. He dropped to one knee before her and presented her with a velvet ring box. He opened it with a flourish, revealing a huge blue diamond solitaire set in ethereal platinum. Her heart nearly stopped. "I love you with all my heart and soul, Janine. Marry me. I promise to love, cherish and spoil you rotten for the rest of my life."

He'd seen her at her best, and he'd seen her at her worst—he loved her, anyway. She couldn't think of a better recommendation than that.

She said simply, "Yes."

If you enjoyed what you just read,
then we've got an offer you can't resist!

Take 2 bestselling
love stories FREE!
Plus get a FREE surprise gift!

COMING NEXT MONTH

#521 FATHER, LOVER, BODYGUARD by Cassie Miles
Captive Hearts

Amanda Fielding remembered nothing of the robbery or blow to the head that caused her partial amnesia. When she woke in the hospital, she gazed into the dark, sexy eyes of Dr. David Haines—her former lover. David swore to protect her from the danger stalking her—and she knew she'd finally have to tell him about their baby...

#522 WANTED: COWBOY by Kelsey Roberts
The Rose Tattoo

Barbara Prather ranted on about Cade Landry, her cowboy protector—but she couldn't seem to get enough of him! As the only witness to a murder, Barbara had an assassin on her trail. Cade kidnapped her to save her life—but was his interest professional...or personal?

#523 HER EYEWITNESS by Rita Herron

Blinded in the line of duty, police officer Collin Cash had a transplant to regain his sight—and woke to a vision of murder. The dead man's widow stood accused—and only Collin could prove her innocence. When Sydney Green discovered Collin's identity, would she accept his help...and his heart?

#524 THE BRIDE'S SECRET by Adrianne Lee

Nikki Navarro would do anything to find the family she'd never known—even take on Chris Conrad, the dark and sexy owner of Wedding House. Nikki was the spitting image of the bride whose portrait graced the master suite—and only Chris could protect her from someone determined she would never know if she was, in fact, the bride's secret...

Look us up on-line at: http://www.romance.net